THE KILLINGS AT
KINGFISHER HILL

Agatha Christie

The Killings at Kingfisher Hill

THE NEW HERCULE POIROT MYSTERY

SOPHIE HANNAH

HarperCollins*Publishers*

HarperCollins*Publishers*
1 London Bridge Street
London SE1 9GF
www.harpercollins.co.uk

Published by HarperCollins*Publishers* 2020

1

A catalogue record for this book
is available from the British Library

ISBN 978-0-00-826452-9   HB
ISBN 978-0-00-826453-6   TPB

Set in Sabon by Palimpsest Book Production Ltd,
Falkirk, Stirlingshire.

Printed and bound in Great Britain by
CPI Group (UK) Ltd, Croydon CR0 4YY

MIX
Paper from
responsible sources
FSC™ C007454
www.fsc.org

This book is produced from independently certified FSC™ paper
to ensure responsible forest management.
For more information visit: www.harpercollins.co.uk/green

*This book is dedicated to Helen A.,
my friend and fellow Agatha superfan.*

Acknowledgements

As always I would like to thank the 'gang'—James and Mathew Prichard and everyone at Agatha Christie Ltd, David Brawn, Kate Elton, Fliss Denham and the team at HarperCollins, Julia Elliott and her colleagues at William Morrow in the US, and all the dedicated and talented teams who publish my Poirot novels all over the world— thank you!

I'm hugely grateful also to my amazing agent Peter Straus and everyone at Rogers, Coleridge & White, to my family and friends, and to my lovely readers and fellow Poirot-and-Agatha fans. Thank you to Emily Winslow for her incisive editorial feedback, to Kate Jones for all her amazing help in the last year and a half, to my Dream Authors who are all amazing and ace and teach me so much, and to Faith Tilleray, my website and tech guru. Special thanks to Helen Acton, who suggested I might like to use her name for a character in this book and bravely declared her willingness to be either murderer or victim, goody or baddie. Thank you also to Claire George, who suggested the name of another character: Marcus Capeling—a great name which I loved as soon as I heard it.

And last but most, thanks to the Queen of Crime, Agatha Christie, whose books never stop delighting and surprising me, no matter how many times I read them.

Contents

CHAPTER 1

Midnight Gathering

It is not midnight when this tale begins, but ten minutes before two on the afternoon of 22nd February 1931. That was when the strangeness started, as M. Hercule Poirot and Inspector Edward Catchpool (his friend, and the teller of this story) stood with thirty strangers in a dispersed huddle—no one too close to anybody else, but all of us easily identifiable as an assembly—on London's Buckingham Palace Road.

Our group of men and women and one child (an infant carried by his mother in a bundle arrangement that presented a rather mummified appearance) were soon to be travellers on a journey that felt peculiar and puzzling to me long before I knew quite how extraordinary it would become.

We were congregated by the side of the motor-coach that was to take us from London to the famed Kingfisher Hill country estate near Haslemere in Surrey, a place of outstanding natural beauty according to many. Despite all of us passengers being present well in advance of the coach's scheduled departure time, we had not yet been permitted to board. Instead we shivered in the damp February chill, stamped our feet and blew on our gloved hands to warm ourselves as best we could.

It was not midnight, but it was the sort of winter day that is light-starved at dawn and remains so deprived for its duration.

There were seats for thirty passengers on the coach, and thirty-two of us in all who would be travelling: the driver, the swaddled infant in his mother's firm grip, and the rest of us occupying the passenger seats on either side of the central aisle, including a representative of the coach company.

It struck me, as I shivered by Poirot's side, that I had more in common with the babe in arms than with any other members of our group. Thirty of our band of thirty-two knew why they were going wherever they were going on that day. Poirot was one in that lucky position. The coach's driver, also, knew his reason for being there: it put food on his table—a compelling motive if ever there was one.

The baby and I were the only people present who had not the faintest notion of why we were about to board the garishly-painted motor-coach, and of the two of us, only one perceived his ignorant state as a problem. All I knew was the coach's destination: Kingfisher Hill, a private country estate of some nine hundred acres, with a golf club, two tennis courts and a swimming pool designed and built by celebrated architect Sir Victor Marklew that boasted warm water all year round.

A country home within the quiet and leafy confines of the Kingfisher Hill Estate was out of the reach of all but the wealthiest of people, but that did not prevent Londoners of all denominations from talking about it endlessly. I might have been eager to enter those blessed gates for the first time had Poirot not been so determined to withhold from me the reason for our visit. As it was, the sense that I was being kept even more in the dark than usual proved too great an irritant. Was I, perhaps, on my way to meet a future Queen? It was sometimes said at Scotland Yard that the inhabitants of Kingfisher Hill were mostly royal person-ages and aristocrats, and anything seemed possible on a journey of Poirot's devising.

The coach departed promptly at two o'clock, and I cannot think that the events which took place before the driver called out his cheery 'Away we sally, ladies and gents!' occupied as much as a quarter of an hour. I can therefore confidently locate at ten minutes before two the moment that I noticed her: the unhappy woman with the unfinished face.

I might as well tell you that my first title for this chapter was 'An Unfinished Face'. Poirot preferred the original and protested when I told him I had changed it.

'Catchpool, you have in you the tendency of unreasoning contrariness.' He glared at me. 'Why give this most impor-tant chapter a name that will create confusion? Nothing significant occurred at midnight, on that day or any other!

It was the broad light of the day when we waited in the cold, nearly freezing to blocks of ice and receiving no explanation of why the doors of that char-a-banc could not be opened to us.' Poirot stopped and frowned. I waited while he disentangled two separate sources of annoyance that he had unintentionally woven together in his invective. 'It was decidedly *not* midnight.'

'I do say that in my—'

'Yes, you do say so. It is your duty, *n'est-ce pas?* You have invented, from no necessity, the requirement to state *immediatement* that a particular condition did not pertain. It is illogical, *non?*'

I merely nodded. It would have sounded pompous to offer the answer that was in my mind. Poirot is the finest detective at work anywhere in the world, but he is not an experienced teller of stories in written form, and he is, very occasionally, wrong. Broad daylight was an unfair description of that particular afternoon, as I have already said, and midnight—not the hour but the word—has everything to do with the matter at hand. If the words 'Midnight Gathering' on the cover of a book had not caught my eye before we set off on our travels that day, it is possible that no one would ever have known who was responsible for the killings at Kingfisher Hill.

But I am getting ahead of myself and must return us all to the cold outdoors. I understood why we were being made to wait in the relentless headwind, even if Poirot did not. Vanity, as so often where people are concerned, was the explanation—specifically, the vanity of Alfred Bixby

Esquire. Bixby was the owner of the newly minted Kingfisher Coach Company and wished us all to observe the beauty of the vehicle that was about to transport us. Since Poirot and I had arrived, Bixby had been attached to our side as if by a gravitational force. So tickled pink was he to have the great Hercule Poirot among his patrons, he was prepared to ignore everybody else. This was a circumstance of which I could not count myself among the beneficiaries; my proximity to my friend ensured that every word addressed to him was also endured by me.

'Doesn't she look splendid? Blue and orange like the kingfisher bird! Bright as a button! Look at the shape of her! Beautiful, I'd say. Wouldn't you agree, M. Poirot? Nothing like her on the road. The last word in luxury, truly she is! Look at those doors! Fit together perfectly. A spectacular feat of design and engineering. Look at them!'

'Very fine indeed,' I told him, knowing we would only be allowed to board once we had admired the vehicle sufficiently. Poirot made a gruff noise in his throat, unwilling to feign approval.

Bixby was a thin, angular man with bulbous staring eyes. Spotting two women wrapped in hats and coats walking on the other side of the road, he drew our attention to them and declared, 'Those ladies are too late! Ho-ha! They should have reserved their seats in advance. If you want to travel with the Kingfisher Coach Company, you can't afford to leave it to chance, or there'll be no room for you. Ha! Sorry, ladies!' he bellowed suddenly.

The two women must have heard him, but paid no attention as they walked purposefully onwards. They would barely have noticed our presence had Bixby not called out to them. They had no interest in the Kingfisher Coach Company, nor in this four-wheeled blue and orange representative thereof. Bixby's frankly desperate and undignified behaviour made me wonder if his firm was as successful as he kept telling us all that it was.

'Did you hear that? Mr Bixby just had to turn away two ladies,' a man near me said to his companion, who replied, 'Quite right too, if they weren't expected. He said we're all here, didn't he, after he'd marked us off on his list? I don't know why people don't plan ahead.' Irritable as I was that day, it irked me that Bixby's inelegant deception had fooled at least two people.

I nodded along and made appreciative noises at what I hoped were the correct moments as he explained how his firm had come into being: something about most people not taking the initiative and not being able to imagine something that didn't already exist . . . something about owning property at Kingfisher Hill himself, profits from a previous venture, the inconvenience of getting to London despite it being relatively close geographically . . . something about not letting fear stop him, even with the national and global economies being in their present catastrophic state . . .

I remember thinking, 'Well, if Alfred Bixby owns a house at Kingfisher Hill then it can't be all royalty and aristocrats,' seconds before I saw a woman standing alone at the outer edge of our group and noticed her expression of horror, at which point all other considerations left my mind.

'An unfinished face,' I muttered. No one heard me. Alfred Bixby was busy inflicting upon Poirot a list of the many failures of Ramsay MacDonald and his 'Russia-favouring government of knaves and reprobates' and his words smothered mine.

I estimated that the woman was around twenty years old. She was wearing a smart green hat and coat over a faded, almost colourless dress that looked as if it must have been washed more than a hundred times. There were scuffs on her shoes.

She was not entirely unattractive, but her skin looked dull and bloodless, and her features all had the same look to them: as if someone had stopped short of adding the final touches that would have given her a more conventional visual appeal. Her lips were thin, pale and recessive, and her eyes brought to mind two dark holes in the ground. In general, her face seemed to yearn to have more detail and shape added; elements needed to be brought out that were sunken in.

All of this is incidental, however. What fascinated and alarmed me was that she looked frightened, disgusted and unhappy to her core, all at once. It was as if she had suffered, only moments ago, the most dreadful and distressing shock. Her eyes were fixed on the motor-coach—a wide-eyed, maniacal stare that no amount of disapproval of those particular shades of blue and orange in such close association could explain. If the vehicle had not been inanimate, I might have suspected that, while the rest of us were distracted, this woman had witnessed it committing a crime of unparalleled barbarism.

She appeared to be alone, standing at the outer edge of our little crowd. I did not hesitate in approaching her.

'Excuse me. Forgive me for intruding, but you look as if you've had a nasty shock. Can I be of assistance?' So extreme was the horror on her face that I did not stop to wonder if I had imagined a problem that did not exist.

'No, thank you.' She sounded vague and seemed distracted.

'Are you quite certain?'

'Yes. I . . . Yes. Thank you.' She took four or five steps away from me and closer to the coach.

I could hardly insist on helping her if she was determined to forbid it, so I returned to Poirot and Alfred Bixby, but kept an eye on her movements, which soon grew more agitated. She started to walk round and round in little circles, her mouth moving silently. At no point did the terrible expression leave her face, not for a second.

I was about to interrupt Bixby's monologue and draw Poirot's attention to the object of my concern when I heard a loud, disdainful female voice to the left of me say, 'Do you see that young woman over there? What on earth is wrong with her? Perhaps her mother dropped her hard on her head when she was a baby.'

The mother of the bundled infant gasped and held her child closer to her body. 'There's no need to be insulting, miss,' said an old man, which remark inspired a general murmur of agreement. The only people who seemed not to notice all of this activity were the woman with the unfinished face and Alfred Bixby, who was still talking to Poirot, though Poirot was no longer listening.

'She does appear to be disturbed,' someone said. 'We ought to check that her name is on the passenger manifest.'

This provoked a chorus of observations:

'Mr Bixby said we're all here.'

'Then what's keeping him from opening the doors? Driver! You're the driver, aren't you? May we board now?'

'I suppose if her name is on the list then she cannot be an escaped lunatic from a nearby asylum, though her behaviour indicates otherwise,' said the loud, rude woman. She too was young—around the same age as the woman with the unfinished face. Her voice was severely at odds with the viciousness of her words. It was a strikingly musical and feminine voice—light, bright, almost sparkling. *If a diamond could speak, it would sound like her,* I thought.

'That gentleman was speaking to her a few seconds ago.' An elderly lady gestured in my direction, then turned to face me. 'What did you say to her? Do you know her?'

'Not at all,' I replied. 'I simply noticed that she looked . . . disturbed and asked if she needed help. "No, thank you," she said.'

'Now, then, ladies and gentlemen,' said Alfred Bixby, eager to redirect our attention to his pride and joy. 'Is it time to reveal the luxurious interior of this brand new beauty? Why, I believe it is!'

As several people rushed forward in their eagerness to climb on board and escape the cold, I stood to one side and watched as the woman with the unfinished face backed away from the coach's open doors as though afraid they might swallow her up. I heard Poirot's voice behind me. 'Let us proceed, Catchpool. I have taken enough of your English fresh air for one day. Oh—you observe *la pauvre mademoiselle.*'

'What the devil is the matter with her, Poirot?'

'I do not know, my friend. It is likely that her mental faculties are impaired.'

'I don't think so,' I told him. 'When I spoke to her, she appeared sane and lucid.'

'In that case, she has since deteriorated.'

I walked over to her once more and said, 'I'm terribly sorry to intrude again, but . . . I am quite certain that you are in need of help. My name is Edward Catchpool. I'm a police inspector with Scotland Yard, and . . .'

'No!' Her mouth contorted around the word. 'You *cannot* be. It's impossible!' She backed away from me, knocking into the woman with the baby. She seemed aware of nothing and no one but me. The first time I had spoken to her, she had been too preoccupied by her own fears and torments to notice me. Now she seemed entirely fixated on me to the exclusion of all else. 'Who *are* you?' she demanded to know. 'Who are you, really?'

*

Poirot came quickly to my defence. 'Mademoiselle, I can assure you that it is true. Inspector Catchpool and I, we travel together. I am M. Hercule Poirot.'

His words had a visible effect. All at once, her demeanour changed. She looked around. She seemed to notice for the first time that her behaviour had attracted many avid spectators. Then she hung her head and whispered, 'Forgive me, Inspector. Of course you are who you say you are. I don't know what came over me.'

'What's the matter with you?' I asked her bluntly.

'Nothing. I'm perfectly all right.'

'I find that difficult to believe.'

'If I needed help, I'd ask for it, Inspector, sir. Please, you mustn't trouble yourself on my account.'

'Very well,' I said, dissatisfied. 'Shall we?' I gestured towards the motor-coach, curious to see if she would behave sensibly henceforth. In spite of her erratic behaviour, I was convinced of the soundness of her faculties. She was not afflicted by any mental infirmity. The problem was an emotional one.

'I . . . you . . .' she stammered.

'Let *us* take our seats, Catchpool,' said Poirot firmly. 'You and me. This young lady wishes to be left alone.'

At this, the woman with the unfinished face looked distinctly relieved and, with her and Poirot united against me, I admitted defeat. As we climbed on board, having left our valises with all the others, she retreated. Perhaps her name was not on Alfred Bixby's manifest and she was not and never had been bound for Kingfisher Hill. Now that I came to think of it, she did not seem to have any suitcases with her and was carrying no bag or purse. She might have put herself among us to hide from somebody. I decided that, since I would never know, there was no point in speculating further.

Once inside, I saw that most of the coach's seats were empty. There was a simple explanation for this: many people had dropped back, eager to overhear my questioning of the woman with the unfinished face. Now that was concluded, everybody had remembered how cold they were. There was a build up of impatient bodies in the aisle behind me. 'Forward march,' someone muttered.

'Yes, do hurry, Catchpool,' said Poirot.

I followed his instruction and walked on along the aisle, only to come to a sharp halt a few moments later. In my peripheral vision, I had glimpsed a book that was sitting open on one of the coach's seats, with its cover facing upwards and its title clearly visible. Could it be . . . ? No, how could it possibly?

Exclamations of impatience erupted, not least from Poirot, as I stepped backwards, forcing those behind me to do the same, in order to get a closer look at the book's cover. I had indeed made a mistake. The title of the book was *Midnight Gathering*. I blinked and looked again. Yes, definitely *Midnight Gathering*. Yet I had been left with the powerful impression that I had seen two quite different words.

'What's that bunny up to?' I heard an American voice call out from the logjam that I had created in the aisle. 'We're all waiting here!'

'*Alors, on y va*, Catchpool,' said Poirot behind me.

A woman's hand reached out and snatched the book from the seat. Her swift action broke my trance, and I looked up. It was the rude woman with the diamond voice. She clutched the book close to her body and glared at me, as if by merely looking at it I might have tarnished it beyond repair.

'I'm sorry, I didn't mean to . . .' I mumbled. She glared more fiercely. Her face had much in common with her voice. With the addition of kindness and compassion to either or both, the effect would have been charming. I felt a jolt of recognition: this young lady, with her exquisitely sculpted cheekbones, delicate features, blue eyes and fine golden hair, was in every way my mother's favourite type—in a physical sense at least. All of the women she insisted I ought to want to marry looked more or less like this one, minus the furious grimace.

On the third finger of her left hand, the owner of *Midnight Gathering* wore a ring: a large ruby. *Sorry, Mother, too late,* I thought to myself. *She's already promised to another chap. I hope he's not the sensitive sort or he'll never survive the ordeal.*

I turned away from her and was about to advance along the coach's aisle when she did the most peculiar, petty thing. She moved as if it was her intention to replace the book in its former position, and then she very pointedly stopped just before doing so. She allowed the hand in which she held it to hover in mid-air above the seat between us. Her meaning was unambiguous, and she aimed a spiteful smile at me, knowing that I knew it. What an unpleasant woman! She was thoroughly enjoying her silent persecution of me. Her smile said, *I don't mind anybody else seeing the book— only you.* It was my punishment for having been a nosy nuisance. Well, there she perhaps made a fair point. I had probably peered rather intrusively.

Once Poirot and I were seated side by side towards the back of the coach, he said, 'Tell me, Catchpool, what did you see that was so interesting to you that you felt compelled to keep us all trapped in the aisle for so long?'

'It was nothing. I made a mistake. And it wasn't long—the whole thing was over in seconds.'

'What mistake?'

'Did you see the book that woman was reading?'

'The beautiful, angry woman?'

'Yes.'

'I saw a book, yes. She held it very tightly.'

'I think she feared I might tear it away from her,' I told him. 'That was what I wanted to get a second look at—her book. It was called *Midnight Gathering*. When I first saw it, I was certain I saw the words "Michael Gathercole" as the title. It must have been the M and the G.'

'Michael Gathercole.' Poirot sounded interested. 'The solicitor Michael Gathercole? That is curious.' He and I had become acquainted with Gathercole the previous year during an eventful stay in Clonakilty in the Irish Free State. 'Why would the name of Michael Gathercole, an unremarkable practitioner of the law, be the title of a book, Catchpool?'

'Well, it wouldn't. And it wasn't. I was mistaken. We needn't discuss it further.'

'It is more likely for Gathercole to have written a book and for his name to be on its cover as the author,' said Poirot.

'Gathercole has nothing to do with anything. Some other person wrote a book called *Midnight Gathering*.' *Please*, I thought, *let this be the end of it.*

'I think I comprehend why you saw a name that was not there, Catchpool—and why it was this name in particular.'

I waited.

'You are preoccupied with the unhappy woman who accuses you of impersonating Inspector Edward Catchpool of Scotland Yard. She tells us that she is not in need of help, but you disagree, and so you are alert to danger. To harm. *Alors*, in the part of your mind that does not perceive its own workings, you make a connection between this incident today and the events of last year in Clonakilty, where danger was present and terrible harm was done.'

'You're probably right. She hasn't got on yet, has she?'

'I cannot tell you, *mon ami*. I have not been keeping watch. Now, we have important matters to attend to.' He produced a small, folded piece of paper from his coat pocket. 'Read this before the coach departs. It is unwise to read while in motion. It makes for the bilious stomach.'

I took the paper from his hand, hoping that whatever was written on it would tell me why we were going to Kingfisher Hill. Instead, I found myself looking at an excessive number of the tiniest words I had ever seen on a page. 'What is this?' I asked. 'A set of instructions? For what?'

'Turn it over, Catchpool.'

I did so.

'Now do you see? Yes, instructions. Rules. The rules of a game played with a board and a number of round discs with eyes on them—the game of Peepers!'

'Eyes? Human eyes, or the letter "I"?'

'Eyes, Catchpool.' Poirot fluttered his own open and closed. He looked absurd, and I would have laughed had I not felt so frustrated.

'What's this about, Poirot? Why do you have the rules for a board game in your pocket?'

'I do not.' His green eyes glittered. 'You have them in your hand.'

'You know what I mean.'

'I have brought with me more than the rules of Peepers. I have too the game itself—it is in a box inside my suitcase!' He made this announcement triumphantly. 'I tell you to read the rules now because, as soon as possible, you and I will play Peepers together. We become the great experts and enthusiasts of Peepers! You will note that it says two players is the minimum number.'

'Please explain,' I said. 'I don't like board games. I detest them, in fact. And what does this Peepers game have to do with your determination to take me with you to the Kingfisher Hill Estate? Don't tell me the two are unconnected. I shan't believe you.'

'You do not detest Peepers, Catchpool. It is impossible, for you have never played it. Keep the open mind, I beg of you. Peepers is not like chess.'

'Is it like the Landlord's Game? I cannot abide that one.'

'You refer to the Monopoly game, *n'est-ce pas?*'

'Yes, I've heard it called that as well. Appalling waste of any intelligent person's time.'

'Ah! *Pourrait-il être plus parfait?*' Poirot had never looked more delighted. 'Those are the very words you must say when we arrive at the home of *la famille* Devonport!'

'Who are the Devonport family?' I asked.

'You must say it so that everybody hears it: that you *detest* the Monopoly game.'

'What are you talking about, Poirot? I'm not in the mood for'—I had been about to say 'games'—'your usual antics.'

'I do not have any antics, *mon ami*. Now, read the rules, please. Do not delay. Soon we will be moving.'

Sighing, I started to read. Or rather, I looked at the minuscule words and did my best to concentrate on them, but, hard as I tried, I could not take them in. I was about to say so when I heard Alfred Bixby's indignant voice rise above the general murmurs of conversation around me. 'I'm afraid this is your last chance, miss,' he said. I was in an aisle seat and so was he and I saw him as he leaned forward; he was sitting in one of the front seats immediately behind the driver and level with the doors, and was addressing his remarks to someone outside. 'No Kingfisher

Coach Company coach has ever been as much as a minute late in departing, and that's a tradition I intend to keep up! You're not the only pebble on the beach, young lady! I've got twenty-nine other passengers to think of who don't want to be late—one with an infant! So, are you joining us for the journey or not?'

'It's her,' I muttered as, a moment later, the woman with the unfinished face appeared in the aisle. She cowered there as if afraid Bixby might rise from his seat and give her a walloping. For his part, he looked as if he wished to do that very thing. 'Driver, close the doors,' he said. The driver did as instructed and started up the engine.

The woman, whose face showed traces of tears, stood immobile at the front of the coach. 'Take your seat, miss, please,' Bixby said to her. 'There's only one left. It's not as if there are dozens to choose between!' He rose to his feet and pointed. 'There—seventh row.'

'I think that perhaps you were right, Catchpool,' said Poirot. 'The behaviour of *la pauvre* begins to interest me. See how she thinks most intensively. There is a puzzle in her mind. Until she solves it, she cannot know . . .'

'Know what?'

'If she wishes to accompany us or not. Her indecision causes her great distress.'

As the disapproving noises of the other passengers started to rise in volume, the unhappy woman hurried forward and sat down. Seconds later, we set off, and it wasn't long before Bixby was on his feet again. He walked up and down the aisle, intent on telling every single one of us how deeply he regretted that we had very nearly had to experience a delay to what would undoubtedly turn out to be the most comfortable and blissful journey of our lives. I missed the odd word thanks to the excessively loud growl of the engine. Bixby made no mention of this unfortunate circumstance—no apology or explanation—and I deduced from his silence on the matter that the din would accompany us all the way to Kingfisher Hill.

He had taken his little speech almost to the back of the coach, and we had been travelling for no more than ten minutes, when I heard a loud squeal of distress. It had come from several rows in front of me. Immediately after the noise, the woman with the unfinished face appeared in the aisle again. 'Stop, please!' she called out to Bixby. Then she turned and addressed the driver, 'Stop this coach. I must . . . Please, open the doors. I cannot stay here, sitting there.' She pointed at her seat. 'I . . . unless someone will take my seat in exchange for theirs, you must let me get out.'

Bixby shook his head. His upper lip curled. 'Now, you listen to me, miss,' he said as he walked slowly towards her.

Poirot rose to his feet and put himself in the aisle between the woman and Bixby. 'Monsieur, if you will allow me to intervene?' he said with a bow.

Bixby looked uncertain, but he nodded. 'As long as it doesn't lead to a delay, M. Poirot. I'm sure you understand. These good people have homes and families waiting for them.'

'*Bien sûr.*' Poirot turned to face the woman. 'Mademoiselle, you wish to sit in a different seat?'

'Yes. I must. It's . . . it's important. I would not ask otherwise.'

A sharp, bright voice that I recognized only too well said, 'M. Poirot, please be kind enough to grant her wish and give her your seat. I should much rather sit beside a world-renowned detective than a gibbering fool. She's done nothing but gasp and shudder for the last fifteen minutes. It's fatiguing in the extreme.'

So *la pauvre mademoiselle*, as Poirot had called her, had been sitting beside the owner of that wretched book all this while! No wonder she didn't want to stay there any longer. She had probably made the mistake of glancing at the book's cover and received a thorough savaging.

'What is wrong with your seat?' Poirot asked. 'Why do you wish to move?'

She shook her head wildly. Then she cried out, 'You won't believe me, but . . . I will die if I sit there. Someone will kill me!'

'Please explain to me what you mean,' said Poirot. 'Who will kill you?'

'I don't know!' the woman sobbed. 'But I know that it's *this seat*. Next to the aisle, seven rows back, on the right. Only this seat, and none of the others. That's what he said. Nothing will happen to me if I sit anywhere else. Please, sir, let me take your place and you take mine?'

'Who said this to you?'

'The man! A man. I . . . I don't know who he was.'

'And if you sit in this particular seat, what did the man say would happen?' asked Poirot.

'Haven't I just told you?' the woman wailed. 'He said I'd be murdered! "Mark my words,"' he said. '"You heed this warning, or you won't get off that coach alive."'

CHAPTER 2

The Seat of Danger

After making her astonishing announcement, the woman with the unfinished face clammed up so determinedly that further debate proved impossible. Ignoring the outraged splutterings of Alfred Bixby ('The very idea, M. Poirot! A murder on a Kingfisher Coach Company motor-coach? Such a thing would never happen!'), Poirot ordered the driver to stop so that he could take the unhappy woman outside and attempt to get to the bottom of it all.

I had started down the aisle, intending to join them, but a sharp look from Poirot told me that I was not invited. The driver had parked the coach by the side of whatever road we were on. I am familiar with most parts of London, but I did not recognize this nondescript row of houses and shops. There was a milliner's, and one building that stood higher than the rest, with a large sign attached to its front that read 'McAllister & Son Ltd. Disposal of Premises—Clearing Sale of Entire Stocks at a Remarkable Discount'. None of us knew how long we would have to wait while Poirot conducted his private conversation outside. Whispering had broken out all over the coach, and the tone of most of it was anxious.

'Catchpool.'

I looked up to find Poirot in the aisle beside me.

'Come outside, please.'

'I thought you wanted me to—'

'Follow me.'

We walked around the side of the coach and found the cause of our delay hunched over and shivering by a wall.

'Here is Inspector Catchpool!' Poirot presented me to her as if I had not already introduced myself. As he did so, I realized that I was still holding the rules of Peepers in my hand. Hurriedly, I folded the paper and put it in my pocket.

She looked up as I approached. 'No,' she said. 'It wasn't him. It definitely wasn't him. I'm sorry, I must have got it all mixed up in my memory.'

'What's this about?' I asked Poirot. 'Who was not me?'

'The gentleman who told our friend here that she would be murdered if she sat in the seat immediately to the right of the aisle in the seventh row.'

'What? Are you suggesting—'

'I suggest nothing, Catchpool. Mademoiselle, did you not tell me *less than two minutes ago* that the man who gave you this warning was the very same man with whom you had conversed before we all boarded the motor-coach? This man, Inspector Catchpool, who stands before you now?'

'Yes, I said so. But as soon as I saw his face again, I knew I'd been wrong,' she wailed.

'There is a resemblance, though, between Catchpool and the man who said you would be murdered if you sat in that particular seat?'

'Yes, sir! They're both tall, with the same colour of hair. But . . . the other man had funny eyes.'

'Funny in what way?' asked Poirot.

'I don't know! I can't explain it.'

'Before, when we were waiting to depart, you demanded to know the identity of Inspector Catchpool, did you not?' The woman nodded.

'Was that because you thought then that he was the man who had given you this strange warning?'

'*No!*' she cried, apparently alarmed by the suggestion. 'No, I . . . I don't remember what I was thinking then. It seems so long ago.'

'Less than thirty minutes have passed since then,' Poirot told her. 'I do not find dishonesty impressive, mademoiselle, and there is something I find less impressive still: dishonesty that includes the pretence of the amnesia! You cannot confabulate an adequate story. *Eh bien*, it is most convenient for you, this sudden loss of memory!'

'I've been honest all my life,' the woman sobbed. I felt a pang of sympathy for her. 'There are things I do not wish to tell you—things I *cannot* tell you. The truth is . . . I did not think Inspector Catchpool could be who he claimed to be because . . . well, because I was afraid of what might happen to me! On the coach. It all seemed so unlikely.'

We waited for her to say more.

'I have been scared ever since the man warned me I

24

might be killed! Well, who wouldn't be? A complete stranger appears from nowhere to tell you you'll be murdered if you sit in a particular seat on a coach . . . Who wouldn't be scared when it came to it? That was why I was in the state I was in. And then *he* comes from nowhere'—she pointed at me—'and starts asking me questions. What was I supposed to think? I'll tell you what I thought. "Is this the man who's come to murder me if I sit in the wrong seat? Is he only pretending to be a policeman?" Not that I believed what the first man had told me, not entirely. That's to say, why on earth should anyone wish to kill me? I've never harmed a single soul.'

'And why do it in the enclosed space of a moving vehicle, surrounded by people who would surely witness the crime as it was committed?' Poirot murmured. 'Mademoiselle, please explain to me: if you believed there was even the smallest chance you would be killed, why did you not decline to board the motor-coach?'

At this question, she seemed to tremble with fear. 'I . . . I . . .'

'Calm yourself, mademoiselle. Tell the truth to Hercule Poirot and all will be well. That I promise you.'

'Well, I . . . I just didn't believe it could be true!' she said. Then a great torrent of words tumbled out of her. 'And my aunt's expecting me, and I'd bought my ticket and didn't want to let her down. She's expecting me this afternoon and she hasn't been well at all. I'm the only person she's got. And I told myself there'd be plenty of other seats for me to sit in, but I was scared even so. Who wouldn't be? And I said to myself, "Get on that coach, Joan," but I couldn't bring myself to do it. Then I spoke to you and Inspector Catchpool, M. Poirot, and you very kindly tried to help me but I didn't want to tell you what was troubling me. I didn't want to be a burden to anybody. And that's when I had my idea.'

'What idea?' I said.

She looked at me. 'I was too frightened to get on board when you did, so I stood aside. Then I thought, "What if I wait . . . and wait . . . and wait? That would be a good way to test it."'

'Ah!' said Poirot. 'Yes, I see. But please explain to Inspector Catchpool.'

She looked at me fleetingly, then averted her eyes. 'Well, I thought I could make it work out so that I was the very last to board,' she said. 'Then the seat of danger would most likely be taken and that would have been all the reassurance I'd have needed . . . but then I got on and that seat *wasn't* taken!'

I was not at all convinced by this. I said, 'If the threat was attached to that one seat and no other, you could have been the *first* onto the coach and sat anywhere else, quite easily. That, surely, would be the only certain way to avoid what in fact happened: boarding at the end and finding that the seat of danger, as you call it, was the only one left. Incidentally, how on earth is *that* mysterious circumstance explained? Even assuming there is somebody who wishes to kill you and planned to do it during our journey today, and his plan relied upon you sitting in that seat, our prospective murderer would have had to persuade all those who boarded before you to leave that seat unoccupied!'

'Calm yourself, Catchpool.' Poirot placed his hand on my arm.

'It's absurd, though,' I protested. 'I'd like to hear her explain why she didn't run a mile in the opposite direction as soon as she saw that the only seat still available was the very one she'd been warned about.'

'That is a pertinent question,' Poirot agreed. 'Mademoiselle?'

'I didn't feel as if I had a choice,' she whimpered. 'I wanted to get off, but the doors were locked and I didn't want to cause any more fuss than I had already. Everyone looked so angry. And . . . oh, you won't believe me, but when I saw that there was only one seat free and it was that one, I . . . well, I almost thought I must have dreamed the whole thing: the man, the warning, all of it.'

She shivered and pulled her green hat down, then left her hands over her ears as if to shield them from the cold. 'I felt as if I must be going mad! How could it be that I had been warned of this by a stranger, and now I was going to have to sit in that very seat? It seemed utterly impossible. As you say, Inspector Catchpool—he would have needed to arrange it so that all the other people sat in seats that weren't that one. How could anyone make that happen? They couldn't. They *wouldn't*. And so it seemed to me, only for a moment, that maybe I was losing my mind a little and had dreamed the whole thing. Or maybe it had been a . . . a premonition.'

'*Je comprends*, mademoiselle.' Poirot passed her a handkerchief so that she could wipe her streaming eyes. 'Because it did not make logical sense, you entered a state of panic and your brain ceased to function properly. If it was a premonition then perhaps you were doomed, and you did not have the energy in that moment to resist.'

'*Yes*, M. Poirot. You put it all so well.'

'Premonitions are usually of terrible things, *n'est-ce-pas?*' He smiled. 'Not merely of *warnings* of terrible things.'

She looked confused for a second, then said, 'I didn't think I could save myself, if it had been decided that I was going to die. But the fear wouldn't leave me alone and . . . well, that's why I stood up again, I suppose, and said what I said.'

'Indeed,' said Poirot briskly. 'What is your name? Your full name.'

'Joan Blythe.'

'And your aunt lives at Kingfisher Hill?'

'Pardon? Oh—no. I'm getting off two stops before that, at Cobham.'

I had not known that there were to be stops along the way, but now it made perfect sense. Many people on the coach looked highly unlikely to keep country homes at Kingfisher Hill or to be visiting anyone who did.

I was surprised to hear Poirot say next that he and I were also travelling to Cobham. A flash of warning in his eyes ordered me not to disagree. Did this mean that our plans had suddenly changed—and only because of Joan Blythe and her implausible story?

'What is the name and address of your aunt?' Poirot asked her.

'Oh, you mustn't go to her about this, M. Poirot. Please— she would worry dreadfully. This has nothing to do with her, nothing whatever. I beg of you, please do not involve her in this horrible affair.'

'You will tell me her name, at least?'

'I . . . I would rather not, if you don't mind, sir.'

'Do you live with your aunt?'

'I do. I have for nearly a year now.'

Was the new plan for us to leave the coach at Cobham and follow Joan Blythe to the home of her aunt? Or did Poirot merely wish her to believe that we might? I hoped for the latter; I was looking forward to seeing how the other half lived at Kingfisher Hill. The former, too, might have its advantages—chief among them that I might avoid having to learn the rules of Peepers.

Poirot took a new approach: 'Tell us about your encounter with the person who so closely resembles my friend Catchpool—assuming that this man who warned you was neither a premonition nor a figment of the imagination. When and where did you make his acquaintance?'

'I . . . I can't say that I remember when it was. Perhaps five or six days ago. As for where, well, it was . . . it was on the Charing Cross Road. That's where it was!'

I was certain that she was lying. Maybe not about all of it, but there was something to the way she said 'the Charing Cross Road'.

'I was in town to collect some things for my aunt. I came

out of a shop and there he was. I've already told you what he said to me.'

'How did he commence the conversation?' Poirot asked. 'Did he know your name?'

'Yes. I mean . . . well, he didn't say so or address me as Miss Blythe or anything, but he must have known who I was, mustn't he?'

'What did he say to you first of all?' Poirot asked.

'I don't remember.'

'Endeavour to recall the scene, mademoiselle. Often we can remember more than we imagine we will.'

'I can't, I just . . . All I can recall is him saying about me taking a trip on a motor-coach soon, and that I'd be wise to avoid sitting in the seat that was seven rows back and . . . well, as I've told you!'

Poirot seemed lost in thought. Eventually he said, '*Eh bien*, let us resume our travels.'

'No!' Joan Blythe's eyes widened in alarm. 'I cannot sit there, I've told you!'

Poirot turned to me. 'Catchpool?'

'You want me to swap places with Miss Blythe,' I said, resigned.

'*Non*. I could not allow you to take such a risk. I, Hercule Poirot, will sit in this seat of danger, and we will see if a killer reveals himself!'

I was surprised and grateful. In almost all minor matters, Poirot volunteered me to suffer inconveniences that he wished to avoid for himself. It was heartening to know that, in matters of life and death, he applied different rules.

I would have worried equally about him, of course, except that I did not believe for a moment that any murders were going to take place between here and Kingfisher Hill.

Poirot patted me on the back. 'It is decided! Miss Blythe, you will have my seat and I shall take yours. Catchpool, sit beside Miss Blythe and ensure that she arrives at Cobham unharmed. Can you do as I ask?'

I could—and it looked as if I was going to have to.

I wasn't the only one being churlish; Joan Blythe was no happier than I was about our new seating arrangements and she didn't try to hide it. Once we were on the move again, her fear seemed to leave her and her mood turned to moroseness. 'M. Poirot believes me even if you don't,' she said.

'I have not said that I don't.'

'I can see it on your face. You . . . you really do not look at all like him, now I come to think on it.' Her voice took on an apologetic tone as she said this. She sounded almost ashamed. Then, earnestly, she said, 'I'm not a liar, Inspector Catchpool.'

I wondered. That assertion could have two very different meanings. The first was obvious: 'I'm not a liar—by which I mean that I have told you nothing that is not true.' I favoured the second: 'I'm not a liar by nature or inclination, which is why it pains me to have needed to lie to you today.' Yes, if I had been putting good money on it, I would have plumped for that second meaning.

'May I ask you a question, Miss Blythe?' I said.

31

She closed her eyes. 'I'm so tired. I would rather not talk any longer.'

'One question. Then I'll leave you be.'

She gave a small nod.

'You said to Poirot, "My aunt's expecting me and I don't want to let her down." That was the reason you gave for being determined to travel despite the warning you were given. Then later, when Poirot asked you if you live with your aunt, you said that you did. You told him you had lived with her for nearly a year. Then you said, "She's expecting me this afternoon and she hasn't been well."'

'That is all *true*,' said Joan Blythe miserably. She sounded as if she was pleading with me—as if my asking about it could somehow render it untrue.

'You did not say, "She's expecting me *home*," as I think most people would who lived with an ailing relative. You sounded very much like a visitor who had promised to call on her sick aunt.'

'But I do live with her. *I do!* I'm not a bad person, Inspector. I've never committed a crime and I've always done my best to do what's right.'

'Shall I tell you what I think? I believe your fear is real and . . . yes, I believe it might well be mortal fear. And I'm sure you are as uncriminal as you claim to be, and perhaps you are in grave danger . . . but you've also told me some lies since you and I first met. That makes it much harder for me to help you, which is why I wish you would tell me the whole story—the unadorned truth.'

'Please, can we not talk any more? I'm so tired, I can

hardly keep my eyes open.' She leaned her head back and closed her eyes. Gradually, her breathing slowed. If she was not asleep, then she was certainly in the calmest state that I had seen her in since I first noticed her. This I found interesting: that her fear was for herself and nobody else. She was not worried that, by swapping seats with him, she might be endangering the life of Hercule Poirot. On one level this made perfect sense: she was afraid only of the very precise scenario that she had been advised to avoid— the particular combination of her and the seat of danger; these were the two things that must not come together. And she alone had been warned about the seat; no such 'premonition' had appeared to Poirot.

And yet she could have hurried onto the coach as soon as its doors opened and sat in any one of twenty-nine other seats. Assuming she had taken this mysterious stranger at his word, that would have been a way to ensure her safety, would it not? Here she was, sitting beside me and no longer in a state of agitation—behaving very much as if she believed her problem to be solved—when she could have boarded *before* me and sat herself down in this very seat before I chose this pair for Poirot and me.

It made no sense. Unless . . .

I imagined how Poirot might answer all of my points: she was afraid, as anyone would be, to enter a vehicle in which she might find someone intent on ending her life. She knew she needed to travel to her aunt, which was why she dithered and generally behaved as if she needed to get herself onto that coach yet very much did not wish to. Then when she saw others boarding before her, she had the idea of waiting to see which seat would be left if she were to be the last one on. Yes, that hypothesis worked.

And then she saw that the one unoccupied seat was the one about which she had been warned and . . . this was the part I could not fathom. How did she go from being too scared even to approach the vehicle and secure a 'safe' seat to being willing to sit in *the exact seat* about which she had been warned?

That was assuming that her whole story wasn't a lie from top to bottom—which I reminded myself might be the case.

By the time she opened her eyes again twenty minutes later, I had reflected further upon her story and had more questions for her. I started with a simple one: 'Why were you in London today?'

She turned and looked out of the window. We had left the busy streets behind and were now surrounded by greenery. Soon it would start to get dark.

'I was meeting a friend.'

'I can't help thinking it odd that you have no cases, no handbag—'

'That's not true. The driver took my case when he took the others. All my effects are inside it.'

'You had no suitcase when I first saw you.'

'It was there,' she insisted. 'I left it near some others. I . . . I must have walked away from it. If you don't believe me, wait until we get to Cobham. Then you'll see.'

'This mysterious stranger who approached you . . . what

was his mood and manner? Was he trying to help you or scare you?'

'Oh, I was scared, all right. Frightened out of my wits, I was.'

'Indeed, but can you know for certain that his *intention* was to scare you?'

She looked suddenly angry. 'I know it because that was exactly what he did—I've never felt a terror like that before, Inspector. So, yes, I'm certain!'

'What if he was trying to save your life?' I pressed the point. 'What if he *has*, in fact, saved your life? Have you considered that?'

'I don't want to consider anything. Please stop asking me questions that I can't . . . Please stop!'

'Of course.'

The last thing I wanted to do was to cause her further distress. My mind, however, remained fixed on the problem. If his aim had been to help her, it followed that he must have known several facts—that she was to travel on the two o'clock Kingfisher Company coach from London, and that another passenger on that same coach planned to kill her, but would or could only do so if she sat in the aisle seat of the seventh row. Did that mean that the stranger knew where Joan Blythe's would-be murderer planned to sit?

The woman with the diamond-bright voice and the golden hair . . .

How could this not have occurred to me before? She had been sitting right next to her and had spoken unkindly—and in a deliberately loud voice, it now seemed to me—about Joan Blythe before we all boarded the coach. Could she be the one with murderous intentions? Yet I had heard her say that she would much prefer to sit beside Poirot, and now she was doing just that.

'*Midnight Gathering*,' I murmured.

A small gasp came from beside me. I turned, and started at the sight of Joan Blythe's face. Her expression was the same one she had worn when I had first laid eyes upon her: one of utter horror, as if she had seen something ghastly. 'What's the matter?' I asked her.

'You . . . you said something . . . I did not quite hear it.' Despite our proximity to one another, the noise of the engine made it difficult to hear precisely what even one's immediate neighbour was saying if one was not also looking at them.

'"*Midnight Gathering*",' I repeated. 'Do those words mean something to you?'

'No. No, they don't,' she gabbled, frantic with fear. 'What are they? What is this about? Tell me what you mean! Why would you say those words?'

'The lady sitting next to you was reading a book called *Midnight Gathering*. She seemed to object to people looking at it—to me looking, at any rate. Given her temper, I wondered whether she might be the prospective killer your mysterious stranger had in mind.'

I said all of this with a slight smile. I fancied that a more lighthearted approach from me might coax her into perking up or even admitting that she'd invented the whole thing—though there was no doubt that her fear was real. I could hardly breathe for the weight of it, sitting between us.

And then, as quickly as it had sprung up, it seemed to dissolve into nothing. Her body sagged, her eyes dulled and she sounded almost bored as she said, 'I didn't see any book.'

I made a mental note of all this so that I could report it to Poirot later. Once Joan Blythe had learned that *Midnight Gathering* was the title of a book, she had lost interest in it entirely and been frightened no longer.

One thing I knew beyond doubt: the words 'midnight gathering' had great significance for Joan Blythe. For some reason that she was determined not to reveal, they filled her with terror.

CHAPTER 3

Richard Devonport's Letter

The rest of the journey as far as Cobham was uneventful, and there we made our first official stop. Joan Blythe aimed a dejected 'Thank you' in my direction before alighting. She had told me the truth about one thing, at least: she *did* have a suitcase with her. I watched as the driver returned it to her.

It was even colder here than in London. My breath froze in the air as I stood by the coach opposite an establishment called The Tartar Inn, waiting for Poirot. I got a shock when he finally joined me. He looked quite unwell, as if he had been drained of all vitality. Evidently he had suffered since he and I had last spoken.

'Goodness me, Poirot, was she as unpleasant as all that?'

'Was who unpleasant?'

'The lady with the book.' I looked to see if she was among those who were stepping off the coach now. Not all of them were asking the driver for their cases; some wanted only to stretch their legs. The Kingfisher Coach

Company's vehicles were not as comfortable as Alfred Bixby believed them to be.

'She had put away her book by the time I arrived at her side,' said Poirot. 'As to whether she is unpleasant . . . no ordinary word is adequate.'

'What do you mean?'

'She has given me much to think about, Catchpool. Do not ask me any more—not until I have had a chance to reflect and arrive at an opinion.' He produced a splutter of annoyance. 'One reason that I find travel so *désagréable* is that one cannot efficiently move the little grey cells of the brain when one's body is being thrown about in an infernally noisy contraption with wheels!'

'You look positively sickly,' I told him. A sudden panic gripped me. 'Poirot, have you consumed anything? Can we be certain that you haven't . . .'

He chuckled, and my dread dissolved. 'It is that you think Hercule Poirot has been poisoned by that devil, the elusive seventh-row killer? *Non*. I shall arrive at Kingfisher Hill in excellent physical condition.'

'So we are still going there?' I said. 'I thought our plans had changed.'

'Never. I merely wished to give to *la pauvre mademoiselle* that impression. Where is she?' Poirot looked around. 'Do you see her?'

'No. She must have hared off in a hurry. Damnation! I was on the lookout for you and took my eyes off her.'

'What did you hope to see? A motor car driven by the infirm aunt?' Poirot smiled. 'It is likely that no such person exists. Still, it was an interesting tale.' He nodded slowly, as if confirming something to himself.

Once the driver had reunited all the Cobham people with their suitcases, he and Alfred Bixby made for the Tartar Inn. Several of our number followed them, and Poirot and I decided that the chance of victuals and warmth was an unexpected blessing that we should not pass up. After the endurance test that had been our afternoon so far, I was ravenous.

We walked through the public bar into the Tartar's sitting room. 'Ah!' Poirot exclaimed with relief, pointing at an available table with chairs around it. It was the last one left. I hurried to secure it for us.

'Give me a comfortable chair over a bar stool any day of the week,' I said. 'I don't know how people sit on those things for as long as they do. If your legs are as long as mine it's a torture—and I am reliably informed that it's equally painful for those with legs that are too short. Here, with any luck, we'll get service at the table.'

'Keep your eyes on Monsieur Bixby,' Poirot said. 'If he ends up—how do you say it?—*in his glass*, he might permit his char-a-banc to depart without all of its passengers.'

Bixby looked as if he was nicely settled in, with a large measure of ale set before him. I hoped there was nobody waiting on the coach who was hoping to depart promptly.

'And, Catchpool?'

'Mm?'

'These might be preferable to wooden stools, but they are not comfortable chairs. Most decidedly not. When we reach Kingfisher Hill, *that* is when we will sit in the comfortable chairs.'

A waitress came over to take our order, after which refreshments were brought that were rather stodgy but no less satisfying for it. That was my feeling, anyway; Poirot made his usual murmurings about the atrocious English cuisine.

'Well, then, *mon ami*,' he said, once we had warmed up and dealt with our hunger and thirst. 'You have much to tell me, of that I am sure.'

Acquaintance with Hercule Poirot has done wonders for my memory. Knowing that he likes me to report to him in the most thorough fashion, I now always make a point of remembering and storing away every detail. I told him all about my conversation with Joan Blythe, from start to end, and he listened intently. When I had finished, he smiled and said, 'I do enjoy the way you construct these yarns of yours, Catchpool. Now tell me: did you have time also to peruse the rules of Peepers?'

He could not have deflated my spirits more thoroughly if he had tried.

'No, I did not. And it wasn't a yarn, it was a factual account of the conversation I had with Miss Blythe.'

'You do yourself a disservice, my friend. Your telling of it added so much to the bare facts. It added the mood and the interpretation, the fear that burned in her eyes in response to the words "midnight gathering"—ah, *c'est merveilleux*! You do indeed make the yarn. I did not intend the word in a derogatory sense.'

41

Mollified, I said, 'Can you make any more sense of it than I can, Poirot? When I told Joan Blythe that *Midnight Gathering* was the title of a book, she was no longer afraid. But that has to mean that the words frightened her for some other reason—one that had nothing to do with the book.'

'And why does this cause you the disquiet?' said Poirot.

'Well, because . . . because it still makes no sense even if that's true! Imagine this: imagine that the words "Tartar Inn" are enough to strike dread into your heart.'

'They are and evermore shall be,' said Poirot drily. 'Both the chairs and the food—'

'For whatever reason, those words frighten the life out of you. You have also been told that you will be murdered if you sit in a particular seat. Later, you discover that the woman in the adjacent seat had a book in her possession called *Tartar Inn*—the very words that fill you with terror—and your response is to become immediately *less* afraid, not more so? That makes no sense to me.'

Poirot nodded decisively. 'Now I see to where you are driving, Catchpool. Ah, yes, now I see. I agree, we cannot yet know the meaning of this detail. It is an unanswered question. Even so, much about the peculiar situation of Joan Blythe is clear.'

'No, it isn't,' I said. 'What on earth do you mean?'

'*Mon ami*, do you not understand that—?'

Our conversation was interrupted at this juncture by Alfred Bixby. 'M. Poirot, Inspector Catchpool. Not wishing to hurry you, but we're hoping to be on our way again before too long. There's a little chap whose mother tells me he's growing rather impatient. Mind you, if you ask me, it's her that's out of sorts and not the baby. He looks the picture of contentment to me, I haven't heard so much as a peep out of him—but I know better than to tell a doting mother that she's wrong about her own son. Hoha!'

I told Bixby that we would return to the coach in a moment. Once he had moved on to the next table of Kingfisher Coach Company passengers, some of whom were still eating, Poirot said, 'It is of great interest to me that the angry lady with the book was unduly harsh both to you and to Mademoiselle Joan. Great interest.'

'She did not tell you her name, then?'

He gave a small, mirthless laugh. 'No, Catchpool, she did not. She told me a considerable amount, but not her name—for reasons that will become obvious when I tell you what passed between us.'

'Evidently you did not enjoy your conversation with her. I'm eager to know why you disembarked at Cobham looking as if you had escaped the jaws of hell.'

'Very soon I will tell you why. First, though, if you will indulge me . . .'

'If you bring up the rules of Peepers again—'

'There is a letter I would like you to read,' Poirot said gravely, his hand lingering near the pocket of his waistcoat. 'A letter from a Monsieur Richard Devonport of Kingfisher Hill.'

'Hadn't we better get back to the coach? I shall read it once we—'

'Many of our fellow travellers are still at their tables. There is time,' Poirot said firmly. He passed me a neatly folded sheet of cream-coloured paper. 'I had not intended to show this to you until much later, but now I believe I must. I received this most extraordinary letter two days ago.'

This provoked my curiosity. I unfolded the paper and began to read:

Dear M. Poirot,

I should so much have liked to say that I am delighted to introduce myself to you. Your reputation is formidable, and, if things were different, nothing would give me greater pleasure than to begin with those very words. Sadly, nothing has delighted me since the tragedy that befell my family in December of last year and the grave injustices that have followed it—though whether those can correctly be termed injustices rather depends upon one's definition.

I am no doubt confusing you already, so let me start with more essential matters. My name is Richard Devonport. I am the younger son of Sidney Devonport, of whom I am sure you have heard. Recently I have also become the manager of his investments, though until the middle of last year I worked for the Treasury, and I would encourage you to approach any contacts you might have there if you are in need of a testimonial as to my good character.

On the sixth of December last year, my older brother

Frank Devonport (Francis was his name, but everybody knew him as Frank) was murdered in our family home at Kingfisher Hill. I loved my brother dearly, M. Poirot, and admired him greatly. He was a unique and brilliant man. Since his death, I am rather ashamed to admit that I have been wallowing in grief and confusion, and therefore until now have felt myself quite unable to take useful action such as requesting your help. I might have wallowed for many more months or even years, were there not a growing urgency about the case that cannot be ignored—at least not by me.

A woman has confessed to my brother's murder, M. Poirot. She confessed almost immediately and is to be hanged on the tenth of March. That does not give us much time, assuming you are willing to offer your assistance. I would of course reward you handsomely for your service. Your name has been in my mind for several weeks. Repeatedly I have thought to myself, 'Only a man of Hercule Poirot's calibre can save Helen now.'

Helen Acton: that is the name of the woman who insists that she is the murderer of my brother Frank. Perhaps you have read about the case in the newspapers. Helen is also my fiancée. In the normal run of things, that would mean that she and I are engaged to be married, but I regret to say that I have not lived in the realm of normality for some time now. I regret even more deeply to inform you that no facet of my involvement with Helen is straightforward or ordinary.

M. Poirot, it is well nigh impossible to explain

adequately in one letter all that you will need to know in order to prevent further tragedy. Most of it can wait, assuming you decide that you wish to help me. There is one more thing that I must tell you in this letter and it is the most important thing of all: Helen did not murder Frank. She is innocent of the crime for which she is to be hanged, completely innocent. At the same time, she is determined to tell anyone who will listen that she is guilty.

Why should anybody conduct themselves in such a perverse fashion and endanger their own life by doing so? I am convinced of two things: only the correct answer to that question can save Helen from Holloway Prison's gallows, and only you, M. Poirot, possess the necessary intellect and understanding of human nature to obtain that answer.

I hope and pray that you will look favourably upon this heartfelt plea and write to me without delay to inform me of your acceptance of this undertaking.

Yours most sincerely
Richard Devonport, Esq.'

'Good gracious,' I said. 'What a peculiar letter.'

'This is why I wanted you to see it,' said Poirot. 'When we left London, there was only one puzzle to be solved: the one presented here by Richard Devonport.' He took the letter from me, folded it and put it back in the pocket of his waistcoat. 'But since that time we have acquired two more mysteries. Each of these conundrums involves, as

Monsieur Devonport says in his letter, a tragedy or a possible tragedy—or both! The combination of all three gives to Poirot a heavy anxiety. I cannot carry the burden alone, Catchpool. It is too much.'

'Hold on,' I said. '*Three* mysteries?'

'*Oui, mon cher.* There is the betrothed of Richard Devonport, Mademoiselle Helen. Did she or did she not kill his brother Frank? If she did not, then why has she confessed? That is Mystery Number One. Then we have Number Two: the strange affair of Joan Blythe who speaks of mysterious warnings of her own future murder and is assuredly deeply afraid of something.'

'And Number Three?'

'You do not yet know of Number Three—although this will be remedied when we return to the char-a-banc. Now that Mademoiselle Joan no longer travels with us, we may sit together again.'

I guessed that Mystery Number Three had something to do with Poirot's conversation with *Midnight Gathering*'s owner: Diamond Voice, as I thought of her.

'There's a fourth puzzle,' I said as we stood up to leave the Tartar Inn.

Poirot rubbed the small of his back and winced, staring resentfully at his chair. 'What fourth?' he said.

'Peepers. What does it have to do with anything? I assume we're going to Kingfisher Hill to speak to Richard Devonport, but . . .'

'Yes, indeed. I responded *tout de suite* to the letter I have shown you and announced my willingness to intercede.

Monsieur Devonport suggested that I come to his Kingfisher Hill home at my earliest convenience, but he wanted to converse first by telephone. When we spoke, he told me that there would be a condition applied to my visit.'

'I hope you asked his permission to bring me with you,' I said.

Poirot regarded me sternly. 'I am not the *imbecile*, Catchpool. Though the same condition applies to you as it does to Poirot: we are not to mention to anyone in the household our true reason for being there.'

'What?' I said, astonished. 'Is this a joke?'

'*Non, c'est serieux.* I tell you in earnest: Frank Devonport's murder, the name of Helen Acton, Richard Devonport's belief in her innocence—none of these things are to be mentioned once we arrive at the house. The matter is never spoken of by the family. We must proceed as if we are unaware of it all.'

'That is beyond ludicrous,' I said.

'I do not find it as strange as you do,' said Poirot. 'When something so devastating and tragic has occurred, I can imagine that a certain *entente* might come to exist between the members of a family. Above all, Richard Devonport impressed upon me that no one must ever know that I was summoned by him. He believes that he would be disowned if that fact were to come to light.'

'Poirot, this is irregular in the extreme.'

'*Non, non*, Catchpool. You make the customary error.'

'What error?'

'Your belief that the ways and the habits, the anxieties

and the neuroses of the Devonports are so extraordinary. I would expect to find something similarly incomprehensible in most families. Think of the impositions of your own mother, Catchpool. The *vacances à la mer* that neither one of you enjoys—is that not both a senseless tradition and one that cannot be broken?'

My mother had nothing to do with the matter at hand and nor did the regular seaside holidays that she and I took together, so I ignored Poirot's provocative digression.

'Assuming that Richard Devonport is correct and his fiancée is innocent,' I said, 'how are you to uncover the truth if you're forbidden to refer to Frank Devonport's murder? The arrival of Hercule Poirot at the family home can have only one possible meaning. Everyone will know it.'

'Once more, you are in error, my friend. Poirot, he comes to Kingfisher Hill in order to meet the genius Sidney Devonport and his good friend Godfrey Laviolette. It is of those two men that I must pretend to be the ardent admirer! Sidney is the father of Richard and the late Frank, and Monsieur Laviolette is Richard's godfather.'

'And what have Sidney Devonport and Godfrey Laviolette done to earn your esteem?' I asked.

'You cannot guess?' Poirot chuckled. 'Together they invented . . .' He waved his finger at me, as if I were an orchestra and he the conductor.

I groaned. 'Not Peepers?'

'*Oui, c'est ça*. And this is where I enter the stage, as the passionate player of the board games. This I have been for many years!'

'Hardly,' I said, though I could not help smiling. Poirot sounded utterly convinced by his own story.

'It is so,' he said solemnly. 'Yet never before have I encountered a game so stimulating to the intellect as this creation of Messieurs Devonport and Laviolette. This, then, is why Poirot comes to Kingfisher Hill—as an enthusiast of the games, and to meet his heroes.'

'Yes, but chinwagging with some chaps about a silly game isn't going to get you anywhere, is it? How do you propose to advance your true purpose?'

'It is quite the challenge, is it not?' Poirot smiled. 'Partly it is the difficulty that appeals to me. I am not allowed to refer to the matter apart from when alone with Richard Devonport. Of course, it is possible that one or more people might mention the tragic affair to me of their own volition. If that were to happen, well, there I would have the opportunity.'

'But Richard Devonport told you it is never mentioned,' I reminded him.

'Among the family it is not. Sometimes it proves easier to confide in a stranger.'

'And if nobody confides? How—?'

'Stop the how-how, Catchpool. You come at it from the wrong direction. Why do you ask me *how* before I know how? When I have done it, that is when I will know how I did it. Then I will tell you.'

'You had better tell me the rules of Peepers as well, if I am to be required to play it and behave as if it brings me great joy.' I shuddered. 'I take it you know the rules—you are not relying on me to relay them to you?'

'I have made a brief study of them, yes. You do not need to know them or play the game.'

This was the most welcome news I had received in some time.

'I have had a better idea.' Poirot beamed at me. '*I* am the devotee of the board games. You, my friend, are a businessman.'

'A . . . Poirot, I am not any sort of businessman. I'm a police inspector.'

'I am aware of your profession, Catchpool. Sidney Devonport is not aware of it and does not need to be.'

'I refuse to pretend—'

'On the contrary.' Poirot gave me his most imperious look. 'You accept.' He seemed to soften slightly. 'Catchpool, I beseech you—do me this kind favour and affect an interest in the business of the games. You could ask such questions as how Peepers might be produced in large quantities so that, within five years, no home in the civilized world will be without a . . . a set? A copy? Is it correct to talk about a "copy" of a game?'

I was prevented from answering by the sound of footsteps, loud and fast. I turned and found Diamond Voice immediately behind me. She was breathless. Her mouth opened and closed but only gasps came out. If she had registered my presence, she showed no sign of it. Poirot was the sole focus of her attention.

'M. Poirot, come at once!' She reached out her hand to him and I saw a smear of blood on the side of it. 'Come!'

Poirot and I were already moving towards the Tartar Inn's doors, following her. 'To where, Mademoiselle?'

'The coach. Something terrible has happened. Oh, please, hurry!'

CHAPTER 4

The Missing Manifest

I had never seen Poirot move with such speed or urgency as he did now. My legs are longer than his, but still I had trouble keeping up. He started to murmur as we got closer to the motor-coach, and I made out the words '*Notre Seigneur*'.

I thought I knew what he was praying we would not find. I feared the same thing: that Joan Blythe had been murdered after all and that we were about to discover her body.

She had sat in the very seat against which she had been warned—not for long, but perhaps for long enough. I had not believed her dramatic story before; now that I was afraid for her, I found it easier to believe. But had I not seen Miss Blythe walk away from the coach? She could, of course, have returned to it while Poirot and I were inside the Tartar Inn. Why she would ever do such a thing was a different matter.

We found the coach half empty, with only about fifteen

people inside. The majority of those who were travelling on from Cobham must still have been at the Tartar Inn. I was dimly aware of the presence of the mother and baby as I climbed aboard and looked for signs of catastrophe.

The mother said something inconsequential about it being too cold on the coach and an inn being no place to take a baby. She was aggrieved and seemed not to care that blood had been spilled. 'Has something happened?' I demanded of her, for she was the only one looking in my direction.

'*Qu'est-ce qui se passe?*' Poirot asked a man seated near the front, who looked distinctly nonplussed. 'Somebody has been hurt?'

'I am not aware of anyone being hurt,' the man told him.

Diamond Voice was behind us. 'It's all the way at the back', she said. 'The last row.'

I rushed down the aisle, with Poirot behind me. 'She's not here, dead or alive,' I called out.

'Miss Blythe?' he said.

'Yes. There's no sign of her. Though there is something here . . .'

'What is it that you see?' Poirot panted. 'Move aside, please.'

I squeezed myself into the space between the back two rows of seats on the left, and we surveyed the item together. It was a piece of fabric that looked as if it had been torn from an item of clothing or a fancy tablecloth. It was white, around seven inches by four inches, with lace along one edge. It was smeared with spots of blood.

'Madame!' Poirot waved the bloodstained fragment in the direction of an elderly lady who was sitting immediately in front of where it had been left. 'Can you tell me how this piece of petticoat came to reside here?'

The woman recoiled. 'I'm sure I don't know anything about it, and I would rather not have anything so unpleasant as blood or torn clothing brought to my attention, thank you very much.'

'You must tell Hercule Poirot, madame: how many people have been to this part of the vehicle since we stopped? I will need you to make the identifications—'

'You have no right to order me around, you pompous little man! I know of no Erckle . . . whoever it was you said.'

'*Hercule Poirot*. I am he, madame. Please tell me at once: has a person been attacked? Have you witnessed, since we stopped here, any acts of violence or anything untoward that might cause blood to be shed?'

'I most certainly have not.'

By now, everyone on the coach was muttering about the fuss Poirot was making. It made me suddenly aware that, when we had first boarded the coach in our state of panic, all the seated passengers had appeared perfectly calm—as if nothing out of the ordinary had happened in our absence.

'*Mesdames et messieurs!*' Poirot called all those present to attention, and asked them the same questions: did they see anything? Had anyone been attacked or harmed? Where had this bloodstained material come from?

One by one, everybody told us the same thing: they had

seen nothing alarming or worthy of note. Several people had walked up and down the aisle at various points, wishing to stretch their legs without venturing out into the eye-stinging wind, but there had been no acts of violence—at least none that had been observed. Everyone agreed that the young lady who had caused a silly fuss earlier by insisting on swapping seats with someone had most certainly not returned to the motor-coach since leaving it.

That, in isolation, was comforting—Joan Blythe was most likely unharmed. I was on the point of suggesting that we look around outside, in case the attack had taken place there, when Poirot grabbed me by my wrist and whispered fiercely, 'Catchpool.'

'What is it?'

'Regard!' With the hand that was not clutching my arm, he made a gesture that was intended to suggest the coach in its entirety. 'Poirot has been the incredible fool! Do you not see? Then look now! Observe what is missing, what is not here to be observed!'

'How can I—?'

'*Elle aussi est disparue—notre tueuse,*' he said in an urgent whisper. 'She was behind us, urging us forward in haste, and now she is not here. Of course!' He made a low moaning sound as he sank into a seat in the back row.

'Did you just say . . . ? Doesn't the word "*tueuse*" mean "killer"?'

'Please lower your voice, Catchpool. A killer belonging to the female sex. *Oui.*'

'Then I understood you correctly. You said that our killer

has also disappeared. To whom are you referring? Oh, do you mean . . . ?' It struck me only then that he must have been talking about Diamond Voice, who was no longer with us. Where had she got to?

'You do not comprehend what has transpired, Catchpool? We have been tricked. Forever will I curse my own stupidity!'

'Why did you call her a killer?' I asked him. 'Was she the one planning to murder Joan Blythe? How?'

Poirot looked bewildered. He raised a hand to stop me. 'You bark at the improper tree, as so often, Catchpool. No, she did not plan to kill Miss Blythe. She planned to kill somebody else, and then she put her plan into action.'

I was struck dumb momentarily. Was this what Poirot had meant by Mystery Number Three? Other passengers were boarding and the coach was filling with loud chatter, but still I lowered my voice and whispered as quietly as I could. 'Do you mean to tell me that the woman who savaged me for glancing at her book has committed a murder? Whom did she murder? And how did you come to know of her crime?'

'She told me.'

'She *told* you?'

Poirot nodded. 'I do not know the name of her victim. I thought, when she first began to tell her tale, that it could not be true. What person who has deliberately taken the life of another would describe her crime in such detail to none other than Hercule Poirot, who is known to bring murderers to justice? That was the argument I made to myself—but now, see what has happened! She is vanished! I do not know her name or where to find her. Wherever she is, she is laughing at me, Catchpool. She outwitted me.'

'Excuse me, gentlemen.' A head popped up from the row in front of us. It was a young man with dark hair and a continental accent—Italian, perhaps. 'I could not help but hear a little of what you say, and . . . if you will forgive the intrusion, I believe I have information that may interest you.'

We made noises of encouragement. On this occasion being overheard might have worked to our advantage, though I resolved to make sure to stick to a whisper in future, at least until the growl of the engine started up again.

'You are M. Hercule Poirot?' asked the Italian.

'I am,' Poirot confirmed.

'A lady was asking Mr Bixby many questions about you after you went outside.' The man gestured towards the Tartar Inn. 'A very beautiful lady with golden hair. She asked to where you were travelling.' He turned to me. 'You too—the inspector.'

'As I thought!' Poirot murmured. 'What was Monsieur Bixby's response to her enquiry?'

'He told her that you and the inspector were going all the way to the final stop: Kingfisher Hill.'

'Was any more said?'

'Yes, it was. She asked if he might have made a mistake. He told her that he had not, and showed her the passenger manifest. After that, she seemed to believe him.'

'This is most useful information,' said Poirot. 'And it gives to me the idea. We must hope and pray . . . Monsieur Bixby!'

'Yes, M. Poirot?' Our host hurried towards us down the aisle. 'How can I be of assistance? We'll be on our way again in a jiffy!'

'Do you have the passenger manifest?' Poirot asked him.

'Ho, yes. Naturally.'

'Might I see it?'

'It's funny, M. Poirot—you're the second person who has asked for it. There was a young lady—'

'Yes, yes. Please let me have it without delay.'

'Of course. Of course.' Bixby reached into his pocket. He blinked, then frowned. 'I don't seem to . . . Why, it's not here. I don't understand. I certainly had it when we stopped.'

'Might it be somewhere else among your effects?' Poirot asked him. 'I would be most grateful if you could make a more thorough search.'

'I shall do that very thing,' said Bixby, straight-backed and solemn, as if making a vow that would bind him for years to come.

Poirot and I watched as he looked up and down the coach, in all of his pockets and under every seat. Finally, he had no choice but to admit defeat. 'I can't understand it,' he said. 'It appears that the passenger manifest is well and truly missing.'

Far from discouraging him, this news seemed to fill Poirot with energy. 'Monsieur Bixby,' he said, 'Is it possible that the young lady who asked to see the manifest when we stopped at Cobham *never gave it back to you?*'

'Well, I . . . I can't see why she'd want to keep it.' Bixby looked to his left and right, then down at the ground. Then he turned in a small circle, as if he might find his list of passengers near his feet.

'Spare yourself the futile effort,' Poirot advised. 'You will not find it. The young lady who took it from you has vanished and taken it with her. You do not, I suppose, know her name?'

'I'm afraid I don't,' said Bixby. 'It will be on the list.'

'Yes, and that is precisely why we no longer have it. Do you have another copy somewhere? In your offices in London, perhaps?'

'No, I don't. Everyone had paid in full, so I only needed the list to bring with me today, so that I could check them all off—and to hand in to the gate porter once we arrive at Kingfisher Hill.'

'I assume you do not know, then, if the woman who has made off with the list originally planned to disembark at Cobham?'

Alfred Bixby shook his head. He looked stricken. 'I wish I could be of more help, M. Poirot. Then he brightened and said, 'Now that I ponder on it, I'd wager that her plan at the outset was to stay on after Cobham. Yes, I am sure of it! When we first came to a stop, she stayed in her seat. I was standing at the front, so I noticed who was getting off and who was staying put, and she didn't move a muscle. I don't mind telling you, M. Poirot, that I noticed her *in*

60

particular.' Bixby narrowed his eyes and nodded meaning-fully. 'What red-blooded fellow wouldn't notice her, if you catch my drift? Ho-ha!'

'Indeed so,' said Poirot.

'She had no plans to go anywhere, but she must have spotted something. She was looking out of the window and must have seen something that . . . well, it altered her bearing completely. Yes, I'd swear to that. She went from seeming rather languid, I suppose you'd say, to being all of a hurry and a fluster: enquiring about your journey, then asking to see the passenger list with everybody's destinations on it. She didn't believe me when I told her that you and Inspector Catchpool were staying on until Kingfisher Hill. So I showed her the proof in black and white, and her response made no sense to me. She said, "So they aren't being met off the coach by their dear old friend."'

'Thank you, Monsieur Bixby,' said Poirot. 'All is as I surmised. Only then, after her exchange with you, did she decide to make Cobham her destination. Until then, she had planned to travel further.'

Once Poirot and I had reclaimed our original pair of seats and the coach had started on the second leg of its journey, I pestered him for answers. I was unclear as to whether our three mysteries were still outstanding and unresolved as far as he was concerned, or whether he had formed some conclusions. Also, I wanted to know what he had done with the white fabric with the blood spots on it.

'The fabric is unimportant,' he told me. 'It was a decoy, that is all.'

'So you *have* solved one of the mysteries?'

'Catchpool, use your sense. How could I have made progress in the matter of Richard Devonport's murdered brother when I am trapped in an icy char-a-banc with no way of getting at the relevant information?'

'All right, don't get your hackles up. You were talking as if you knew something.'

'And Joan Blythe, who is so dreadfully afraid of who knows what—how could I have solved that problem, when she told me so little of the truth?'

'I agree. I did not intend to imply that—'

Poirot spoke over my words. 'As for the other woman, the one who takes a close interest in our itinerary: I do not know whom she murdered or why she chose to tell Poirot, but I *do* know why she took a hat pin or some other sharp object from her reticule and stabbed it into her thumb. You noticed, I dare say, that there was blood on the side of her hand when she came to find us at the inn? The manner in which she said, "Quickly, come at once!"—it was to make us believe that the blood belonged to somebody else, someone in urgent need of help if it was not already too late. *Mais non*, it was not the blood of a victim who waited, injured or deceased, in this vehicle, as she led us to suppose. *It was her own blood, from a self-inflicted wound.*'

'Why would she do that?' I asked.

'You will understand why when I tell you the alarming story that she told me. Now, however, I am trying to tell you what little I know and how I know it.'

He paused, then took up the story again: 'I had told her

that I was travelling only as far as Cobham. This was the same incorrect information that I had given to Mademoiselle Joan, and an instinct warned me that I would be unwise to share too much of the truth with The Sculpture.'

'The Sculpture?'

'Yes, that is how I think of her, since I do not know her name.'

'I think of her as Diamond Voice,' I told him.

'*Je comprends,*' he said. 'It did not strike you that she had the bone structure that could have been the work of a master sculptor? The cheekbones and jaw and forehead that all look as if carved with the greatest skill and delicacy from the rarest and finest of materials? Hers is a powerful beauty. You did not notice?'

'I might have if her manner had been less rebarbative.'

'From what material her character is carved, I prefer not to speculate. This is another reason why my instincts urged me to withhold from her our true destination. She told me that she was going as far as Martyr's Green.'

'Then she would have seen us get back on the coach and known that you had lied to her.'

'Indeed. When I told her that I intended to alight at Cobham, my aim was not to mislead her successfully. As you say, that could not have worked. No, I merely wished to see how she would respond.'

I frowned. 'Why would she respond differently to hearing that you were going to Cobham rather than Kingfisher Hill?'

A small smile appeared on Poirot's face. 'Surely you know

why, Catchpool,' he said. 'The answer could not be more apparent.'

'Not to me, I'm afraid. And you're evidently not ready to tell me. So how *did* she respond to your Cobham lie?'

'Not in the manner that I expected. And then came the even more unexpected: her story of the murder she had committed. I do not think she had resolved in advance to confess, but she wished to goad me. To assert her superiority. She could not resist the urge to boast about her . . . achievement.' He sighed.

'So she is not merely a murderess, but proud of it?'

'Proud is too happy a feeling for her, I think. She was . . . angry. Her fury, it burned—a slow, cold burn, the way ice sears the skin—though I cannot think which of my contributions to our dialogue had this effect upon her. Her boasting felt like an attack: on me and on all that I symbolize to her. Most interesting is that she told me of this crime she had committed only after I had told her that I was leaving the coach at Cobham.'

'Why is that relevant?' I asked.

'You still do not see what is quite evident, *mon ami*? Here is what happened: when you and I disembarked, The Sculpture assumed that our journey was over and she would not see Hercule Poirot again. She remained seated. Languid, as Monsieur Bixby tells us. But then, what does she see through the window of the motor-coach? The two of us, entering the Tartar Inn and remaining there for some time. Where, she wonders, is the dear old friend of whom I had spoken with such affection? Would he not be waiting to take us *immediatement* to his home? She correctly calculates that something does not fit. When Bixby and his list of passengers confirms this, she knows that Poirot, he has misled her! He will return to the coach, she realizes, and now that she has confessed to a crime, what if he follows her when she alights at the next stop, Martyr's Green?'

'So she hooked it with the passenger manifest on which her name was listed, making it vastly less likely that we would ever identify her, and . . .' I broke off.

'Catchpool?' Poirot peered at me. 'Why do you stop like the unwound clock?'

'*Now* I see!' I exclaimed. 'She wanted to make a dash for it at Cobham, but knew that was risky. If she'd left the coach in the ordinary way, she could not have guaranteed that we wouldn't pick that moment to exit the Tartar Inn and catch her in the act. You might have followed her home, and once you had her address—'

'*Précisément*! The jig, it would be up! It would have been only a matter of time before I knew also her name and the name of her victim. All of this she foresaw. What, then, does she do, *la bête ingénieuse*? She must ensure that she has the means of the undetected getaway, *non*? She tears a piece from her petticoat, cuts her own hand and allows the blood to stain the cloth, which she then leaves at the back of the motor-coach. Then she stages her little dramatic production at the Tartar Inn, and she succeeds in fooling us. We rush at once back to the vehicle. Once she sees that our attention is fully occupied by the false clue that she has left for us, she makes her exit—'

'Knowing that by the time we've tumbled to the truth, it will be too late for us to follow her!'

'Never is it too late,' said Poirot with grim determination. 'I will find her. Oh, yes. Even with not one morsel of a clue, I am determined. Wherever is Martyr's Green, she will be known to somebody in its environs.'

'We're not getting off there, are we?'

'No. We will continue to Kingfisher Hill as planned,' said Poirot. 'It is Helen Acton for whom time is in the shortest supply: there are only sixteen days between now and the tenth of March, her execution date. If she is innocent, we must establish the facts that will lead to her life being saved. After that, I will turn my attention to finding The Sculpture.'

My attention, meanwhile, was elsewhere.

'Poirot?'

'Yes, Catchpool?'

'Does it not strike you as peculiar that among our fellow passengers there should be two women who tell us the most unlikely tales, both on the theme of murder, while we are on our way to investigate another murder?'

'It requires an explanation, *certainement*. Fortunately, everything that requires an explanation has one. We simply need to find it. Tell me, how are you able to claim that the confession of The Sculpture was an unlikely tale? You did not hear it.'

'Well, what did she say? I'm sure you remember every detail.'

Poirot's eyes were fixed on the back of the seat in front of him. He gazed at it, as if at a far-off horizon. 'They were the most abstract of details, and yet she told me a great deal. So much, and yet so little.'

'I should very much like to hear those abstract details,' I said, preparing myself for disappointment. Poirot rarely provides timely answers to my most pressing questions.

I was astonished when he said, 'Of course, my friend. I shall tell you without further delay everything that is known to me about what we have called our Mystery Number Three.' And he proceeded to do so. What follows is my rendering of the conversation that took place between Hercule Poirot and the woman to whom we had given so many names: the woman with the book, Diamond Voice, The Sculpture and—the one I found most chilling to contemplate—*la bête ingénieuse.*

CHAPTER 5

An Abstract Confession

'Do you suppose she's an actress?'

Poirot's conversation with The Sculpture had begun with this bold question from her. He understood her to be talking about Joan Blythe.

She continued, 'Could anyone really be as witless as she seems? I think that was a performance from start to finish.'

'You do not believe her fear and unhappiness are real?'

'No. She was playing a part. As for why this particular part . . . that is puzzling. I can't think that he would have asked her to, but perhaps he did.'

'"He"?' Poirot enquired.

'Mr Bixby. I think several people on this coach are actors and not real customers of his business.'

'Might I ask why you say so, mademoiselle?'

'How many times has he so far drawn to your attention the fact that *every seat is taken*, that one cannot leave it

68

to chance if one wants to travel with the Kingfisher Coach Company, that one must book a place well in advance of the desired date of travel? Well?'

'Many times,' Poirot admitted.

'It's all we have heard from him since we arrived at the meeting point in London, and he sounds very much as if he is reciting well-rehearsed lines. Think about this, M. Poirot: why would he bother to tell us at all, if it were true? We would have seen with our own eyes that the coach was full, yet he mentions it over and over again. When a fact is both evident and true—and when nobody is attempting to deny its truth—one does not feel the need to insist upon it so relentlessly. Think what obnoxious company he is, how he inflicts himself on his customers, who cannot possibly want to listen to his endless, tedious speeches. Does he strike you as a man who would do well in business? Of course not. Which means that he must have paid at least half of us passengers to pretend to be paying customers in order to make his firm seem far more successful than it is.'

'I see no evidence for this,' Poirot told her. 'Though it is an interesting possibility.'

'When I say "actors", I don't mean that they've played King Lear at the Fortune Theatre or anything like that,' The Sculpture said impatiently. 'I'm talking about a few shillings stuffed into the pockets of Mr Bixby's acquaintances. It's hardly the most demanding role, is it? Sit on a coach and allow those around you to assume you paid for your ticket as they paid for theirs.'

'If you are correct, why have we heard none of our fellow passengers volubly proclaiming the wonders of Kingfisher coaches and announcing their intention never to travel with any other companies?'

'It's hard to hear much of anything above the noise of the wretched engine,' said The Sculpture. 'It is perfectly possible that Mr Bixby would not have thought to make that additional request of them. You credit him with too much imagination.'

'I might say the same to you, mademoiselle. The arranging of the passengers who are not really passengers—this is a scheme that would take more imaginative flair than our Monsieur Bixby possesses.'

'Again, we disagree,' she said coolly. 'Desperation breeds imagination, even in the minds of the dull-witted.'

'May I ask you a question, mademoiselle? Have I done something to offend you?'

She laughed. 'It is I who have offended you, M. Poirot, whether you realize it or not. You scour my every remark in search of the sycophantic adoration you have come to expect and find none of it. This mystifies you. You are so accustomed to receiving fawning praise that anyone who speaks to you as if they are your equal is interpreted as hostile.'

'You would not define your attitude towards me as hostility?' Poirot enquired in an even tone.

The Sculpture turned in her seat so that she could look more squarely at him. She seemed to him to be weighing up whether or not to say something. 'Your life's work—the

70

mission that you have set for yourself, this vocation that I'm sure you see as noble and sacred—is to bring murderers to justice. Would you agree?'

Poirot considered it. Finally he said, 'I have never thought of myself as having a mission. There are things I believe to be sacred: the right of all men, women and children to live the lives that have been given to them, and not to have those lives ended too soon by violence. The importance of restraining the disorderly elements in a society, so that the world is safe for those who wish only to live in peace and according to the law.' He nodded, satisfied with his answer. 'That is the purpose of Hercule Poirot. The bringing of murderers to justice is a necessary part of it, I grant you, but all that I do, I do for the sake of what I cherish and wish to preserve. It is a terrible tragedy to have as one's foremost purpose in life a preoccupation with that which one detests.'

Poirot had noticed that, as he was speaking, The Sculpture was growing increasingly agitated. When he stopped, her relief was visible. She said abruptly, 'You are revered all over the world for your achievements, but I find your presumption rather naïve—this belief that you can keep everybody safe from harm, that murders should be prevented and murderers dispatched to the gallows.' She waved her hand dismissively. 'Murder is not the only or even the greatest harm one person can do to another, and besides, it cannot be stopped.'

Poirot regarded her gravely. 'Now I begin to wonder if you are the actress, mademoiselle. Do you seriously suggest that we should allow murderers to commit their crimes without interference?'

'It is not a question of allowing,' she said, reminding Poirot of a school mistress giving much-needed instruction to her least favourite pupil. 'They will do it anyway, as they always have. What is your solution? That we kill all the murderers? If that is your answer, then you *do* believe that sometimes the taking of a life is justified. Many murderers would agree with you. I suppose you are travelling to the Kingfisher Hill Estate?'

'No—only to Cobham.' Poirot added an embellishment: 'There my friend Catchpool and I will be met by a very dear old friend of mine, whom I first met as a young *policier* . . .' He stopped and smiled. 'But you do not want to know about my dear friend. Why do you ask if I am going to Kingfisher Hill? Are you?'

'No,' she snapped as if horrified by the idea. 'I'm getting off at Martyr's Green. I thought perhaps you might have a country residence at Kingfisher Hill. It would suit you.'

'I do not.'

'All the puffed-up lords and ladies there would doubtless agree with you that the powerful should be able to put to death anyone who displeases them and call it by the name of justice.'

'You assume the worst of me, mademoiselle.' Thoughtfully, Poirot looked at her. 'At the same time—yes—you endeavour to present yourself in your least favourable aspect. Why? I do not believe that you truly, in your heart, approve of murder.'

'I am not impartial in this matter.' She hesitated for a moment before saying, 'Oh, caution be damned! I will say it, and there will be nothing you can do, since we are strangers to one another.' Lowering her voice, she said, 'I have committed a murder myself.'

'Please, tell me it is not so,' said Poirot. He wished he could believe that he had misheard her over the angry rumble of the engine, but he knew precisely what she had said. And then she said it again:

'It is quite true.' She mouthed the words at him: 'I killed a man.' Then, speaking once more at a normal volume, she said, 'Nobody could have stopped me. I did it deliberately and was quite set on doing it. Afterwards, I felt no regret. I am glad I did it. There, now you know. What are you going to say to *that*?' She smiled at him coldly.

'Whom did you kill, and why?' he asked.

'If I told you that, you might be able to identify the case in question. I cannot risk it. I've only confided as much as I have in the hope that you might make an effort to see things in the round—from the murderer's point of view as well as the victim's.'

'The murderer's point of view,' Poirot repeated slowly. It was hard to produce any words in response to her extraordinary proclamations.

'Yes!' The sullen veneer was gone and she sounded suddenly jubilant. Leaning in towards Poirot, she whispered as if sharing a delicious secret, 'Once you have killed a person, it becomes infuriating to contemplate the likes of Hercule Poirot, with their determination to eradicate and punish something that is an ever-present part of life and always will be—something that, in certain circumstances, can feel natural and even beneficial. The wish to kill is simply a part of human nature.'

Poirot was deeply unsettled. 'May God forgive you for these callous words,' he muttered.

'Well, there's no need to resort to hysterics,' said The Sculpture. 'And remember, God has far more than words to forgive me for. I can't help noticing that you assume He shares your principles—of course you do. What if I were to tell you that He thoroughly approves of murder, and that is why it's as prevalent as it is throughout the world?'

Poirot thumped his knee with his closed fist. 'You are teasing Poirot. You must be. No one could say these things and believe them.'

She seemed to take pity on him. 'You are right: I am teasing you a little. I do not approve of murder in all or even most cases. There, is that better? I do wonder, though . . . do you and your sort really need to make quite such a fuss about it when it happens?'

'Ah, so you admit that you jest!' said Poirot. '*Merci à Dieu!* Then you have committed no murder.'

She frowned. 'I did not say that. I have committed *one* murder. It was my only choice in the situation. I do not approve of killing people all over the place any more than you do, but in this instance it was necessary and I . . . yes, I will say it: I am glad I did it.'

Poirot was starting to feel a sickness in the pit of his stomach. It was clear that she was playing a game of sorts, but he feared that, on the essential point, she spoke the truth.

'I can tell you a little of the story if you would like to hear it,' she offered. 'I think I can render it in the abstract so that there is no chance of you finding me after today. I should actually enjoy hearing the thoughts of an expert on murder. It is something I have never been able to discuss with anybody and . . . well, you are not just anybody, M. Poirot. What do you say? Shall I tell you all about it?'

Poirot shuddered, which seemed to thrill her. 'Oh, do say yes! I feel that you and I might have the most fruitful discussion on a topic that is of great import to us both. Such exchanges are rare.' Now her manner was that of an over-excited child, though Poirot expected that the cold, gloating superiority might return at any moment.

Feeling complicit in something monstrous—yet telling himself, as comfort, that it might all be lies, or that she might unintentionally let slip information that he could later use in the service of justice—Poirot said, 'Very well. Tell me your story. Let me ask first one question: in your bag, you have a book, *n'est-ce pas*? A book by the name of *Midnight Gathering*.'

'Ah! Has your prying inspector friend filed a report on me? Why do you ask about the book?'

'You are fond of crime, mademoiselle. Did you steal it?'

'Did I steal *Midnight Gathering*? What an extraordinary question. No, I did not.'

'And if I do not believe you?'

She searched his face carefully, then gave an uncertain

laugh. 'If you must know, the copy in my bag was originally a gift from . . . Well, I shall tell you no more, as it's none of your concern. If you are not careful, I will change my mind about telling you anything at all. You have one last chance, M. Poirot. I can't think why you should wish to distract me with talk of books when I'm eager to tell you about'—she lowered her voice—'the man I killed. Shall I give up on you as a hopeless scatterbrain, or may we speak of murder now?'

With little appetite for what he imagined he was about to hear, Poirot invited her to tell her story.

The Sculpture took a few moments to prepare herself. Then, as soon as she began to speak, her face lost its hard contours and her eyes filled with tears. For the first time since making her acquaintance, Poirot was able to see her as someone capable of feeling pain, not only of inflicting it on others.

'There was a man,' she said. 'I loved him very much. More than I have ever loved anyone, before or since. And I murdered him.'

She pulled a handkerchief out of her bag and dabbed at the corners of her eyes. 'Those are the bare bones of it. There is more, of course, but never forget, when you hear the rest of the story, that my love for him was as strong when I killed him as it had always been. It was in no way diminished.'

'This is not as unusual as you may think,' Poirot told her. 'Some murderers hate their victims, but those who kill loved ones are as numerous, and suffer all the more.'

'Yes, I can see that.'

'Did he betray you?'

'Yes. At least, I think he did. He would have denied it, and you would probably have taken his side. I think most people would. In any case, his betrayal of me was not the reason I killed him. I did it for . . . for the sake of my family. You see, he'd committed a crime. He stole from my father—a lot of money. Afterwards, my father insisted that I was to have nothing to do with him. He was evil, an enemy, no longer allowed to come to our house. My parents were not willing to see him or speak to him. They refused to listen to his side of the story—and do not tell me, M. Poirot, that a thief cannot have a defence that is worth attending to!'

'I had not thought to do so. However, your father's anger is understandable, is it not? I take it he trusted this young man?'

'He would have trusted him with his life before the theft of the money, yes. The thing is, the man would never have stolen from anybody if the predicament had not been dire. His theft was not for his own benefit. He worked for my father, you see, and my father rewarded him generously. But while he was doing well financially, he had a friend whose family had lost everything when the stock market fell apart two years ago. *Everything.* And his father was sick and very old, and . . . well, our thief, if we can call him that, could not bear to see to his friend consumed by the fear of ending up in a workhouse—and, being in charge of my father's investments and business affairs, he thought

. . . well, he *knew* that my father would not miss a certain amount. There would be no hardship for our family, none at all, if he were to take this money and give it to his friend. So that was what he did. But he didn't see it as *giving* the money, or even theft, really. He saw it as a loan, and that was certainly the spirit in which his friend accepted it. It was offered not as charity but in the form of a challenge.'

'What challenge?' asked Poirot.

'The thief and his friend were great believers in enterprise. In that respect, they and my father were all cut from the same cloth. They all believe—believed—that anyone can start with not very much at all and go on to build empires and create riches beyond the wildest dreams of most. The agreement was that the friend would borrow the money and use it shrewdly to produce more money.'

'With the stock market as it was two years ago—as it remains to this day—this is not so easy,' Poirot observed.

'No, it is not,' The Sculpture agreed. 'But the man I loved had always had this belief that . . . well, that absolutely anything was possible, and that if you wanted something enough, you could always find a way to get it. He made other people believe it too. I wish . . .' She looked down at her hands. 'I wish you could meet him, M. Poirot.'

'You say this now, yet only minutes ago you said you were glad to have killed him.'

'I mean that I wish you could have met him before . . . while we were all still happy.'

'I see. Please, continue with your story,' said Poirot.

She dabbed at her eyes a few times, then said, 'Together, the thief and his friend made several extremely risky investments. Most of them failed, as risky investments tend to, but one succeeded beyond anything they had hoped for— and it was enough to enable the thief to put back quite a bit more than he had stolen from my family, and for his friend to ensure a life of comfort for himself and his elderly father. There was plenty left over too, and the thief and his friend used it to set up some excellent schools in which pupils are treated with respect—as if they are proper people who matter. That ought to happen in ordinary schools but rarely does. And then . . .' She choked on the words.

Poirot noted that it was not easy for her to tell this story and wondered why she was putting herself through the ordeal. 'Then the thief made a terrible mistake: he told my father, told both of my parents, what he had done.'

'Ah! He preferred the honesty to the concealment.'

'He was an honourable man, M. Poirot. He valued integrity above all else and had always planned to tell the truth as soon as the money was returned. He knew how my father admired him and could not allow that admiration to continue based on a false premise. Of course, he anticipated that my father would be angry at first, but he believed that if he apologized and described the precise circumstances . . .' She was speaking quickly now, and breathlessly, as if trapped in a nightmare she was desperate to escape, appearing to have forgotten that these were past events. 'He thought that if he made it clear that he would not have rested easy until every single penny taken had been returned . . . But my father is an unforgiving man, and my mother agrees with my father about *everything*. She cannot even bring herself to say that a book or play that he likes is not to her taste, for fear of one of his tyrannical outbursts. And so the thief was . . .' She stopped and covered her mouth with her handkerchief. 'Sent away. He was banished.'

'Did your parents know that you loved this man?'

'Oh, yes—but it made no difference to them. My father told me that if I had any more contact with him, ever, I would be cut off without so much as a farthing to my name. I believed at the time that I had no choice but to obey.'

'May I ask . . . before these events occurred, were you betrothed to this thief?'

'No.' She looked amused. 'What makes you ask that?'

'I just wondered. I notice that you wear the ruby ring now . . .'

'Oh, that. Yes, well . . . I am now engaged to be married.'

'To somebody else?'

The Sculpture made an impatient noise. 'I like to think that I am a person of the highest determination and ingenuity, but even I could not succeed in marrying a dead man.'

'The man you intend to marry . . . do you love him?'

Her expression grew solemn and studious, as if she was concentrating on something important. 'Yes, I do. If you're about to ask me if I love my fiancé as much as I loved the thief—though goodness knows why you're interested in that when it is hardly the point of my story—the answer is no, I do not. I hope this doesn't disturb you, M. Poirot. It does not pose a problem for me. My love for the thief could not have been more different in character, and the thief is *dead*.' This last emphasized word provoked more tears. 'I tried as hard as I could to persuade Daddy to forgive him, but it proved impossible! Have you ever tried to persuade a stubborn man that he is wrong and, at the same time, to convince him that you do not disagree with him at all?'

'Is that not a contradiction?' asked Poirot. 'Nobody could do both at once.'

'Oh, yes, they could. *I* did. I said, "Come now, Daddy, you are so wise and fair—everybody knows this. And the wise and fair thing to do here is exactly as you have done so far, because it would have been a mistake to be too lenient when you first heard of the offence. But now, the *next* correct thing to do is to give him another chance, as I'm sure you'll be the first to see. I'm sure, in fact, that you have had this brilliant idea yourself and do not need me to suggest it to you." I thought if I poured on the flattery . . .' She sighed. 'That strategy sometimes works with Daddy.'

'But this time it did not?'

'No. It only made him angrier. He made ever more extravagant threats against me: I would be penniless, without a home, without kin. If I betrayed our family by siding with a thief, he would revenge himself upon me in terrible ways that I could not imagine.'

'You were afraid of him?'

'I *am* afraid of him.'

'I still do not see the shape of the picture,' said Poirot. 'You loved the thief, and you do not love your father. I wonder if, by your own assessment, you have perhaps murdered the wrong person.'

'Oh, I love Daddy,' said The Sculpture. 'I fear him, dislike him and cannot bear to be in his company, but I think I also love him in a way. Mother too, though she sat demurely by his side and uttered not one word of protest when he made those vile threats to me.'

'Even so,' said Poirot, 'what you have told me is not the story of a daughter who murdered her father. Anyone would expect him to be your chosen victim, *non?*—not the thief whom you so loved and admired. What, I beg to know, can have led you to kill him?'

'What indeed?' she said, as if the two of them were trying to solve the puzzle together. 'All of the events I have described took place between November of 1929 and March of last year, when the thief was cut off by my parents. Idiotically, I believed that I had no choice but to cut him off, too. I was not asked for my opinions: they were given to me by my father—forced upon me! The thief was the human embodiment of evil and must under no circumstances be allowed back into our lives. I must stop loving him—my father said those words to me. "You do not love him any more. You see him for the enemy he is. He is dangerous. He is wicked. He is a threat to this family." I had to endure hours of it. Daddy would not leave me alone until he was confident that he had removed all my thoughts and feelings and replaced them with his own. And then five months later, in August of last year, my mother was told that she was dying.'

'I am sorry, mademoiselle.'

'She is still alive now, but she won't be for very long,' said The Sculpture. 'She has an illness that is causing her to waste away before our eyes.' In a falsely bright and jocular tone, The Sculpture went on, 'Anyway, you will never guess what happened two weeks after she received her diagnosis, M. Poirot. It was *such* a delightful surprise. My father summoned me to the room he infuriatingly calls . . .' She stopped. Whatever her father called the room, she had decided against sharing it. 'To his study,' she said instead. 'He told me that, now Mother had only limited time left, the thief was to be readmitted to the fold.'

'I see.' Poirot had not expected the story to take this turn.

'A *delightful* surprise,' she repeated, her voice throbbing with anger. 'I'm afraid I cannot tell you why my mother's impending death made it so urgent for us all to forgive the thief and invite him back into our lives—not without revealing certain particulars that I would prefer not to discuss. All that matters is that Mother and Daddy were suddenly ready to welcome him back—and I was told that I must do the same. And so back he came, and once again he was put in charge of managing my father's business affairs. Not only was I ordered to forgive him—that would have been bad enough—but I was also told that I would be cut off and reviled forever if I did not participate in the pretence that *nothing had ever happened*.'

'*Incroyable*,' Poirot breathed.

'Quite,' said The Sculpture. 'I'm so glad you agree.'

'Please go on, mademoiselle.'

'There's not much more to say. The thief was happy to return and happy to collude in the pretence that nothing unfortunate had ever occurred. He came back at the end of August . . . and a little over three months later, I killed him. There. That's the whole story. The End.'

'Why did you kill him? When the motive is unknown, the story is always incomplete. It is missing its most vital part.'

The Sculpture laughed. 'Pardon me, but have I been under a misapprehension all this time? Are you not Hercule Poirot? Surely I do not need to tell you why I did it. You're the great detective, are you not? I would hate to deprive you of the opportunity to work it out for yourself. I have told you everything that you need to know. Why do *you* think I killed this man I loved so much?'

'You said before that you did it for the sake of your family . . . and I tell you again that this makes no sense to me. To kill a man you love so much for the sake of . . . who? Your parents? You claim to love them also—but did you not love the thief more?'

'Oh, yes. Much more.'

'Then why kill him, and why for your family's sake? Explain it to me.'

'No,' said The Sculpture. 'Making sense of things like this is what you're supposed to be good at. And . . . what if it's not true that I did it for the sake of my parents?'

'You told me that was your reason.'

'Then you should ask yourself: why would I say that if it wasn't true?'

'Mademoiselle, you confuse me greatly.'

'That is certainly not my intention,' she said solemnly. Her eyes, once again, were full of tears. 'I shall be quiet and say no more.'

Poirot wondered if he had ever before had such a discomforting exchange with another human being. He tried every tactic he could think of to persuade her to explain herself, but her resolve did not weaken, and he arrived at Cobham with his bewilderment fully intact.

CHAPTER 6

The Devonport Family

My first impression of Kingfisher Hill was that it was well protected from the outside world. Even knowing it was a private estate, I had not anticipated the outer walls that seemed higher than any wall would need to be in the middle of the tranquil English countryside.

There were two sets of gates with a reinforced look about them, as if designed to withstand a siege. These had to be traversed if we were to cross over from the common outskirts to the hallowed ground within. I remarked to Poirot that it was as if someone feared imminent invasion.

'Not from Hercule Poirot!' He laughed at his own witticism. 'He is an invited guest. Though there is perhaps somebody at Kingfisher Hill who has much to fear now that I am here.'

'You mean . . .'

'Whoever murdered Frank Devonport, if it was not Helen Acton. Ah, you do *not* see. Richard Devonport did not say so in as many words, but he wishes me to find out which member of his family, or which family friend or servant, killed his brother.'

'Those are the possibilities, are they?' I asked. 'Do you know who was there when the death occurred?'

'Apart from Richard himself and Helen Acton, there were seven people in the house when Frank Devonport died: Sidney Devonport, the head of the household; his wife Lilian, their daughter Daisy, her fiancé Oliver Prowd, a servant called Winnifred Lord, and two very good friends of the family—Americans—Godfrey and Verna Laviolette.'

We were through both sets of gates at last, but another step was required, it seemed, before we could think of ourselves as having arrived. The driver parked the coach in a gravelled area where another blue and orange Kingfisher Coach Company coach was already parked, along with an impressive row of motorcars. Most of these had people leaning against them, some of whom were waving. A number of our fellow passengers waved back at them. I wondered if anyone was waiting to collect Poirot and me, and, if not, how long we would need to walk before we reached the Devonport home. Alfred Bixby hopped out of the vehicle to speak to the occupant of a small rectangular booth: a square-faced man whose hairline started halfway down his forehead. This man's job, apparently, was to question those intent on crossing the Kingfisher Hill Estate's threshold.

'Does Richard Devonport believe that one of those seven people killed his brother?' I asked Poirot. 'I suppose he must. Did he give you a steer as to who he thinks it might be?'

'No. And you suppose incorrectly, Catchpool. It is true that if Helen Acton did not commit the murder and neither did Richard Devonport himself, then it must have been one of those seven other people. There exist other possibilities too.'

'That Richard killed his brother Frank—of course.'

'*Oui*. Or that Helen Acton did so, and Richard Devonport refuses to allow this explanation because it so distresses him.'

'That strikes me as more likely,' I said. 'If Devonport himself committed the crime, he'd be a damned fool to solicit the presence of one of the finest crime-solving minds . . .' Seeing Poirot's grimace, I went back and corrected my error: '*The* finest crime-solving mind in England.'

'I have rarely met a man or woman who was not capable of being the damned fool, should the conditions prove favourable for such a thing,' said Poirot. 'Richard Devonport might be not as clever as he believes himself to be.' He leaned forward to watch what appeared to be an altercation between the hirsute man in the booth and Alfred Bixby.

'He wishes to see the list of people Monsieur Bixby brings to Kingfisher Hill, *mais ce n'est pas possible*. The passenger manifest has been stolen. Thanks to The Sculpture, we must now all be detained unnecessarily.'

I exhaled slowly. 'Does this not feel like the longest journey you have ever undertaken?' I said.

'Ah, we are saved! *Le portier*, he has taken pity on our friend Bixby.'

Soon we were able to alight and retrieve our suitcases. 'What now?' I asked as everybody else made their way towards the motorcars and their drivers. Enthusiastic greetings echoed in the air.

'Someone will drive us to the house,' said Poirot. 'It is one of the furthest from the entrance gates. Richard Devonport told me we would be collected.'

'I hope our collector arrives soon,' I said. 'A person can only take so much exposure to this weather before hypothermia sets in.'

'Console yourself with the knowledge that it is worse for me than for you, *mon ami*. My constitution was not designed for such conditions. You Englishmen enjoy the heroic freezing to death.'

'That is quite untrue.'

'Do not tell me that you have not heard of Robert Falcon Scott and his doomed voyage to the Antarctic—was he not an Englishman?'

'Poirot . . . about the book, *Midnight Gathering*.'

'What of it?'

'Why did you ask her about it? The Sculpture. And why ask if she stole it?'

'She did not steal it. Though if she had, it might explain why she was so enraged to find a Scotland Yard inspector casting his eye over it. But no—it was a gift. From whom, I cannot tell you. She came close to revealing the name of the person, and then she stopped. She did not want Poirot to know. The book interests me greatly, Catchpool. Not its contents, you understand. Whether it is an adventure story,

a romance or *un policier*, it matters not. Her anger when you looked at its cover . . . I do not believe it had anything to do with *Midnight Gathering* itself. It was all about its significance in the mind of The Sculpture and nothing to do with the words on its pages.'

'So whoever gave it to her is what makes it significant? Her relationship with the giver of the gift?'

Poirot shook his head and said, 'I owe a debt of gratitude to our old friend Michael Gathercole. If it were not for the initials of his name, that book would have made no impression on you. But thanks to his initials being the same and the 'Gather' in his family name, *c'est parfait*.' He did a little bounce on his heels.

'What is perfect?' I asked.

'The precise way in which events unfold and provide us with the most wonderful opportunity,' Poirot answered enigmatically.

At that moment an American voice said, '"S'cuse me, gentlemen. Moysiers Poy-row and Catchpool?' I turned to find a tall, thin man in a long overcoat standing behind me. It was hard to make out his age. He might have been elderly or as young as forty. He had skin as smooth as if it had been gone over with a steam-iron and thick white hair that jutted out at odd angles. He made me think of a hedgehog, though he was the opposite of small and round— an elongated hedgehog. Anyone making a satirical sketch of him would certainly show his nose as ending in a sharp point, though in reality it did not.

We shook his hand.

'It's a pleasure to meet you, gentlemen. I'm Godfrey Laviolette. I can't tell you how thrilled Sidney and I are to have you here. We've been bursting with excitement, I can tell you. Follow me—the car's over here. I'll bet you're both looking forward to filling your bellies! Nothing like a cold wind to sharpen the appetite, eh? Well, we'll have dinner, and then . . .' He broke off and laughed. 'I said to Sidney, the ladies will have to pardon us gentlemen this evening after dinner. Our conversation's bound to bore them to sleep. They don't understand our passion for our little baby. They say things like, "It's only a game," but we know different—right, gentlemen? With me and Sidney and the two of you all being just nuts about Peepers, we're going to have ourselves a ball!'

So the 'little baby' Laviolette had referred to was that wretched game. A groan rose up inside me but I managed to swallow it before it did any damage to our cover story. Did my supposed business interest in the potential of Peepers necessarily imply that I was 'just nuts' about it? Shouldn't a businessman have a more detached attitude to a prospective investment? It would have been useful to have more precise instructions from Poirot about the part I was supposed to be playing.

Laviolette drove us along a series of wide roads. It was dark and there were trees everywhere, so we were not able to get a good look at the Kingfisher Hill houses, though the distribution of illuminated windows told me that each of these buildings was much larger and had more space around it than the houses I was used to seeing in London.

The effect, as we drove along, was attractive in an unreal sort of way: small and large rectangles of golden light that seemed to dangle from tree branches in the distance or balance upon them.

Godfrey Laviolette had embarked upon the story of his long association with Sidney Devonport. He had prefaced this narration by informing us that, when Peepers had overtaken chess as the most celebrated board game in the world, everyone would clamour to know how its two inventors had first met. It was a complicated tale that centred around an elemental metal called vanadium that was readily available in southern Africa. This chemical element had made the fortunes of both Sidney Devonport and Godfrey Laviolette some twenty years ago. Laviolette explained— and managed to do so without sounding boastful—that he and Sidney Devonport had both more than tripled their wealth since their vanadium-finding days, and without doing a day's work.

'You did not suffer in the recent calamity that befell the stock market?' Poirot asked.

'No, Moysier Poy-row, happily we did not. We are cautious men, Sidney and I. We share an appetite not only for board games but also for small and measured risks. We have never gone crazy in the way that other fellows do. We prefer the slow and steady approach. And this might amuse you: we also share a taste in houses! Sidney's house here, where we're going now—my wife Verna and I used to own it! We sold it to Sidney and Lilian. They were looking at a different house and were nearly ready to sign on the dotted line when we said, "Hey, why not buy ours? We've been thinking of selling." So they did!'

'You did not like living here?' Poirot asked him.

'Oh, we *loved* it at first,' Laviolette said. 'Tell me, gentlemen, how do you find the Kingfisher Hill Estate so far? I know it's dark and you can't see much, but are you getting a feel for the place? Paradise, right? You can't see it now but over there, that's where the Victor Marklew swimming pool is. Sublime! Oh, we're in paradise, all right—and that's the very reason that Verna and I decided to sell up and move on. There's nothing worse than living in paradise and knowing that one day it's bound to change for the worse. It kind of became my motto, if you want to know: never let anybody ruin your paradise. Not if you can help it. Sadly, a lot of the time people *can't* help it. But oftentimes, they can!' He seemed unsure of whether he wanted to put forward a message of hope or one of despair.

'Has the Kingfisher Hill Estate deteriorated since you sold your house?' said Poirot.

'Now there's a fascinating question, Moysier Poy-row. Oh, yes, a fascinating question. Oh, boy! Let's just say that *I* think it has, and my wife Verna agrees, and we're glad we don't own property here any more. Don't tell Sidney and Lilian I said that, will you? I wouldn't want them to think they'd ended up the worse off for our little deal.' He laughed. 'They would disagree with me, anyhow. We're persnickety about different things, Sidney and me—very different things. Sometimes he loves the things I hate and

I love the things he hates. It's why we work so well together on Peepers: two completely different minds. It means we end up not missing any of the angles, if you follow me.'

Silently I begged him not to give us the specifics of either his own approach to the game or Sidney Devonport's.

'The funny thing is, Verna and I are here all the time now, staying as guests in the house we used to own, visiting our good friends! And you know what amuses me? I can enjoy Kingfisher Hill again now in a way that I couldn't in the months before we sold the house to Sidney and Lilian. Now that I'm only a guest and there's nothing here that's *mine*, I don't worry about my paradise being ruined. I can enjoy what there is to be enjoyed without any anxiety.'

'What were you afraid would happen?' I asked. 'Were houses here being sold to the wrong sort of people?'

Godfrey Laviolette laughed loudly. 'Who are the wrong sort of people, Mr Catchpool?'

'In my estimation? Well . . . criminals and people of unsavoury character. I assumed that because of the exclusive nature of the estate, the walls and the gates—'

'You assumed that I must believe in right and wrong sorts of people? Oh, no, not me! You want to know what I think? I don't think you can divide people into categories like that. People do it all the time, sure, but it leads to lazy thinking. If you want to get anywhere, you need to pay attention to the particular man—and you'd be wise to pay more attention to who he wants to be in the future than to who he's been in the past. Even criminals must not

94

all be tarred with the same brush.' Godfrey Laviolette warmed to his theme. 'Some deny their crimes to their dying day, while others confess and try to make good.'

I reflected that, if Godfrey Laviolette was determined to believe only in independent people and not in collections or sorts of people, then it was no wonder that he had sold his house at Kingfisher Hill. Having neighbours in a place like this struck me as significantly different from living on an ordinary street. If you were closeted away behind high walls together, and all sharing the same swimming pool, tennis facilities and golf course . . . well, even with 900 or more acres in which to spread out, that might create a feeling of communality that some would find oppressive. I knew that I personally would dislike the 'club' flavour of this sort of estate and the sense of shared identity that went with it.

After about ten minutes of driving, Godfrey Laviolette took us through another set of gates. A squat, heavy-set mansion with nothing graceful about its design loomed at the end of a straight driveway. Two sturdy lamp-posts stood on either side of it. There was something vaguely threatening about the arrangement, as if the two posts were henchmen ready to intervene on behalf of the house if necessary.

As we drove closer, I saw that the building was not one big, square block of stone, as it had at first appeared. Rather, it had a more layered structure, like a square with a wider rectangle behind it, and a third and even wider rectangle behind that.

'Home at last!' said our driver. 'Welcome to Little Key. Or as I probably should have said: "*Former* home at last".'

I made suitably amused noises, while Poirot made no effort to laugh or smile. Laviolette said, 'Gentlemen, I will admit it: I make that joke whenever I come here, whether I'm alone or in company. I need to work on some more original material—don't you think so, Moysier Poy-row?'

'The name of the house is Little Key?' Poirot asked. 'That is an interesting name.'

'It is—but I can't take credit for it. When Verna and I lived here the place was called Kingfisher's Rest. The new name is much more intriguing, don't you think? Little Key—now there's a house name with an *atmosphere*.'

'So, *la famille* Devonport—'

'It comes from a quote from a story by Charles Dickens, or so I'm told: "a very little key will open a very heavy door", and I don't mind telling you, Moysier Poy-row, the door of this house sure is heavy! Say, do me a favour: don't mention the change of name to Sidney. Or to Lilian.'

'Do you mean to suggest that M. and Mme Devonport do not know the name of their own house?' said Poirot. 'Surely it was they who changed the name to Little Key, after they bought the house from you.'

His eminently reasonable enquiry received no response; at that moment the front door opened and a barrel-shaped man with a broad smile on his face was striding towards us. 'Ah, here comes Sidney!' said Godfrey Laviolette. I could not tell if I was imagining it, but it seemed to me that he was relieved that our conversation on the subject of the house's name had been interrupted.

Immediately to the right of the front door was a large stone plaque with the words 'Little Key' carved into it. The stone was pale grey and the carved grooves of the letters had been painted black. Sidney and Lilian Devonport cannot have failed to notice the prominently displayed new name of their home, I decided. I tried to come up with a likely reason why the change of name should be ruled as unmentionable by Godfrey Laviolette, but no plausible theories presented themselves.

One of the first things I noticed about Sidney Devonport, as he repeatedly slapped me on the back by way of welcome, was that his smile took on an increasingly intimidating air the more one saw of it. It had a mask-like quality: mouth half-open, corners upturned, frozen in a past moment of guffawing joviality that was no longer applicable. I had been in the man's company for less than three minutes when I decided that I would find it difficult to look at his fossilized face for much longer.

'Welcome, welcome!' he said, now giving Poirot's back the same pummelling treatment that I had just endured.

'It is most kind of you to invite us as your guests to Kingfisher Hill . . . and to Little Key,' said Poirot, indicating the stone plaque. I looked at Godfrey Laviolette, who flinched slightly. Sidney Devonport showed no sign of discomfort as he ushered us into his house, telling us that we must be ready for a glass of something, not to mention a hot meal. As we followed him inside, however, his order of priorities changed and the conversation turned to Peepers.

What happened, in fact, was astonishing to me, though I expect Poirot found it easier to comprehend than I did, being somewhat obsessive himself. As we stood in the house's resplendent circular entrance hall—with its balconied landing that started at the top of the curved staircase and wrapped almost the full 360 degrees around, and its excessively long chandelier that looked like a narrowing avalanche of crystal daggers descending from on high—both Sidney Devonport and Godfrey Laviolette started to speak rapidly and often simultaneously (so that at times it was impossible to hear what either said) about Peepers and what they believed was its rival, the Monopoly game. Devonport insisted that Peepers was far superior and would triumph, while Laviolette was afraid that its prospects might be crushed by the fast-growing popularity of the other game. They held forth on the subject as if they might never stop, and I formed the distinct impression that this was an argument they had regularly. Every so often one of them would look at Poirot and me expectantly as if hoping we would take their side, although at other moments it was as if they had entirely forgotten that we were present. Poirot made a range of appropriate-sounding though non-partisan noises, and I did my best to give the impression that I agreed with whoever had aimed a remark at me most recently. On and on it went, with Devonport proclaiming that the people behind the other game ought to be thinking about making changes before it was too late, or else how were its players to know whether it was promoting the unrestricted accumulation of property as a worthy aspiration or taking a critical position on such monopolization?

Laviolette countered that there were already many inventors and re-inventors of different versions of Monopoly, or the Landlord's Game as some called it, and everyone thought that the moral message of the game was whatever they wanted it to be. This complication, argued Laviolette, had done nothing to make a dent in its popularity. Ah, said Devonport, but that did not mean that further complication needed to be introduced to Peepers in the hope of currying favour, especially not when the undeniable appeal of the rival game was in spite of its unclear moral message and not because of it.

On and on it went. Before I had met these two men, it would never have occurred to me that there might be so much to be said about a board game. I wondered several times if this little scene was a test or joke of some kind, but it went on for too long and each point was made with too much zeal for that to be credible.

I nearly cried out in gratitude when the conversation was interrupted by the arrival of a stooped, bony woman. The pale skin of her face and hands looked as dry as fine paper and was covered with lines and creases as if every inch of her had been folded and unfolded hundreds of times. Her eyes were large and grey, and her hair was a darker grey—the colour of iron filings—and arranged in an artful pile atop her head. She came in on the arm of a young man of around thirty, leaning heavily on him as they shuffled slowly towards us. Sidney Devonport hurried over to her and supported her other side. 'Poirot, Catchpool— may I introduce my wife, Lilian, and my son Richard?'

Hearing that she was his wife was a shock to me. From appearances, she could have been his grandmother. She looked at us with dull eyes and a flat expression, and barely greeted us at all.

As for the young man . . . so this was Richard Devonport. He was short and compact with fair hair and a capacious face that seemed to swallow up his small, unremarkable features. As I shook his hand, he gave me a pointed look that seemed to contain both fear and a threat. If I could have done so without giving the game away, I would have put him out of his misery by promising not to breathe a word about the letter he had sent to Poirot.

'Oh, are they here?' a dry and rather aloof-sounding American voice called out from above our heads.

We looked up to the balconied landing, where stood a slim, auburn-haired woman of around sixty years of age. Her bright red lipstick, gold high-heeled shoes, green silk dress and strings of pearls made her easily the most glamorous among us, and her posture looked practised—as if she had rehearsed for hours how to look perfectly elegant in front of the mirror.

'Verna!' said Godfrey Laviolette, opening his arms as if inviting her to leap into them. 'Yes, they're here: Moysier Poy-row and Mr Catchpool.'

I nearly corrected him from Mr to Inspector, then

remembered that I was supposed to be a businessman, not a policeman.

'Gentlemen, say hello to Verna, the love of my life! My dear love, my dear wife!' Godfrey Laviolette, at the foot of the stairs, performed a complicated and undoubtedly celebratory forward-rolling gesture with his right arm, as if Verna descending the staircase were a special occasion.

'Godfrey, don't embarrass these poor fellows,' she said as she swept towards us, her long dress swishing around her feet like waves in a green sea. 'Are we all here, then? Am I the last?'

'Not quite,' said her husband. 'Oliver took his motorcar out to fetch Daisy, who telephoned with some sort of emergency. She seems to have gotten herself into a scrape. He said he would probably be a while.'

'Oh, not too long, I shouldn't think,' said Sidney. 'They will arrive in good time for dinner, which in any case will be delayed because . . .' He stopped, glanced sideways at his wife and obviously decided not to continue.

'Because *what*?' Verna Laviolette sounded ready to be aggravated, whatever the answer turned out to be. Sidney Devonport did not appear to notice her rudeness. With his ossified smile-mask still in place, he was now staring at his son, Richard, who gave a small nod. Some meaningful communication must have taken place between the two men, for Richard moved immediately to stand in front of Lilian, blocking her view of her husband. 'How are you feeling, Mother?' he said. 'Shall I get you a chair?'

Her flat, unfocused eyes came to life in response to this,

as if she had suddenly awoken in a vertical position after a long sleep. She said, 'Do not provoke me, Richard. Why should I want a chair *here* when I could sit in the drawing room? I feel quite well, thank you.' Her voice sounded surprisingly strong, and was deeper than is usual for a woman.

Sidney, while Lilian's attention was focused on Richard, turned back to Verna Laviolette and said quietly something that sounded like, 'It's Winnie.' I might have misheard that part, though I definitely heard what he said next: 'She has given us no end of trouble and her return is now out of the question. She's very upset.' From the movements of his head, I concluded that the second 'she' was his wife. Lilian was upset about somebody called Winnie.

In which case, why had Sidney given Richard the signal to distract her so that he could explain this to Verna? Presumably Lilian was aware of her own distress. Why could it not be mentioned openly in front of her? This question had much in common with another one I had asked recently: why must Little Key's name not be mentioned in front of Sidney and Lilian Devonport when that very name is clearly displayed on a plaque beside their front door?

Verna was evidently thrilled to hear of the problem. Her eyes sparkled as she said, 'Well, well, so no more Winnie. Whatever will you do without her? How *unfortunate*!' she added, in a tone that would better have matched the words 'How *marvellous*!'

I wondered if Winnie was perhaps the cook; her absence was evidently linked to dinner being delayed.

Sidney Devonport dismissed Verna's gloating question with a vague gesture, then loudly announced himself to be 'more than ready for a snifter'. This, I observed, was his way of indicating to Richard that he could stand down from his distraction duties. Richard immediately seemed to lose all interest in pursuing a conversation with his mother.

It was all most peculiar. The most perplexing thing of all, however—and I had to keep reminding myself of it because there was no external evidence to suggest it—was that a woman named Helen Acton, fiancée of Richard Devonport, was soon to be hanged for the murder of his brother and Sidney and Lilian's son Frank, and everybody was behaving as if this tragic circumstance did not exist. There was no air of sadness or solemnity in the air, no circumspect, guarded allusions to the Devonport family being in the midst of a terrible ordeal. It was true that Lilian Devonport could not be said to be in the best condition, and she had perhaps been able to walk without assistance before Frank's death, but otherwise this looked and felt very much like a normal social occasion.

How could Sidney Devonport muster the enthusiasm to welcome two strangers to his home and talk to them at length about a board game when the betrothed of one of his sons was about to swing for the murder of the other?

A discussion started up about where drinks should happen. Richard Devonport and Verna Laviolette favoured the drawing room, but both Godfrey and Sidney insisted that we should congregate in a room they both called 'Peepers HQ'.

'Ah, *oui*,' said Poirot. 'The headquarters of the Peepers operation is something that I have yearned to see for many . . . for the longest time!' I smiled to myself, suspecting that he had been about to say 'many years', then realized that he did not know how long the game had been in existence.

Richard was ordered by his father to show us to our quarters, help us to get settled in and then escort us downstairs again. This he stiffly and dutifully did, while avoiding looking either of us in the eye and speaking only the minimum number of words in a curt, clipped fashion.

Poirot seemed unperturbed by this closed-down manner from the man who had invited us here. He was busy humming a cheery tune to himself and adjusting his lustrous black moustaches, perhaps thinking that there would be plenty of time to question Richard Devonport later. I hoped I was being overly pessimistic in fearing that Devonport might *never* be willing to answer questions. Had he not already specified that he expected Poirot to solve the mystery of his brother's murder and save his fiancée from the gallows without saying a word about the subject to anybody? That was strange enough all on its own, and my experience of life had taught me that, wherever strange things are found, you can usually unearth further and even more peculiar ones if you look hard enough.

It struck me as eminently possible that Richard Devonport might want to include himself in the category of people whom Poirot was not permitted to question directly on the matter of Frank's demise. And how could we get to the bottom of it all if the only avenue open to us was drinking cocktails while discussing a board game?

Having divested ourselves of our effects and splashed some water on our faces, we followed Richard down the stairs. 'And now to enter the headquarters of the world's greatest game!' said Poirot, trotting ahead of me. 'Ah, this is truly the realization of my heart's dream!' I thought he was overdoing his act somewhat, particularly since at that moment there was no one to hear him apart from me and Richard Devonport.

As we reached the bottom of the staircase, the front door started to creak open. Richard stopped. 'This will be Oliver and Daisy,' he said without enthusiasm.

A man walked in, bringing a gust of cold air with him, and removed his hat. He was tall, pale as a ghost, with neat, short black hair that had a pronounced shine to it. Though he was smartly and conventionally dressed, there was a roguish aspect about him. He made me think of a highwayman of aristocratic descent. Richard Devonport commenced the introductions: this was Oliver, Oliver Prowd, good friend of the family and engaged to be married to Daisy Devonport, who was . . .

I did not at that moment take in who Daisy was, though I'm sure Richard told us then that she was his sister. I was prevented from attending to his commentary by the arrival of Daisy herself, who walked into the house a few seconds after Oliver.

I had met her before. Poirot had too. Our mouths gaped open in matching displays of incredulity.

Daisy was The Sculpture: the woman from the coach with the book, the one who had confessed to murder before tricking us and disappearing at Cobham.

How could she be here at Little Key? Yet here she undoubtedly was, *La Bête Ingénieuse*, staring back at us as if she had walked straight into a trap from which she wished furiously to escape.

CHAPTER 7

Confessions for Dinner

'What's the matter, darling?' Oliver Prowd moved closer to his fiancée and put a protective arm around her. *Guarding his treasure*, I thought, unable to banish the highwayman association from my mind.

'Daisy, you look a fright,' her brother Richard agreed. 'Has something happened?' Both men were so aware of the sudden change in her that neither had noticed my shock or Poirot's.

Daisy opened her mouth, but no words emerged. She stared at Poirot as if waiting for a cue.

He hurried forward, his hand extended. 'Mademoiselle Daisy!' he said. 'It is a great pleasure to make your acquaintance. I am Hercule Poirot—you have perhaps heard of me, eh, and seen my photograph in the newspapers? What an enormous surprise it must be to find me here in your family's home! May I introduce my friend, Monsieur Edward Catchpool?'

So this was how he was minded to play it. I fell in with

his plans, assuming there were sound reasons behind them, and waited to see if Daisy would participate in the charade. She shook my hand without once glancing at me and kept her glare fixed on Poirot.

'So, you're Hercule Poirot?' Oliver Prowd said as he stepped forward to make his greeting. To Daisy, he said, 'Darling, he is terribly famous.'

'I know,' she said in a tone that conveyed disgust. 'I have heard of his many successes.'

'*Merci bien.* It is true, there have been many.' Poirot gave a little bow.

'I assume you are not here in your professional capacity,' said Prowd.

'Why would he be?' Richard Devonport cut in quickly.

'Well, he wouldn't. That was my point: he must be here for purely recreational purposes.' The two men exchanged a looked that seemed to me to be loaded with meaning.

Poirot, pretending not to notice, said, 'You are correct in your assumption, Monsieur Prowd. Poirot, he takes the break from work to come here to this place of great significance.'

'Significance?' Daisy Devonport scowled as she spat out the word, while her brother and fiancé passed another meaningful look between them.

'*Oui.* My friend Catchpool and I, we are the most enthu-siastic players of the Peepers game!'

Perhaps Poirot had forgotten by now that I was supposed to be interested only in the game's commercial prospects. Or was I supposed to be both: a businessman wishing to assess the market potential of Peepers and an ardent fan? It would have been useful to know.

'It is the most enormous treat for us to be able to meet our favourite game's two inventors!' he said. 'We hope to learn much about what precisely inspired the invention of Peepers in the *coming few days*.' He stressed these last three words.

Daisy received his meaning clearly: he would have plenty of time to extract the truth from her about the murder she claimed to have committed. Her lip curled in a snarl.

'Darling, whatever is the matter?' her fiancé asked her solicitously.

'Shut up, Oliver,' she said flatly. There was plenty of emotion in her—that much was apparent from her face—but clearly none to spare for him.

'Let us go and find the others,' said Richard, leading the way. Behind him but ahead of Poirot and me, Oliver Prowd tried to walk close to Daisy. To thwart him, or so it seemed, she slowed down and ended up walking beside me instead.

I could understand her bitterness even if I could not sympathize. Had she known on the motor-coach that Poirot had been on his way to her very own home, she would not have uttered so much as a whisper. Could the murder she told him about be the murder of her brother Frank?

The more I considered it, the more likely it seemed. After all, Richard Devonport believed his fiancée Helen was innocent of that crime, and it struck me as highly improbable that Daisy Devonport should have been intimately involved with *two* murders. Besides, when I thought back over what

Poirot had told me of their conversation on the coach, there seemed to be many clues: Daisy had said that she had loved the man she murdered very much, but that her love for him was quite different from her love for her fiancé. Was not love for a brother very different from romantic love?

It all fitted perfectly. Richard Devonport, in his letter to Poirot, had said that he had once worked for the Treasury, but that recently he had left that employment and taken charge of his father's financial and business affairs. And Daisy had told Poirot that the thief who stole from Sidney Devonport had been in charge of those very same affairs. Sidney had entrusted his assets first to one son—a son who betrayed his trust and stole from him—and then, after Frank's death, to his surviving son, Richard.

If my theory was correct, that also meant that Lilian Devonport was dying from a wasting disease. That would explain her visible frailty.

I could hardly believe that we had been so lucky. Thanks to the simple coincidence of us having travelled on the same coach as Daisy Devonport . . . but of course, we were coming to Kingfisher Hill, at her brother's request, and she was coming here too because it was where she lived. The only coincidence was that Daisy had happened to be travelling from London today, at the exact moment that we were making the same journey.

Another lucky accident for us, I reflected as we turned a corner into another, wider corridor with mirrors, paintings and tapestries hanging on the walls, was that Daisy's character was as it was. Most people finding themselves

seated beside Hercule Poirot would not take the opportunity to confess to a murder and assume they could get
away with it. I decided that Daisy must be an unusually
daring and confident young woman. Her present emotional
state seemed to confirm my assessment: rage as opposed
to abject terror. Her cold, beautiful face was set hard.
There was resentment there, but there was also great
resolve. I sensed that she was thinking, *If this is the situation I find myself in, then so be it*. Her anger towards
Oliver Prowd also fascinated me. It told me that she did
not wish to wallow or be cooed over; she desired, instead,
to be left alone so that she could make a strategic plan
for her own benefit.

She must have been wondering, as was I, how long Poirot
would wait before telling her family all about her confession
and Helen Acton's innocence. He could produce the reve-
lation at any moment—as soon as we reached the room
known as 'Peepers HQ'.

Of course! I recalled that Daisy had nearly referred to
its silly nickname in her conversation with Poirot on the
coach. Had she not said that her father had summoned her
to a room that he 'infuriatingly' called . . . something? And
then she had made a quick alteration, to protect herself:
that room, in her narrative, became 'his study'. Of course,
if she had uttered the name of Peepers, Poirot might have
been able to identify her from that alone.

If I were Daisy Devonport, I thought, I would be angrier
with myself than with anyone else. She could so easily have
kept her mouth shut. Instead, thanks to her own reckless

loquacity, we knew nearly everything. She might not have divulged her motive for murder, and I could not for the life of me imagine why the unfortunate Helen Acton should wish to confess to a crime she had not committed, but the way things were turning out—and also taking into account Poirot's effervescently high spirits (he was almost bouncing along the corridor ahead of me now, by the side of Oliver Prowd)—I was confident that all of these remaining questions would soon be resolved and we would have the matter of Frank Devonport's murder nicely wrapped up by the end of the evening.

Goodness me, but we were lucky! If Poirot had not told Daisy the lie that he and I were travelling only as far as Cobham, she would never have uttered so much as a whisper about any murder. Had he told her that we were bound for Kingfisher Hill, she would almost certainly have kept quiet; that would have been too close for safety, even if she had not guessed that his destination was not merely the estate but Little Key specifically.

We arrived finally at Peepers HQ, where we found the others with drinks in hand. They presented an odd little scene. Godfrey and Verna Laviolette were standing with Sidney Devonport near a large window at the farthest end of the room, talking and laughing. Lilian Devonport was seated several feet away from them, facing towards the door. She was slumped in her chair and appeared half asleep. As we walked in she straightened her posture and her eyes cleared. She looked at us—or so I thought at first. Then I realized that it would be more accurate to say that she was looking through us, as if we were transparent. She did not acknowledge our presence with a smile or any words. Nor did she greet her daughter or Oliver Prowd. Her illness was possibly too far advanced for such niceties.

The room we were in was not so much a headquarters for Peepers as a shrine to it. Three different board designs for the game hung on the walls in frames, and an oversized example of a fourth board design lay flat on a table in the centre of the room, surrounded by uneven piles of discs with eyes on them. These had the effect of making one feel rather spied upon. Inside a glass-fronted cabinet, the rules of the game were on display, painted in blue, calligraphy-style, upon a series of stiff boards.

I walked over to the cabinet and tried to concentrate on reading and taking in some of these rules, in case I was later called upon to demonstrate a plausible level of familiarity. Alas, the words danced around my field of vision and I could extract no sense from them. I am sure I was at fault rather than the rule-writers, but I could not persuade my attention to give itself over to Peepers no matter how hard I tried. Instead, I found that my mind kept returning to the puzzle of Joan Blythe, the anguished woman from the coach. I no more believed her story now than I had when I had first heard it, but there was no doubt that Miss Blythe had been afraid of something—perhaps, sincerely, of murder.

Still, the impossibility of the particular story she had chosen to invent still weighed on my mind, as did the fact that the seat she claimed to have been warned against happened to be right next to that of Daisy Devonport, a self-confessed murderer . . .

I got no further than that before Richard Devonport put a drink into my hand. I thanked him in a tone designed to discourage further conversation. With every passing second I was finding it increasingly unbearable to be in a social situation when all I wanted was to sit down with a pencil and paper and list all the questions that plagued me.

Richard looked at me searchingly, as if he yearned for something that I could not provide, before moving away. Over by the window, Oliver Prowd and Verna Laviolette were complaining about Alfred Bixby—his vulgar blue and orange coaches; his puffed-up pomposity; his wealth that, they agreed, must have come from a dubious enterprise; his arrogance in naming his firm 'Kingfisher' as if the name of the estate, the improper use of which reflected unfavourably upon everyone who lived there, was his to do with as he pleased. There followed a lively discussion of 'the committee' and the possibility of compelling Bixby to change the name of his coach company.

Throughout all of this, Lilian Devonport remained in her chair facing away from the rest of us towards the door. She might as well not have been there. Daisy Devonport sat alone in a corner, taking large gulps from the glass she was clutching with both hands. At moments, she looked afraid, then her face would set again in an expression that was as murderous as any I have seen.

Poirot did not approach her. He stood between Godfrey Laviolette and Oliver Prowd and inserted entertaining remarks into the general conversation that made everybody laugh. Verna Laviolette adjusted her position every few seconds as if a photographer had instructed her to try out a variety of different poses for his camera. She looked at me, then over at Daisy, then at Lilian, then fawned over one of Poirot's witticisms.

I had a strong sense that Verna was not fully part of things in the way that the rest of us were, though what I meant by that was hard to define. Even Lilian and Daisy, at their lonely outposts, seemed more fully immersed in the scene, albeit in an isolated way. There was an authenticity about them both that did not apply to Verna, who seemed constantly alert and in surveillance mode, and also clearly wished to be noticed. She watched meticulously as, one after the other, Oliver Prowd and Richard Devonport approached Daisy and made an effort to find out why she seemed so out of sorts. Daisy waved them both away as if they were irritating flies buzzing around her. Richard seemed upset by this. Oliver did not; he simply shrugged and returned to more amiable company. Doubtless he was accustomed to his fiancée's variable humours.

Verna's eyes followed Richard as he walked over to his mother and conducted a brief conversation with her—about the timing of dinner, from what I managed to overhear.

I entertained myself briefly by imagining that Verna was a spy sent by the enemy to infiltrate the Peepers operation. Did the creators of the Landlord's Game even know of the existence of Peepers, I mused, or was the perception of this great rivalry entirely one-sided?

A scrawny maid appeared, wearing an apron that was several sizes too big for her, and announced that dinner was about to be served. Once we were all facing each other around the large oval-shaped table in the dining room, the awkwardness only became more pronounced: Lilian's vacant stare was harder to ignore, as was Daisy's vicious glaring in Poirot's direction. Richard Devonport, seated to my right, fidgeted in his chair.

The conversation would have dried up altogether were it not for Oliver Prowd, who, as the maid was serving the first course of tomato soup, said, 'I heard something the other day, Sidney, that I think will interest you greatly. And you, Godfrey. There is much talk in London of the Landlord's Game having been stolen.'

'Stolen?' the two inventors of Peepers exclaimed in unison.

Prowd nodded. 'The details were confusing and I was in a hurry, so I didn't get the whole story, but it seems that those claiming to have invented Landlord's Monopoly in fact stole the work of someone else—the original inventor, whoever that was. "A scandal in waiting" is how it was described to me.'

'Then the success of Peepers is all but assured!' crowed Sidney Devonport. I watched to see if his smile might expand in response to such welcome tidings, but it neither widened nor narrowed: his was a face that truly did not move. There was, perhaps, some sort of medical explanation: a stroke or seizure?

Godfrey Laviolette had started to say, 'We cannot rely

on the misfortunes of our rivals to—' when his wife interrupted him.

'This soup is as cold as the grave,' she said, looking around to make sure everyone had heard her. 'I don't know what Winnie . . .' She stopped, clapped her hand over her mouth and said through her fingers, 'Oh, I'm *so* sorry to mention Winnie. She's not here, is she? This soup isn't her concoction. And what was I thinking? I should *not* be speaking of graves! Oliver . . . Lilian . . . Please forgive the morbid metaphor.'

No one spoke for several seconds. The atmosphere in the room had tightened. Suddenly, it felt as if we were all much nearer to one another than we had been before. I did not believe for a moment that Verna was sorry to have mentioned either Winnie or graves. Though I had no prior knowledge of her, I would have put money on her being the sort of woman who deliberately made tactless and upsetting remarks precisely in order to upset people, followed by apologies designed to absolve herself of all responsibility for the hurt caused. My mother was that sort of woman, so I recognized the type.

It was Poirot who broke the silence. He cleared his throat and said, 'I agree with you, Monsieur Laviolette. To rely on the failure of your adversary is not the quickest path to success for Peepers. Decidedly not! Only by our *own* efforts can we—'

'You're a fraud, M. Poirot!' Daisy Devonport cried, rising from her seat. Her brother Richard gasped, then cowered. Verna Laviolette tried and failed to suppress a smile.

'Daisy, darling, what on earth do you mean?' said Oliver Prowd.

Daisy addressed her answer to Lilian Devonport. 'Mother, M. Poirot has lied to you and Father. He is here under false pretences. His friend is not *Mr* Catchpool—he is Inspector Edward Catchpool, with the London police. The two of them care nothing for Peepers. Do you honestly believe that a renowned detective, in demand as he must be, would waste his time talking to complete strangers about a *board game?*'

A strange noise came from Sidney Devonport's mouth.

'It is quite true, Father,' Daisy went on. 'M. Poirot is not here because he admires your and Godfrey's precious creation. He is here in connection with an unsolved murder—the murder of your son and my brother, Frank.' Turning to Poirot, she added calmly and slowly, 'Though, of course, it is solved now, isn't it, M. Poirot? As I told you when we met on a motor-coach earlier today: *I* killed Frank. I am the one guilty of his murder.'

The din that followed was unlike anything I had ever heard: Sidney Devonport staggered to his feet, knocking his chair to the ground. He emitted a series of noises—like a wild beast roaring as it was clawed to bloodied shreds—that made me want to run from the room. Lilian had finally come to life and was sobbing loudly into her hands. Richard Devonport turned me and said, 'Then Helen *is* innocent. I knew that she could not have murdered Frank.'

'Whereas you think I could have—and did?' Daisy smiled at him. Her anger appeared to have dissolved. Now she was serene and in command. 'Why would I do such a thing, Richard? You know how much I loved Frank.'

Richard looked at her. 'You said you killed him. Did you not just say so?'

'Yes. I killed him—but *why*?' Daisy's tone was teasing, appropriate to a parlour game. 'Why do *you* think I killed him, Father?'

Sidney's face was a monstrous patchwork of purple and white. He looked as if he was choking on something, struggling to breathe. Godfrey Laviolette guided him back to the table, picked up and righted his chair and sat him in it. 'Let me pour you some water, Sidney,' he said. Verna, I noticed, pursed her lips and shook her head at this. She disapproved of her husband's solicitousness.

Oliver was at Daisy's side. He seized her by the arm and said, 'What are you talking about, darling? Of course you did not kill Frank! Everybody knows who did that. Let us not even mention her name.'

'Everybody thought they knew,' said Daisy lightly. 'Everybody was wrong. As so often.'

Oliver released his grip on her. His face had turned pale and his upper lip shook. 'Daisy, what is this pantomime? Why are you saying this? You know it is untrue.'

'Poor Oliver,' she said. 'Are you going to cry? Are you afraid they will hang me?'

'Why, darling?' he whispered. 'Why now, tonight?'

Verna laughed. 'So it's true? And you knew, Oliver?'

'What? No!' Prowd staggered back. 'It is *not* true. It cannot be. I . . . I saw Helen push Frank to his death!'

Richard Devonport said, 'We must telephone the police at once. They must be told that Helen is innocent. It would be unpardonable to allow the execution of an innocent woman to go ahead now that we know the truth. Inspector Catchpool, can you telephone to London straight away and—'

'The *truth*?' Daisy interrupted. 'You will happily accept my story as true, then, even though you cannot think of a single reason why I should wish to murder Frank.'

'I . . . I . . .' Richard gulped and gaped like a bewildered fish. Poirot had not moved from his chair. He was watching and listening with utmost attention.

'Wait a second,' said Verna Laviolette to nobody in particular. 'Helen confessed. Why pretend she'd killed Frank if she hadn't?'

'Did you persuade her to lie for you?' Richard asked Daisy.

'No, I did not.'

'Are you quite certain of that? You could make anyone agree to do anything.'

Daisy turned to Sidney, 'Is he right, Father? Am I as persuasive as Richard thinks I am? Mother?' She walked over to Lilian and rested her hand on her shoulder. 'Mother, do you know why I killed Frank?' A trickle of red ran from Lilian's mouth down to her chin. I thought at first that it was blood, then realized it was tomato soup. Bile rose up in my throat and I had to look away.

'Enough!' Sidney Devonport bellowed. His face had lost its mottle of purple and white and was now an even, livid red. Despite the rage in his voice and eyes, his inflexible open-mouthed smile remained in place, as if his own face was playing the most grotesque trick on him. 'M. Poirot, is it true what Daisy says? Are you a fraud and a liar? Mr Catchpool—or is it Inspector Catchpool?—is your interest in Peepers the true reason for your visit or have you deceived your way into my home?'

He sounded like a wholly different person from the jovial host who had welcomed us so warmly at first. I felt afraid, though he showed no sign of intending physical violence towards me, and I prayed for Poirot to save us somehow before all the hounds of hell burst out of Sidney Devonport and destroyed us all. This seemed a very real possibility.

Luckily, my friend came to my rescue. 'Monsieur Devonport, I must apologize. Yes, Mademoiselle Daisy is correct. I have not been entirely sincere in my communication with you. The fault is mine and mine alone—please do not assign any blame to Inspector Catchpool here. He did not know our destination or our purpose when we set off for Kingfisher Hill this afternoon. I had been extremely secretive. Let me also say that, although there has undeniably been some artifice on my part, it is nevertheless true that I have the greatest affection and admiration for this wonderful game that you and Monsieur Laviolette have—'

'Silence!' Sidney Devonport roared. We all cowered. A thunderous barrage of questions followed. He demanded that Poirot explain what precisely Daisy had told him on the coach. Poirot indulged in yet more 'artifice', as he called it, and said that Daisy had confessed on the coach to the murder of 'a man she loved', but revealed no more than that. Daisy, I noticed with interest, did not correct Poirot's account. Effectively the two of them—detective and confessed murderer—had entered into a conspiracy of sorts, colluding to deceive Sidney Devonport. I was a collaborator too.

Next, Sidney insisted that Poirot tell him if Daisy had summoned the two of us to Little Key so that we could witness her public confession in front of her family—was that the means by which the murder of Frank had come to Poirot's attention? Why and how else could he have developed an interest, when the case was officially solved and the guilty party was preparing, imminently, to pay the terrible price for her crime?

Richard Devonport stiffened beside me. I felt his fear as acutely as if it was seeping through the air between us and into my own heart: his father must never find out that it was he who invited us here. The importance of this was as obvious to me as it was to him; I now understood perfectly well why the poor chap was so afraid of his father. If I found this version of Sidney Devonport so hellish and horrifying to be around, I could only imagine how much worse it must be for anyone who had lived in his household since birth.

Daisy did not flinch in the face of her father's tirade. She remained calm throughout and gave off a directorial air—as if everyone was doing and saying exactly what she hoped they would. Lilian, Godfrey and Verna all seemed to be frozen in a joint resolution not to move a muscle until it was safe to do so.

Poirot explained that his meeting with Daisy on the coach from London had been purely accidental. The murder of Frank Devonport and Helen Acton's confession and impending execution had been brought to his attention, he said, by 'an acquaintance of Catchpool's and mine in the field of law enforcement'. I heard Richard Devonport's relieved exhalation.

Sidney turned on Daisy and asked her why, if she had been on a motor-coach bound for Kingfisher Hill, did she not stay on it? Why, instead, had she alighted at Cobham, making it necessary for Oliver to take a car out and fetch her?

'That is your first question to me, Father, after what I have told you? You are more interested in my travel arrangements than in why I killed your son?'

'You did no such thing!' Sidney bellowed. He turned to Poirot. 'She's talking rot! Tell me you can see it as clearly as I can. I don't know why she would choose to torment me and her mother with such a wicked lie, but that's what it is—a lie! Helen Acton killed Frank *and she will hang for it*! As for the police . . . no one will inform them of anything, no one is to summon them.' He turned his hostile eyes on me. I did my best to look uninformed and unsummoned. I don't know if I achieved the precise facial expression most likely to deter Sidney Devonport from screaming at me, but I certainly gave it my best effort.

'Do you hear me? *No one!*' he barked at me like a savage

123

dog. Saliva flew from his mouth. Luckily, I was not close enough to be hit. He turned on Poirot once more. 'You will disregard Daisy's lies and you will leave my home *immediately*. Richard will drive you and your . . . epicene lickspittle back to London. Richard—do as I ask, at once. I want these two blackguards *out of this house*!'

So it was that, twenty minutes later, Poirot and I were in a motorcar with our hastily packed suitcases, being driven by Richard Devonport through the darkness and out of the Kingfisher Hill Estate.

The words 'epicene lickspittle'—quite the most unpleasant thing anyone had ever called me—echoed in my head as I waited for Poirot to begin his questioning of our driver. He seemed content to sit in silence, however, and it was Richard who spoke first: 'He cannot stop you.'

'*Pardon*, monsieur?' said Poirot.

'Father. I must obey his every order, but he has no hold over you—either of you. You can and must arrange for Helen to be released. Inspector Catchpool, I am begging you.'

I said nothing. At that precise instant, I did not feel inclined to arrange anything advantageous to any member, friend or associate of the Devonport family. I was thoroughly exhausted, freezing cold once again, and my stomach was painfully empty; all I had eaten since the Tartar Inn was a few spoonfuls of lukewarm tomato soup. I opted to sit in silence and imagine, fresh from the oven, a piping hot leg of lamb slathered in mint sauce. That was what I would ask my landlady, Mrs Unsworth, to cook for me as soon as I arrived home.

'It is not so simple, *mon ami*,' Poirot told Richard Devonport when I failed to answer. 'Your Helen has confessed to this murder, has she not? She has been convicted of the crime and condemned to death. This is not so easy to undo.'

'Do you mean to tell me that you intend to—?'

'What I intend is to speak to the right people and alert them to this new development of a *second* confession for the murder of Frank Devonport. I shall also speak to Mademoiselle Helen at the earliest opportunity. Tell me—do you think that she might decide that she is, after all, innocent of murder once she learns that Mademoiselle Daisy has confessed?'

'I don't know,' Richard said gravely. 'I certainly hope so. But what if . . . ?' He left the question hanging.

'What if she does not forswear her original story in which she is guilty? *Eh bien*, then it becomes complicated. With luck, and with my intervention, there could be a delay to the processes of the law. There would need to be an investigation, of course, to establish the truth. May I ask you a question, Monsieur Devonport?'

'Go ahead.'

'Do you believe that your sister Daisy is a murderer, as she claims?'

Richard did not answer immediately. After nearly a minute, he said, 'I would never have thought so, but I would not like to say it is impossible. Daisy does many things that

125

ordinary, decent people would not do. I find her entirely impossible to fathom, if you want to know the truth. With Oliver, her ever-adoring lapdog, and with me, she has always been sweetness and light one minute and rude and cold the next, knowing she can get away with it, but the way she spoke to Father and Mother at the dinner table . . . If I had not seen it with my own eyes . . .' He shook his head to express his disbelief. 'Her whole life, she has treated them with the greatest deference and respect, even when they least deserve such treatment. She had no choice! She has always feared their disapproval and their threatened punishments as much as I have—as much as I *do*. They were the only people, the only thing on earth, that could restrain her. But after her performance tonight . . . Suddenly she was the powerful one and they were the victims. It was extraordinary.' His voice was a mixture of admiration and resentment. After a pause, he added, 'Though I suppose it makes sense, when you think about it.'

'What makes sense?' asked Poirot.

'She confessed to murder when she happened to sit beside you on a coach and had no idea you were coming to Kingfisher Hill. No doubt she did it to be outrageous. She loves to shock and to be the centre of attention. How sure she must have been that her confession would have no unpleasant consequences for her. Then when she arrived home and found you there, she saw that there was nothing to stop you from telling us all that she had admitted to killing someone. She realized that Father could find out imminently that she and not Helen had murdered his favourite son. That made her unusually brave—or reckless, depending on your perspective. She refused to suffer the humiliation of seeming weak and defeated in front of all of us—she is very proud and vain, my sister—so she confessed before you had a chance to incriminate her.'

'Perhaps you are right,' said Poirot. 'Sometimes when what we have feared for so long is no longer avoidable, we can find in ourselves a reserve of courage that we did not know we possessed.'

'Not me,' Richard Devonport muttered. 'My sister has declared herself guilty of the murder of my brother, yet still I am petrified that Father might find out that it was I who invited you to Little Key.'

'There is no need for him to find this out,' Poirot assured him.

'Thank you. I cannot tell you how grateful I am to have your help. Yours too, Inspector Catchpool. And in spite of everything I have said about Daisy, truly I can't see her killing anybody. I think she must have some strange and complicated reason for behaving in this inexplicable way. Nothing about her is straightforward.'

'Yet you wish me to use her confession to free Mademoiselle Helen?' asked Poirot.

'I am *certain* that Helen is innocent,' he said.

'How can you know this for sure?'

'Speak to her and you will be as sure as I am. She had no reason to want Frank dead. None whatsoever. She . . . she loved him dearly.'

'Let us suppose that both women are innocent: your

sister and Helen Acton. That means that Frank was killed by someone else, does it not? Who do you think could have killed him? Who had a reason to do so?'

'I don't know! No one.' His answer was a little too quick and insistent. 'My concern is for the innocent. I don't want either Helen or Daisy to hang, and I don't believe that one of them must.'

'What do you mean?' I asked him.

'If two people confess to the same murder, and both insist that they did it—they and nobody else—and there are no witnesses to anything, then surely nobody can be hanged,' said Richard Devonport. The relief in his voice made it plain that this was his favoured outcome, and no matter that the murder victim was his own brother. 'Each confession would cancel out the other one and there would be no way to discover what really happened. No way at all.'

CHAPTER 8

The Chronology

Two days later, Poirot and I were in the village of Chiddingfold, taking afternoon tea in the home of Inspector Marcus Capeling of Surrey Police. Our enquiries had come up with the name of Capeling as having been in charge of the investigation into Frank Devonport's murder. Happily, he had at once expressed a willingness to talk to us, and, upon our arrival, had turned out to be a congenial fellow. He looked far too young to be a police inspector.

His wife had greeted us at the door with what had struck me as excessive delight, and I soon understood why. She was one of those women who puts plates loaded with all sorts of baked treats in front of you and then cajoles until all present have eaten enough to rupture their stomachs. Poirot and I were not so much welcome guests as necessary repositories for her unbridled catering.

Mercifully, a neighbour had burst into the Capelings' sitting room, just as I was being coaxed through a third fruit scone, with news that the Dunbar baby—'a little cherub if ever there was one'—was now ready to receive visitors, and Mrs Capeling had hurried away with a quantity of wrapped cake slices that would alarm any sensible newborn.

Once the two women had left, Poirot said to Capeling, 'Tell us about the murder of Frank Devonport. Do not omit a single detail, please.' We had already described to him all that had taken place on our journey from London and during our brief stay at Kingfisher Hill. Capeling had said, 'Well, blow me down!' so often that I had lost count.

'You know that Helen Acton confessed to the murder immediately?' he said now.

'I know that she confessed,' said Poirot. 'I did not know that it was immediate.'

'Oh, yes. As one of my men said at the time, "She was busy confessing while poor old Frank's body was still warm." Stuck to her story ever since, too. And soon she will pay the price for what she did.' Capeling frowned and rubbed his chin. 'If indeed it was she who committed the crime. Now that Daisy Devonport has confessed, I'm starting to wonder if I might not have been right all along. Daisy, though . . .' He shook his head. 'I find it difficult to believe she killed her brother, but then again, she's a hard one to make sense of—probably the most interesting character of all the Devonports—and I have been wrong before, M. Poirot. Many, many times, in my daily life and in my work.' He said this quite cheerfully, apparently undisturbed by manifold errors both personal and professional.

'My sincere condolences, *mon ami*. That cannot be a pleasant experience, I am sure.'

'Ah, well.' Capeling shrugged. 'You say you have informed the Home Office of the latest developments? Daisy Devonport's confession, I mean.'

'Yes, I have spoken to my friends there,' said Poirot. 'It was the first visit I made on my return to London.'

'Ah. I only ask because . . . well, I have heard nothing.'

'Everything is in hand,' Poirot told him. 'The execution of Helen Acton is to be delayed and a new investigation of the murder of Frank Devonport will commence. I am afraid that, for a reason I am sure you will understand . . .' Poirot paused tactfully.

'Oh, quite. Quite.' Capeling looked relieved. 'I expect the Home Office will send it up to Scotland Yard? The Devonport family . . . well, they're not any old Jack or Jill. The case was only assigned to us local police because it seemed so straightforward—until one met the people involved, that is. It was thought that to keep it as a Surrey police matter might put a limit on any damage to the family's name. Keep it out of the London newspapers, you know.'

'Indeed,' said Poirot, 'However, now that this solved case is once again unsolved, Scotland Yard will take it on from here.' He gestured extravagantly in my direction, like a magician celebrating the reappearance of a formerly vanished object. 'Inspector Catchpool will lead the investigation and I will offer to him what assistance I can, *n'est-ce pas*, Catchpool?'

131

'Something like that,' I agreed. He and I both knew that it would be the other way round. In truth, I wished that Poirot could lead the charge officially and be seen to do so by all involved. I was not looking forward to our return to Little Key, when I would have to brandish my Scotland Yard credentials and explain to the Devonports that, having thrown me out of their home only days ago, they now had no choice but to admit me once again and answer many upsetting and intrusive questions. That I would be accompanied by Poirot, my partner in deceiving them, would not help to secure a warm reception. I had put all of these points to Poirot on the way to Chiddingfold and he had waved them aside, accusing me of unwarranted pessimism: 'All will be well, *mon cher*. Place your trust in Poirot, who has never let you down.'

Now he said to Marcus Capeling, 'Inspector, you said a moment ago that you might have been right all along. Right about what? Did you not believe that Helen Acton was guilty, even when she said so?'

'No, I did not. Not at first. She insisted upon it, though, and so I thought . . . well, why would she risk her neck if she was innocent?'

'Nevertheless, your first opinion was that she *was* innocent?'

'Yes. Yes, I'm afraid it was.'

'What made you think so?'

'Her grief after the tragedy, for one thing. If you'd seen her, M. Poirot, you'd have thought the same, I'm sure. Never have I seen a plainer case of a woman who wished with all her breaking heart that the man she loved was alive and not dead.'

'The man she loved?' Poirot sat forward in his chair. He spoke quickly. 'Don't you mean to say the *brother* of the man she loved? She is engaged to be married to Richard Devonport, is she not? Richard Devonport is alive.'

Capeling's eyes widened. 'No, no, M. Poirot. *Now* Helen Acton is betrothed to Richard Devonport, that is quite true. But that came later, after Frank's death.'

Poirot and I looked at one another, unable to believe what we were hearing. His eyes appeared more vividly green and jewel-like than usual, I noticed—like two emeralds under a bright light, though the Capelings' small sitting room was dimly lit. Many people don't believe me when I describe what happens to Poirot's eyes at significant moments in the puzzle-solving process he so loves, but it is quite true. I have seen it happen many times: his eyes take on a peculiar green glow, as if lit from within.

I cleared my throat and said to Capeling, 'Do you mean to tell us that Helen Acton and Frank Devonport were, well . . . what, precisely?'

'Why, when Frank died they were engaged to be married,' said Capeling. 'By all accounts they were inseparable and wildly in love. All the family said so.'

'Then how does Richard Devonport fit into the picture?' I asked.

Capeling shook his head. 'That's the strangest part of it all. You see, before Frank died, Helen Acton did not know Richard Devonport at all. And he did not know her.'

'Yet they ended up betrothed to one another?' Poirot sounded as baffled as I felt. 'And this happened *after* she confessed to killing his brother?'

'Oh, it's even queerer than that, M. Poirot. There are so many aspects of the situation that defy explanation, I hardly know where to begin. You see, before he introduced Helen to his family as his fiancée, Frank had been estranged from the other Devonports for some time—just as Daisy told you. You know the story. He stole from the family coffers in order to help a friend in need. I daresay Daisy told you who the friend was? The man she plans to marry: Oliver Prowd.'

In my head, I drew more lines of connection between the Devonports and the various members of their circle. I had already added a new one to my mental picture that led from Helen to Frank, making him not only her murdered almost-brother-in-law but also her murdered almost-husband. Now I created a new line on my imaginary diagram, one that linked Oliver Prowd directly to Frank Devonport. Prowd was no longer simply Daisy Devonport's fiancé; suddenly he was also the good friend of Frank Devonport and the recipient of the stolen money. Which meant that . . .

My mind blurred, then went blank. Too many scones had impaired my deductive functions, but I got there in the end: what this meant was that Daisy Devonport, according to her, had both murdered her brother, Frank the thief, *and* agreed to marry his accomplice and the beneficiary of his crime.

Why would Daisy kill one of the people involved in the

theft and consent to marry the other? Unless her motive for killing Frank had nothing to do with the stolen money. Equally likely, I reminded myself, was that she had not murdered Frank at all and was lying about having done so.

'Ah, so you didn't know that Oliver Prowd was the friend Frank Devonport stole for?' said Capeling.

'*Non*. Richard Devonport, I now see, has told us very little. He did not tell us that Helen Acton was engaged to be married to his brother at the time of Frank's murder.' Poirot shook his head. 'Having invited Hercule Poirot to his home and asked urgently for his help . . . Ah, but Monsieur Richard does not believe my help to be necessary any more. He is certain that no one will hang for the murder of his brother now that there are two confessions, each one contradicting the other. *Alors*, he feels no obligation to furnish me with the additional information. He claims to know no reason why anyone at all should have wished to kill Frank. Yet kill him somebody did!'

'The response from the Home Office so far suggests that Richard Devonport might be correct in his assessment,' I told Capeling. 'Helen Acton's execution has been delayed— and if she and Daisy Devonport both continue to swear to their different versions of what happened, it could well be cancelled altogether . . .' I turned to Poirot. 'I say, imagine if they *both* wanted Frank dead and worked up this whole plot in advance, knowing that if they both confessed, it would be impossible for the blame to land decisively on either of them.'

'Oh, Catchpool. Anyone would think that you joined the police only today and have not yet received the basic training. Have you forgotten that Daisy Devonport went to considerable effort to conceal her name and identity from me when we first met—and also her destination? She never wished for her confession to reach the police or the Home Office in time to save the life of Helen Acton.'

Privately I thought, *But what if Daisy is cleverer than we think?* 'What kind of man asks for his brother's murderer's hand in marriage?' I asked Marcus Capeling.

'A man who believes she's innocent, I suppose,' came the reply.

I turned to Poirot. '*Sidney* Devonport certainly thinks Helen Acton is guilty, and Richard is plainly terrified of his father. He cringes with fear whenever Sidney opens his mouth, jumps to his every whim . . .'

'What is your point, *mon ami*?'

'Are we to suppose that Sidney has no objection to Richard's engagement to Helen Acton? Or that Richard has been willing to defy him on that matter alone while deferring to him in everything else?'

'We do not at present know enough about the Devonport family members and their relationships with one another,' said Poirot. 'It is too early to make suppositions.'

'Do you know about Oliver Prowd's father?' Capeling asked. 'Otto, his name was.'

'Mademoiselle Daisy mentioned him, but not by name. He had a role in the story that she told me.'

'It was not only for Oliver Prowd that Frank Devonport

stole all that money,' said Capeling. 'It was also for the sake of Oliver's father, Otto, who was old and sick. The two of them, father and son, had lost all their money when the stock exchange had its little setback. Frank wanted to help them both. When Otto Prowd died, he was once more a wealthy man—that was thanks to Frank Devonport. He and Oliver invested the stolen money and struck gold. Otto was able to live out his last days in comfort. He died knowing that Oliver would have no money worries for the rest of his life. Well, not unless he made some very unwise decisions.' Capeling wagged his finger suddenly and said ruefully. 'Which is always possible where money's involved.' It sounded as if he might have been speaking from experience.

'Was Daisy Devonport engaged to Oliver Prowd when her brother Frank died?' Poirot asked.

Capeling nodded. 'She was. Although it had not been long, I don't think. Maybe only a matter of weeks.'

'I see. So the plan for them to marry was not something that happened after the fact, as it were.'

'Not at all—but why do you ask?' said Capeling.

'It is useful, always, to understand the chronology of human relationships,' Poirot told him. 'How everything fits together. There are many questions I would have liked to ask Richard Devonport—many that I *did* ask him between Kingfisher Hill and London—but he declined to answer, did he not, Catchpool?'

'Yes, he snapped shut like a clam shell,' I said. 'Once he had satisfied himself that neither Helen Acton nor Daisy could now hang for Frank's murder—'

'I don't see that as being true at all,' Capeling interjected.

'I agree with you,' I said. 'Nothing is guaranteed. This is a highly irregular situation. However, it is what Richard Devonport believes. And it's why he told Poirot and me that he could not answer questions about his family and concentrate on driving the car at the same time.'

'An excuse,' said Poirot.

'He tried various others too,' I said. 'At one point he professed to be too exhausted by the events of the day and suggested that further discussion would be impossible for him. Personally, I think he has a theory about who *did* kill his brother but for some reason doesn't want to tell us. He doesn't believe it was either Helen or Daisy, that's for sure.'

'Yes, it is interesting,' said Poirot. 'Who else in the household would he wish to protect? His mother, perhaps . . .'

I thought of an idea I preferred. 'Or his father. When one fears a parent to the extent that Richard Devonport fears Sidney Devonport, one might be unwilling to risk an accusation of murder in case the accused is found not guilty and returns home to punish the accuser.'

'A very interesting notion, Catchpool.' Poirot gave me an encouraging smile and I felt inordinately pleased. 'Inspector Capeling, I have made arrangements to talk to Helen Acton first thing tomorrow, but in the meantime, my curiosity gets the better of me: did she include in her confession a motive? I assume you asked her why she would kill this man she loved and to whom she was betrothed?'

'Oh, she was very clear about the why of it,' said Capeling. 'She said, and insists to this day, that she did it because she loved his brother, Richard, more. Now, if you'll pardon my saying so, I have always found that hard to believe. Partly because, as I've told you, Helen and Richard did not know each other before Frank died. And . . . well, not that I'm an expert on women's tastes, but anyone would have had to concede that Frank Devonport was a fine specimen: tall, handsome. Handsome as a movie star—that's what my wife said when I showed her a photograph. I can't see any woman falling for his short, plain and quite unremarkable brother instead. It's not only down to physical appearances, mind you. Frank, by all accounts, was a man of real character, a born leader. Charismatic is what everyone said, everybody I spoke to. And you've met Richard. He's a timid little mouse, isn't he? Scurrying around in the background, hoping not to be noticed. No, I can't see that the future wife of Frank Devonport would lose her heart to his brother. Although I could be wrong. I suppose people want all sorts of things for all kinds of reasons, don't they?'

'Nobody would believe that murdering a chap's brother was the way to win his heart,' I said.

Poirot shook his head. 'Remember, Catchpool, we know nothing of the strength or weakness of the Devonport brothers' fraternal bond. Did Richard seem to you eager for Frank's killer to be identified and brought to justice? To me, he did not.' He turned to Marcus Capeling. 'Twice you have told us that Helen Acton and Richard Devonport did not know one another. Please explain, and be precise. Do you mean that their acquaintance was merely superficial, or—?'

'Oh, I can be precise.' Capeling chuckled. 'I can get it down to hours. Probably minutes and seconds if you'd like.'

'Minutes and . . . and seconds?' Poirot smoothed down his moustaches. I braced myself for whatever we were about to be told. I expected it to make as little sense as everything else that had befallen us since we had waited on Buckingham Palace Road to board that infernal orange and blue motor-coach.

'Oh, yes, M. Poirot—it was mere hours before Frank died, you see, when they met.'

'*Mon ami*, do you mean to suggest—?'

'Yes,' Capeling said. 'Richard Devonport and Helen Acton made one another's acquaintance for the very first time on the day of Frank Devonport's murder.'

Poirot rose from his chair and walked over to the window, where he stood and looked out at the row of small cottages opposite the Capelings' house. It was some time before he spoke again. A low-pitched muttering emanated from him, punctuated now and then by muffled exclamations. As I watched the back of his singular, egg-shaped head, I half fancied that it grew larger before my eyes as the finest brain in the land swelled with new thoughts, deductions and questions.

Eventually, he asked Capeling, 'Did you tell Helen Acton

that you did not believe her story? When she told you that she had known Richard Devonport for *only one day* . . .'

'Less than that,' said Capeling. 'It was a matter of hours. A small portion of a day.'

'Yet she claimed to have been driven to kill for his sake?'

'Not exactly for his sake, M. Poirot. She said only that she loved him, and . . . did what she did to Frank in order to be free to marry Richard.'

I made a scornful noise. 'Why not simply break off her engagement to Frank Devonport if Richard was the one she loved? There was no need to kill him for that reason alone. Helen Acton is a liar and that's all there is to it. She might have murdered Frank, but if she did it was for a different reason.'

'All I can tell you is what she told me, Inspector,' Capeling said. 'What she kept telling me, every time we spoke: "I did it because I did not love Frank any more. I loved Richard. He was the one I wanted." Those same words, over and over. Once I had learned the truth from others about the timing of her association with Richard Devonport, I spoke to her again and . . . well, I put it to her that she and Richard had met only on that very day—the day Frank died.'

'What did she say to that?' Poirot asked.

'She did not deny it. But she also would not confirm it. And I got the same response from Richard Devonport when I asked him about it.'

'About when they first met?'

Capeling nodded. 'Neither of them would answer me on

the matter of whether or not they first clapped eyes on each other on that day. All I can tell you is that everybody else present swears that they did.'

'We will come to the details of the day in a moment,' said Poirot. 'Inspector, did Helen Acton claim—has she ever claimed—that for Monsieur Richard she experienced love at first sight?'

Marcus Capeling smiled. '"Did my heart love till now? Forswear it, sight! For I ne'er saw true beauty till this night".'

'*Romeo and Juliet*,' I said reflexively. I had studied it at school and its lessons had stayed with me: pursue your romantic urges with no thought for what society will allow and there is a good chance that you will end up in a disadvantageous situation.

'No, Helen has never said anything about love at first sight to me,' Capeling answered Poirot's question. 'Nor to anybody else, as far as I am aware. If I had to guess . . . well, I would say that she and Richard must have known each other already, before Frank died, but for some reason did not wish to admit it.'

'How soon after the death of Frank did Mademoiselle Helen become engaged to his brother?' Poirot asked.

'Two weeks. Richard visited her twice in jail—he was keen to do so once he heard that she had named her love for him as the why of it all. In fact . . .' Capeling broke off.

'What?' said Poirot.

'I've remembered something: I was there when Richard

142

was first informed of Helen's . . . stated reason for the crime she had committed. Never have I seen a man look more astonished or appalled.'

'Appalled?' I said.

'Well, yes,' said Capeling. 'Imagine how you would feel upon discovering that the reason your brother was dead was *you*. I'd have felt terribly guilty if I'd been in Richard's position.'

'Would you have wanted, or agreed, to marry your brother's murderer two weeks later?' I asked him.

'My friend Catchpool is notorious for never agreeing to marry anybody,' Poirot told Capeling. 'He has driven his mother to the end of her wits.'

'Oh, you should get yourself married, Inspector!' Capeling glanced down at the remaining scones on the table in front of him and smiled. 'You too, M. Poirot. As a married man, I'd be the first to recommend it.'

'So Richard Devonport was appalled to be loved by the woman who killed his brother,' said Poirot thoughtfully. 'Yet soon afterwards, he puts a ring on the finger of this same woman . . .'

'A ring on her finger,' Capeling echoed. 'It's funny that you should say that, M. Poirot.'

'What is funny?' Poirot asked.

'At the time of Helen Acton's arrest she was wearing the ring Frank had given her: a solitaire ruby, it was. Very striking.'

'A ruby?' I looked at Poirot. 'Inspector, you have just described Daisy Devonport's engagement ring. Don't you remember, Poirot? She was wearing it when we travelled together on the coach.'

Poirot nodded.

'This is what I'm trying to tell you,' said Capeling. 'When I first met Daisy Devonport, she was engaged to be married to Oliver Prowd and wore the ring he had bought for her: an emerald with diamonds around it. Helen Acton, meanwhile, was wearing Frank's ring: the ruby solitaire. But after the first time Richard visited her at Holloway Prison, Helen asked the guards to find her ruby ring among her effects and send it on to Richard at Kingfisher Hill. A matter of days later, when I visited the Devonport family, Daisy's emerald and diamond ring was no longer on her finger. Instead, there was the ruby solitaire that Frank had given Helen!'

'Yet Mademoiselle Daisy remains betrothed to Oliver Prowd,' said Poirot. 'This is most extraordinary. *C'est merveilleuse!*' He clapped his hands together.

'Why is it marvellous?' I demanded. 'I don't think it's marvellous at all. Frankly, Poirot, I don't know why you're bothering.'

'Don't you?' His eyes glinted that bright green again. 'It gives me great pleasure to bother, Catchpool.'

'But you'll never make sense of any of it! It's impossible: a riddle without an answer. Helen Acton is lying and Daisy Devonport is lying. Richard Devonport has told us so little that he might as well have lied—in fact, he probably has. And now this business with the rings and people deciding to marry when they barely know each other—never mind that one has been condemned to death, which generally makes marriage impossible! And as for Joan Blythe . . .' I made a disgusted noise.

'Aha. I wondered when you would mention her,' said Poirot. He smiled at Capeling, as if I was a joke to be shared between the two of them. 'You always come back to her, *n'est-ce pas*? You believe she is connected to our other mysteries.'

'All I know is that she started it. She was the beginning of everything ceasing to make the slightest bit of sense. And all that has happened since—all that we have seen and heard of, Poirot, without exception—has made even less sense!'

'And this lack of sense infuriates you,' said Poirot softly. '*Je comprends bien*. But you are in error, my friend, in so many ways. Later I shall explain to you why and you will feel much better.' He turned to Capeling, 'Inspector, let us speak of the indisputable facts of Frank Devonport's death. Start at the beginning, please, and tell me what is known.'

'Very well,' said Capeling. 'I shall start with the morning of the day of the murder. You probably know the date: it was December the sixth last year. Frank had previously been sent into exile by his family as a consequence of a theft—you know that already. Banished, he was, with no hope of a reprieve. Well, when his mother Lilian was diagnosed with an illness that her doctor told her was not survivable, when she knew she only had limited time left, it seems that she and Sidney Devonport softened their position somewhat and decided that it was time for Frank to return. He was at the time working as a schoolmaster in Lincolnshire. He and Oliver Prowd had put that excess money they should never have had in the first place—profits from the stolen money they invested—into opening a handful of schools—did you know that?'

'No,' I said, only to be corrected by Poirot, who told Capeling that, yes, Daisy Devonport had mentioned it to him on the coach and that he had in turn told me about it. I must have forgotten that detail.

'Very successful these schools were too,' Capeling went on 'When Frank died, they were sold to the philanthropist Josiah Blantyre for a handsome sum.'

'You raise an important question,' Poirot said. 'Who benefitted financially from Frank Devonport's death?'

'Sidney and Lilian Devonport, as his next of kin.'

'And did you enquire as to the financial position of Sidney and Lilian Devonport?' I asked, thinking of people I knew at Scotland Yard who might not have bothered to do so after Helen Acton had confessed so readily.

'Oh, indeed I did,' Capeling said proudly. 'It was enough to start my eyes watering, I don't mind telling you. The Devonports, senior and junior, have got so much money between them that someone could take away three quarters of it and they wouldn't notice. Well . . . they might *notice*,' he amended. 'I'm sure they keep a close eye out, after what Frank did. But they would still be immensely wealthy, is my point. No member of the Devonport family has any money worries that would induce them to kill anybody, and that's for certain.'

'Please return to last year, the sixth of December,' said Poirot. 'Start at the beginning.'

'Frank arrived at Little Key with his fiancée Helen Acton at around ten o'clock in the morning,' said Capeling. 'When I interviewed them afterwards, Sidney and Lilian Devonport told me that they had felt a certain amount of trepidation about the meeting: the return of their banished son to the family home. They had exchanged letters and spoken over the telephone, but, as I'm sure you can imagine, the prospect of seeing Frank again in the flesh felt rather momentous to them. After communication had been re-established by letter, Frank had given them the news of his engagement to a woman they did not know. What is more, he proposed to bring her with him. A stranger! Lilian made a point of telling me that she had nothing against the young lady—not before that terrible day, I mean to say—but both she and Sidney would have preferred Frank to arrive alone for his first visit after the period of estrangement.'

'Did they communicate this to Frank?' Poirot asked.

'No,' said Capeling. 'They assured me that they offered Helen their warmest welcome and kept their preferences to themselves.'

'They did not wish to endanger the *rapprochement*.'

'Indeed they did not, M. Poirot. But let me tell you who they made *un*welcome that day: everybody else. Some good friends of the family were staying with the Devonports at the time: Godfrey and Verna Laviolette, whom you've met, of course. Well, they and the rest of the Devonport family were told that Sidney and Lilian would need to be alone with Frank and Helen when they first arrived, and I have the impression that no one is ever willing to argue with Sidney Devonport when he gets a bee in his bonnet about something—so they were ejected from the house, one and all.'

'Ejected,' Poirot repeated in a neutral voice.

'That's right. They went to the home of a neighbour, though not a near neighbour. It was a house on the other side of the Kingfisher Hill Estate: Kingfisher's View, that was its name. Daisy Devonport complained to me that it had taken an age to walk there and back.'

'Kingfisher's View?' I looked at Poirot. 'Wasn't that the name of Little Key when it belonged to the Laviolettes, before the Devonports changed it?'

'*Non*. Little Key was originally called Kingfisher's Rest.'

'Oh, yes. You are right. Why do you suppose everybody on the estate feels compelled to name everything they own Kingfisher this or that? Kingfisher's Rest, Kingfisher's View, the Kingfisher Coach Company. It's a bit much. The Devonports must be the only residents with some imagination.'

'*Mon ami*, only a moment ago you complained that they are all liars with too much of the imagination! Continue, please, Inspector Capeling.'

'Sidney and Lilian had their reunion with Frank and they met Helen. All went well from what I understand. The only other person in the house at the time was Winnifred Lord, a servant. The Laviolettes and Richard and Daisy Devonport were at Kingfisher's View, and Winnifred—Winnie, as I believe she is commonly known—was going to fetch them once Sidney had given permission for them to return. She did this at around two o'clock in the afternoon—though, before that, at a quarter to two, Oliver Prowd had returned from London, and he went straight to Kingfisher's View as he had been instructed. Then they all waited there—Richard, Daisy, Oliver and the Laviolettes—until they were summoned.'

'So, to summarize: Frank Devonport and Helen Acton arrived at Little Key at ten; and then Oliver Prowd, the Laviolettes and Richard and Daisy Devonport arrived at two o'clock or shortly afterwards,' said Poirot.

'I believe Oliver stayed a little longer than the others at Kingfisher's View,' said Marcus Capeling. 'But, yes, he too arrived at Little Key in due course. After that, nothing remarkable happened until the murder itself, as far as I am aware and going by what I was told. Frank, Richard and Daisy were all overjoyed to see each other again, from all accounts, and spent much of the afternoon in lively conversation, catching up on each other's news. The Laviolettes, who were Frank's godparents, were delighted to see him. It was a happy occasion—everyone says so. And then, at twenty minutes before six o'clock . . .' Marcus Capeling stopped. His expression had grown more solemn.

'Go on,' Poirot urged.

'At twenty minutes before six, Frank Devonport fell to his death from the landing, high up in that enormous entrance hall. He'd been pushed over the banana-leaf balcony. Fell and cracked his head open on the hard floor beneath.'

'Banana-leaf?' I said.

Poirot gave me an impatient look. 'Do you not observe what is in front of your eyes, Catchpool? The iron of the balcony has the pattern of many little leaves.'

'I did not notice, no.'

'They're banana leaves,' Capeling repeated. 'Verna Laviolette told me all about it. The balcony was designed by a friend of hers and her husband's. It was a later addition to the house once they'd bought it. The original balcony was ugly, she said. I didn't ask her about the balcony, you understand. But she seemed to want to talk about it. All that mattered to me was whether a woman of Helen Acton's height and frame could have pushed Frank Devonport over it and to his death. My men and I soon saw that it was easily possible. Frank was tall and the balcony is not especially high. Helen would only have needed to give him a hard shove to the back and he'd have gone flying over. Well, as he did.

'I shall never forget all that blood,' Capeling went on. 'When I first arrived at the scene—only for an instant, mind you—I thought I was looking at a large dark-red rug with a man lying on it.' He shook his head to banish the image.

'So, you established that Helen Acton was also on this high landing when Frank fell,' Poirot said.

'Oh, yes, there's no doubt about that,' said Capeling. 'Helen was up there, all right. She wasn't the only one—Sidney and Lilian were up there too, and Daisy, and Verna Laviolette. As soon as Frank hit the ground, Helen came running down the stairs like a rocket on fire and announced that she was the one who'd done it. Ask Oliver Prowd—he'll tell you. They all will. Nearly all of them heard her, though it was Prowd she landed on at the bottom of the stairs. She grabbed him by the arms and said, "I killed him, Oliver. God help me, Frank's dead and I'm the one who killed him."'

CHAPTER 9

The Training of the Brain

Before we left Marcus Capeling's house, Poirot asked him for a pencil and some paper, which he supplied. Once we were alone and on our way back to London, Poirot offered both to me.

'What am I supposed to do with these?' I said tersely. Then I felt ungracious and tried to soften it with a joke. 'If you're thinking that you and I might design a board game together, I'm afraid you will have to find a different partner.'

'We can now forget about the board games, my friend. Never again shall I ask you to think about Peepers. Not even when we return to Kingfisher Hill. We are now in the advantageous position in relation to the Devonport family. The truth about us is known and we need pretend no more.' As an afterthought, he said, 'Peepers needs much consolidation and revision if it is ever to succeed as a commercial enterprise. I do not think this will happen. The vanity of its creators will prevent it. Even when they speak of making the improvements, what they suggest is superficial. They cannot see that the entire structure of the game needs to change.'

'Why don't you offer them your services?' I suggested. 'They would probably make more money from the game with you as co-designer than they will otherwise, even if they had to split the profits three ways.'

'Undoubtedly they would. They will make *no* money without my intervention. Of course, they are both rich men who require no more wealth than they presently possess— that is perhaps part of the problem. If I were to share with them my vision for Peepers, they would make their fortunes all over again. However, the board game design, it does not interest Hercule Poirot especially. Now, take the pencil and paper.'

'Why?'

'You said before that you do not understand why I bother with the murder of Frank Devonport. If it were up to you, you would not wish to bother, *n'est-ce pas*? You are full of the nonchalance.'

'Not nonchalance. Frustration. I don't believe we stand a chance of making sense of the whole mess. Oh, I know you will never give up. But if you want my honest opinion, I think in this instance we're going to fail.'

'But Hercule Poirot never fails. You know this, Catchpool. Once I put my mind to the solving of a puzzle, it is imme-diately in no doubt that the puzzle will be solved.'

'You are assuming that the future can always be accu-rately predicted from the past,' I said.

'Not at all,' said Poirot. 'My assumption is quite different:

the results I have achieved in the past were *only achieved* because I applied to those problems the highest levels of expert knowledge and deduction as well as the strongest resolve and determination. That is why my record contains only successes. I know, therefore, that if I continue to provide all of those elements—and, note, Catchpool, that they all are supplied *by me*, not by the circumstances of the case in question—then it is certain that I will achieve more successes in the future.' He smiled.

'Well, I hope you are right,' I said.

Poirot beamed at me. 'You will not comprehend this, Catchpool, but in my heart I already have the pleasure and satisfaction of having answered every last question and solved the mystery of the death of Frank Devonport most decisively.'

'What?' This surprised me, even knowing Poirot as I did. 'Are you telling me that you already know—?'

'No, no. You misunderstand me. I do not yet have all of the answers. Like you, I have mainly the questions. But when Marcus Capeling told us about Daisy Devonport and the two engagement rings—first the emerald and diamond from Oliver Prowd and then the ruby that was once Helen Acton's—a feeling of overwhelming confidence swept over me. At that moment I *knew* that all would be well.'

'That's a coincidence,' I said. 'It was those confounded rings that sent me in the opposite direction. They convinced me that perpetual confusion was all we would ever get from the Devonport family.'

Poirot smoothed down his moustaches with the index

and middle fingers of both his hands. 'There is a moment in each case—there always has been, from the commencement of my career in the Belgian police—when suddenly, before the mystery is solved, I see enough of the picture to know for sure that it *will* be solved. In that instant—and it is a glorious feeling, Catchpool . . . in that instant, *I feel the very same emotions that I would feel if I already knew the answer.*'

'I see,' I said doubtfully.

'Once I have the feeling of triumph that accompanies the perfectly resolved puzzle, then I am forced to justify it. Do you see? I am bound by my duty to myself to create, in my mind, the resolution that proves the emotion correct. I hope you will experience this for yourself one day, my friend. Truly, it is the only way to succeed.'

'It might help me to get closer to the exalted state you describe if you would explain about the rings. Why should a barrage of new, confusing details about women's jewellery be a source of such delight to you? Why did you declare it to be "*merveilleuse*"?' My friend winced at my appalling French accent, for which I could not blame him.

'I could put the question to you only the other way around,' he said. 'Why were you not happy to have such striking new details added to the incomplete picture that we are attempting to make complete? I tell you, it is all in the attitude one adopts, my friend. To you, the stories about the engagement rings were yet one more complication. Yet another obstacle to us arriving at the truth, pushing us farther away from it.'

'Precisely,' I said with feeling.

'But, *mon ami*, there is truth to be found. It exists! There is nothing human that cannot be made sense of once one knows all of the relevant facts. *Alors*, whenever a new detail is given to us, we must be grateful. Each new morsel of information is to be celebrated! And even more so when one is given a piece as striking as the story of the rings. Here there is additional cause for celebration because this story stands out so prominently. It becomes a point of focus in the still-forming picture precisely because it is, at the first glance, so baffling. Once one has a point of focus, all of the other details start to arrange themselves around it.'

I mumbled something about that not having happened yet. Of course, Poirot had an answer at the ready: 'If you resent it for not happening before it can possibly happen, you push it further away. Me, I prefer to trust that it will happen when the time is right. When we speak to Helen Acton tomorrow, we will gather more details for our picture!'

'Tomorrow? I'm expected at Scotland Yard tomorrow.'

'Then I will leave it up to you to amend those expectations,' said Poirot firmly. 'You will accompany me to Holloway Prison first thing in the morning. All has been arranged.'

'You still haven't explained to me why I'm holding this pencil and paper,' I said.

'You need it to make your list,' said Poirot. 'Often this is what cures you of the petulant mood.'

'I'm not in a petulant mood,' I told him. 'What list?'

156

'All of the things you do not understand.'

'I don't want to make a list. I don't understand *anything* about this latest mess that we've stumbled into. The list would be endless.'

'If you do not feel better after making the list, I will apologize for having wasted your time,' said Poirot. 'Unless it proves useful to my deliberations, in which case I will not apologize—though I doubt that it will. Your lists are usually not comprehensive. Nor are they made in the proper methodical way.'

'Is that so? Well, on this occasion, my method will be not making the list at all.'

'Distinctly, the ill humour,' Poirot muttered under his breath.

After that, we spoke hardly at all for the remainder of the journey back to London. Alone in my rooms that afternoon, I snapped the pencil he had given me and tore up the sheet of paper. I ate a delectable loin of pork cooked for me by my landlady, Blanche Unsworth, then sat in front of the fire with a large measure of brandy and attempted a crossword puzzle, but the clues proved more difficult than usual to decipher and I soon gave up.

Later still, full of admiration for my Belgian friend and mystified by the hold he seemed to have over me, I took some paper from my own supplies and used my own pencil to do what he had asked of me. 'List' I wrote at the top of the page, and as I did so I saw Joan Blythe's unfinished face in my mind and knew that she had to be item number one.

1. What is the explanation for the Joan Blythe incident? Was somebody trying to kill her? If so, who and why? Did the man who warned her not to sit in that particular seat on the coach intend the warning helpfully, to save her life, or did he intend to threaten and scare her? Who was he? Why did she board the coach at all, knowing her life was in danger? And, if she was resolved to do so, why did she not hurry aboard early enough to ensure that she would have a choice of seats? When she finally got herself on board and saw that the only seat left was the very one about which she had been warned, why did she not then make a run for it?

I laid down my pencil with a heavy sigh and considered giving up. This was not one question, it was many. Poirot would mock me for my inadequate list-making abilities.

I started to write again.

2. Does the Joan Blythe puzzle have any connection to Frank Devonport's murder?
3. Why did it scare her so much when I mentioned the words 'midnight gathering', and why was she no longer afraid once I told her that those two words were the title of a book that Daisy Devonport was reading?
4. Why did Poirot ask Daisy about the book? Why did he think it was important?

5. Who killed Frank Devonport? Was it Daisy Devonport, Helen Acton or someone else?

6. If neither Helen nor Daisy murdered Frank, why are both claiming that they did?

7. How could Helen have fallen in love with Richard Devonport in a few hours, and so passionately in love that she decided to kill Frank (if she did)? Is that at all plausible? (Probably not—but she might have met Richard long before that day, unbeknownst to anybody else.)

8. Why did Helen think she could only rid herself of Frank and marry Richard if Frank was dead? Did she believe this to be the case or did she want Frank dead for a different reason (assuming she killed him)?

9. Why did Daisy swap her emerald and diamond ring for Helen's ruby ring, and did Oliver Prowd not object to this? (Richard Devonport suggested that Oliver would tolerate any behaviour from Daisy.)

10. Why did Richard want to marry Helen when she had killed his brother? (Obvious answer: because he does not believe that she is guilty, and never has.)

11. Why did Sidney Devonport allow Richard to get engaged to a woman who had killed his other son? (Does he too believe Helen Acton to be innocent? Or does he care so little about Richard, or Frank, or both? Perhaps he assumed that Helen

would soon hang and therefore it would not matter, but that seems odd from a man in the habit of exerting strong control over his family in other respects.)

12. Why did Sidney Devonport want Richard to distract Lilian before he told Verna Laviolette about Winnie? Why would Winnie not be returning to Little Key? Before she left, what was her role in the Devonport home? Servant/cook?

13. Why did Godfrey Laviolette ask us not to talk to the Devonports about the house changing its name from Kingfisher's Rest to Little Key?

14. Why did Verna Laviolette apologize to Oliver Prowd and Lilian Devonport after mentioning the word 'grave' at dinner? (Possibly because Lilian is dying and Oliver's father recently died.)

15. Why do the Devonports pretend all is well and try to conduct their social life as if nothing has happened when their son has been murdered and his former fiancée is about to hang for the crime (or was about to, until Daisy Devonport also confessed)?

16. What did Godfrey Laviolette mean when he referred to 'paradise' at Kingfisher Hill being ruined? What made him and Verna decide to sell their house to the Devonports?

17. What is the explanation for the strange behaviour of Verna Laviolette? Is it strange or am I being fanciful in thinking it so?

I could not think of any more questions to add to the list, so I folded it and put it in my pocket. As I did so, there was a knock at the door and my landlady, Blanche Unsworth, appeared in the sitting room.

'Goodness me, it's cold in here,' she said, rubbing her arms. I was about to say, 'Don't be silly, there's a roaring fire in the grate,' when I saw that it had burned out. I had been too immersed in my list-making to notice.

'I'm sorry to disturb you, Edward. A gentleman telephoned for you from Scotland Yard, said he worked with you—a Sergeant Giddy?'

'Could it have been Gidley?'

'Yes, I think it was. That's right. Sergeant Gidley.'

'I'll come now.' I rose to my feet.

'Oh, no, he's not still on the telephone. He wanted me to give you a message, but . . .' Her face took on a wounded, hard-done-to expression. 'Why didn't you tell me you'd been put in charge of a murder case? You know I like to hear your stories.'

'Stories aren't stories until they have endings,' I said. 'This one doesn't yet. The case was only assigned to me very recently.'

'Well, that's what Sergeant Giddy wanted to talk about—this new case of yours, the Devonshire case.'

'Devonport.'

'Yes, that's it. A lady came to Scotland Yard to see you about it: a Miss Winnifred Lord.'

Aha! So here was Winnie, the Devonports' never-to-return servant.

161

'She wishes to speak to you at your earliest convenience,' said Mrs Unsworth. 'Says she knows who killed Frank Devonshire and she knows why, too, and it's not the reason you all think. She left a telephone number. I've written it down and left it next to the telephone.'

'But . . .' My mind had started to race. 'Did she not give the information to Sergeant Gidley? Why did he let her leave?'

'He said she wanted to speak to you and no one else. I don't blame her! I'd also want to speak to the man in charge if I had important information in a murder case. I wouldn't want to natter away about something so important as murder to the first person I ran into.' She stared at me pointedly. 'I should want to speak to *you*, Edward, and no one else.'

I had a terrible feeling of foreboding on behalf of poor Winnie, whom I had never met. Who else might know that she knew—if indeed she did—the facts of Frank Devonport's murder, apart from Sergeant Gidley, Blanche Unsworth and me? Was she in danger? I had to find her, and soon.

She knows who killed Frank and she knows why, too, and it's not the reason you all think.

Did that mean what I thought it meant?

I hurried to the telephone and dialled the number that Mrs Unsworth had taken down. A woman answered: Winnifred Lord's mother. Speaking to her did nothing to reassure me that my fears were misplaced. I was told that Winnie had been to Scotland Yard earlier in the day, since which time she had not returned, as she had promised to, and her mother had received no word from her.

The following morning I had a quick wash, dressed and ate a cursory breakfast, all within the space of twenty minutes, much to Mrs Unsworth's chagrin. I have long suspected her of fabricating the most devious schemes to keep me at her breakfast table for as long as she can. Well, on this occasion she failed.

I had arranged for a police driver to call at half past nine and take me from the lodging house to Holloway Prison, collecting Poirot on the way. After Holloway, we would proceed to Kingfisher Hill and Little Key. How on earth I could ever be respected there as a figure of authority after Poirot's and my attempt to pull the wool over everyone's eyes, I had no idea. It would be easier if no one made mention of Peepers, but there was little chance of that.

Poirot was ready and waiting for me on the street when I arrived, looking more dapper than ever. At the sight of him I had to remind myself that we were not on our way to a jolly day at the Ascot races but rather to my least favourite prison. I have visited many in the course of my work for Scotland Yard and have found none to be pleasant, but Holloway is the worst of all. I have never been able to tolerate the suffering of women very easily, and within those walls there is little else to be found. I detest everything about the place, starting with its outward appearance. If one deliberately blurs one's vision, the building's exterior resembles a large, indistinct mass of

163

people with mouths open in protest and arms thrown up in furious protest.

The interior is no better. The strangest thing about being inside a prison is that one expects to meet evil face to face, but in fact there is little of the purest evil to be found inside this or any jail. What one encounters instead, over and over again, is hopelessness and regret: the traces of stale betrayals, tempers fatally lost and horrible compromises in impossible situations.

I said some of this to Poirot. He replied, 'Today will be different, for we bring hope to Helen Acton. We bring the news that her life, temporarily, is saved, thanks to Daisy Devonport.'

'She will have received that news already.'

'This is true.' He soon brightened up again. 'Then we will bring to her even better news! If she tells us the truth, she need *never* pay with her life for that murder.'

'Well, unless the truth is that she did, in fact, murder Frank. Also . . .'

'What, Catchpool? Please speak up. I would very much like to hear every single one of your reservations.' He appeared to mean what he said with no hint of sarcasm.

'I was only thinking that since Helen Acton confessed to Frank Devonport's murder, perhaps she very much wants to pay with her life, whether she in fact killed him or not.'

'Suicide by hangman? It is possible, yes. In due course we will find out.' Poirot said all of this in that brisk way he has when he is eager to move on to another topic. 'Now, tell me, *mon ami* . . . these words of Winnifred Lord's that were reported to you by Blanche Unsworth who heard them from Sergeant Gidley: "I know who disposed of Frank Devonport, and I know why, and it's not the reason you all think".'

'"Disposed of"?' I said.

'Indeed. Those were the exact words of Winnifred Lord. I have spoken to Sergeant Gidley in person this morning. Did you not wonder why I waited for you on the street? I had been out very early, not only to visit Sergeant Gidley but also Winnifred Lord's mother in Kennington.'

'All before ten in the morning?' I raised an eyebrow.

'I detest the excessively early rising, Catchpool, but sometimes it is necessary. *Oui.* Winnie Lord has still not returned. Her mother is extremely distressed. She has not heard from her since she left the house yesterday to go to Scotland Yard. I attempted to calm the mother but was unsuccessful. In the end the most I could do was promise to bring her daughter's disappearance to the attention of the police. This I did when I spoke to Sergeant Gidley. He told me precisely what Winnifred Lord told him—the only thing she told him, for it was you she sought for the telling of the whole story. But to Sergeant Gidley she said those words: "I know who disposed of Frank Devonport and I know why, too, and it's not the reason you all think." Now, when you and I spoke on the telephone last night, you seemed to think that those final words—"It's not the reason you all think"—might have significance?'

'Well, yes. As far as I am aware, no one has any notion at all of why anybody should have wanted Frank Devonport dead. The only reason that has been offered up for consideration is the one that Helen Acton has provided: she wanted Frank out of the way so that she could marry Richard. Therefore "the reason you all think" must be that one, which means—unless I'm mistaken—that Winnie Lord believes Helen Acton is indeed the guilty party, but that she is lying about her motive.'

'I knew it!' Poirot cried in triumph. '*Mon ami*, you are mistaken. I know you so well that I perceive your incorrect conclusions even when you do not state them! Think about it for one second, I entreat you. "I know who disposed of Frank Devonport, and I know why, too, and it's not the reason you all think." Those were the words of Winnie Lord, yes? Now, imagine, purely for the sake of our little experiment, that it was Alfred Bixby, the impresario of char-a-bancs, who committed the murder. This is quite impossible, I know, but humour me. Monsieur Bixby secretly entered the house, hid somewhere on the landing and pushed Frank Devonport to his death. Imagine that Winnie Lord knows this, and knows, furthermore, that his motive was revenge. Let us say that Frank Devonport once insulted the Kingfisher Coach Company.'

'All right,' I said, curious to see where he was going with this.

'Now think again of the words of Winnie Lord: "I know who disposed of Frank Devonport"—she means that she knows it was Alfred Bixby. "I know why, too"—because he insulted the Kingfisher Coach Company. "And it's not the reason you all think". This could easily mean that "you

166

all", *we* all, believe the motive for murder to be a desire to marry Richard Devonport—because we have the wrong culprit in mind. *And Alfred Bixby's reason was quite different!* Do you see, Catchpool?'

'I do. I'm not convinced, Poirot. Philosophically it works, but if Frank's murderer were anyone other than Helen Acton, I do not believe that Winnie would have said the part about "It's not the reason you all think." She would simply have said, "I know who killed Frank and it's not who you think it is" or "I know who killed Frank and why they did it".'

'*Non, non,*' Poirot said gently. 'We cannot know this, my friend. Please consider: if Helen Acton is indeed guilty and Winnie Lord knows this, why would she say to Sergeant Gidley, "I know who did it"? Is she not more likely to say, "You've got the right person but she's lying about why she did it"? I put it to you that "I know who did it" weighs as heavily on the side of Helen Acton's innocence—or at least, Winnie Lord's belief that she is innocent—as "It's not the reason you all think" weighs on the side of Mademoiselle Helen being guilty.'

I was finding it harder, the more I thought about it, to extract any meaning from the words at all. I had been turning them over in my mind for so long that they were losing any resonance and usefulness they had once possessed.

'Tell me, did you make the list I asked you to make?' said Poirot.

Without a word, I produced it from my pocket and handed it to him.

We travelled in silence while he read it. I prepared myself for criticism, and was pleasantly surprised when he began, 'This is not a bad effort, Catchpool. Not bad at all. You have listed many interesting questions. You have only failed to include three or four of the most important questions. This is much better than I expected. A more orderly person would have assigned to each individual question a number of its own, of course, and here you have at the top of your list many questions relating to Joan Blythe, all grouped together—'

The pleasure I had felt at first had deserted me. 'What important questions have I failed to include?'

'Well, for a start, there is a *vital* question that pertains to Winnie Lord and what she told Sergeant Gidley. Though perhaps you made this list before receiving the message from Sergeant Gidley yesterday evening?'

'I did. So that needs adding to the list: what does Winnie Lord know? Who does she believe the murderer to be, and for what reason does she think the murder was committed?'

'*Non, mon ami.* You are right, this does need adding, but it is not the question I had in mind. Ah, if you would only recognize what that most important question is . . .' he said wistfully.

'Yes, just imagine.' I feigned a wistful sigh. 'If only there were some way for me to know what this elusive question might be so that we could discuss it now.'

'Ah, you tease me.' Poirot chuckled. 'I see also that you have omitted essential questions about Kingfisher's View and the book, *Midnight Gathering*—'

'The book features prominently in the list,' I said.

'But the two most important questions about it are missing, along with their obvious and fascinating answers,' said Poirot. 'Also missing is an item that I was sure you would remember to include: the demeanour and temperament of Daisy Devonport.'

'What about her demeanour? When? On the coach or when we met her at Kingfisher Hill?'

'All of the times,' said Poirot. 'The personality and psychology of Daisy Devonport—this is what is most deeply interesting to me in this whole affair.'

'I find her dull and rebarbative,' I told him. 'I think she's spoilt, manipulative and thoroughly unpleasant and I should be happy if I never had to encounter her again. As for an essential question about Kingfisher's View that's missing . . . do you mean Kingfisher's Rest, the original name of Little Key? If so, it's on the list. Number thirteen, I think.'

'I know what is on your list. I have the paper in front of me and I am looking at it now. Why do you assume that my words do not accurately reflect my meaning? I said "Kingfisher's View" because that is what I meant. Kingfisher's View: the house to which the Laviolettes and Richard and Daisy Devonport were sent on the day of Frank's death so that Sidney and Lilian could spend some time alone with Frank. Inspector Capeling told us that it was not near to Little Key, do you remember? "Not a near neighbour," he said. And did he not also say that Daisy had complained about the distance between the two houses? In which case . . .' Poirot made a beckoning gesture, as if he was trying to coax the right answer out of me.

For once I thought I had it. 'In which case, why was that particular house chosen and by whom? Who decided to send the Laviolettes and Richard and Daisy to Kingfisher's View in particular, and why? Is that house owned by friends of Sidney Devonport, perhaps?'

Poirot clapped his hands together in delight. 'Precisely, Catchpool. You have hit on the head the nail!'

I felt briefly elated, until he added, 'It proceeds most satisfactorily, the training of your brain.'

CHAPTER 10

Helen Acton

Holloway was as dismal as ever. The advantage of visiting with Poirot was that we were treated like royalty and shown immediately to a comfortable, well-appointed room in which coffee of a surprisingly good quality was provided, along with a plate of biscuits of varying levels of appeal. Some were symmetrical and biscuit-coloured; others were misshapen and of a greyish hue. Poirot and I both avoided one that looked as if it had an indentation in it from a thumb or large finger. I thought nostalgically of the scones baked by Marcus Capeling's wife, and of the fool I had been yesterday to imagine that one might consume too many of them.

Helen Acton was brought to us by two prison guards. I noticed at once that she was not bound, handcuffed or constrained in any way. She smiled at us—a smile that was demure and moderate, welcoming and cautious—as she entered the room and sat in the chair that we had set out for her. Before leaving us alone with her, one of the guards said, 'Open the door when you're finished. I'll be waiting outside. Don't worry, Miss Acton won't give you any trouble.' As he said this, he grinned at her and his expression seemed to me to contain a great deal of respect. She responded to him with a smile.

I was surprised. Female prisoners, on the whole, were treated poorly and often with great brutality by male prison employees. It was one of the many things I hated to witness inside institutions such as this one, and it gave me a convenient opening for our conversation with Helen Acton. 'You seem to be on friendly terms with the guards here,' I said.

'Yes, they treat me well,' she replied. Her hair was dark brown and cut in a short, plain style. She had a kindly, intelligent face with a large forehead and round brown eyes that were alert and watchful. Her clothing was as plain as the attire of women prisoners all over England.

'You are lucky, mademoiselle,' said Poirot. 'You have received news of the postponement of your execution?'

'I have,' she said.

'And you know the cause?'

'Yes. Daisy has confessed to killing Frank.' She leaned forward. 'M. Poirot, she did not kill him. I did. You must do all that you can to protect Daisy.'

'If she is innocent, why did she confess?' I asked.

'I don't know. Why would she do such a thing? I can think of no reason.' She spoke as if the three of us were jointly charged with solving the puzzle. 'It cannot be to save my life—Daisy and I are . . . well, we are strangers. She might have been Frank's sister but I did not know her.

She has no reason to wish to save the life of the woman who killed the brother she adored, so why does she insist upon this lie?' She looked from me to Poirot. 'It is very important to me to know. Will you find out for me, M. Poirot?'

'Oh, I intend to find out the truth, mademoiselle. Be assured of that.'

Helen Acton seemed not entirely satisfied with his answer. 'May I speak frankly?' she said.

'Please.'

'I have very little left in this world that matters to me. Almost nothing. I will be put to death—not when I expected to be, but later. That is as it should be. I killed Frank and I must pay for what I did. But . . . having been resigned to my own death for so long, and even happy about it, I am now greatly agitated by this news about Daisy. I cannot bear the thought that I might die without knowing what it means. That might not make sense to you but it is how I feel. Frank loved Daisy most of all the Devonports. She mattered to him. For his sake, I need to know why she is saying that she killed him.'

'I understand,' said Poirot. 'As I say, I shall find out the answers to your questions about Mademoiselle Daisy. When I have them, I will bring them to you and lay them all before you.'

'Thank you.'

'In return, I hope that you will tell me and my friend Inspector Catchpool here the full truth about the death of Frank Devonport.'

Helen Acton's expression changed from gratitude to alarm.

'Is it really such a dreadful prospect to tell us the truth?' I asked her. 'You have just told us that Daisy mattered to Frank and that you need to know the truth for his sake. When you said it, you sounded very much like someone who was fond of Frank Devonport. This is also suggested by the fact that, until he died, you were also engaged to be married to him. May I tell you what I believe? I think you loved Frank a great deal, and I think you still do.'

She stared at me intently. After nearly a minute of silence, she said in a voice that was hoarse with emotion, 'I do. I will always love Frank. Thank you . . . No one has asked me that before. They have all asked me endlessly if I killed him and why I killed him, but never if I loved him.'

'Yet in spite of this love, you claim that you murdered him,' I said.

'Yes.'

'Do you regret doing so? If you could wind back the clock and return to the sixth of December last year, would you behave differently?'

'You are the first person to ask me that question too,' she said. 'Yes, I regret it profoundly. I should not have done it. If only I had not done it. I . . .'

'What?' I said.

Tears rolled down her face. She shook her head wildly. 'All I can tell you is that I intended to kill Frank and I did kill him.'

'Why?' Poirot asked. 'Tell us why you killed the man you loved.'

She did not reply. Neither of us tried to persuade her to do so. There was something immovable and wholly resolute about her.

'So you are happy to die,' I said, changing the subject back to what I knew she was willing to talk about.

'Yes.'

'You regret your crime and wish to atone for it with your own death.'

She nodded. 'I hope and pray that I might be reunited with Frank. Oh, I do not truly believe it will happen. He is in Heaven and I have no hope of ending up there, I know that. But I also know, or at least I have been told, that the Lord is all forgiving, and I have prayed for so many hours and begged for His forgiveness. It is all I do in here. And sometimes I allow myself to hope that my prayers have been heard.'

'Mademoiselle.' Poirot stood up and walked slowly around the table that separated us from her. 'You sound sincere but your words make little sense to me. May I ask, how do you feel about Richard Devonport? Is he not the man to whom you are presently engaged to be married?'

'Ah, Richard.' She gave a small smile. 'I wondered when we would have to talk about him. Yes, I have promised to marry Richard, though it is a meaningless promise given where I am and what is going to happen to me.'

'Do you love Monsieur Richard?' Poirot asked her.

'No, I do not.' Her words fell heavily in the hollow air.

We waited.

'You asked me for the truth, didn't you? The truth is, I have never loved Richard. I wanted to confess to killing Frank and I needed to provide a reason, and . . . and the police believed me. People are so stupid. I did not know Richard until that day, the day Frank died. That afternoon, I spent somewhere between one and a half and two hours in his company, for much of that time with Frank present and lots of other people, too—and the police believed that this would be long enough for me to fall madly in love with Richard? How could they think that? Frank was tall and handsome, gregarious and brave. There was no physical resemblance between Frank and Richard, none whatever. Neither was there a similarity of character. Richard is timid and mousy and he looks like a suet pudding.' She closed her eyes. 'I'm sorry, I should not have said that. I don't mean to be unkind, only to say that no one would know Richard was in a room, let alone fall in love with him! It is quite ludicrous to believe that any woman who had known and loved Frank could ever love Richard.'

'Yet you are engaged to be married to him,' I said.

'He proposed. I don't know what he was thinking, but . . . well, it was convenient. I agreed, knowing what awaited me and that I would never have to go through with it. What harm could it do? It made my story look all the more true.'

'If you did not and do not love Richard Devonport, you must have murdered Frank for a different reason,' said Poirot.

'Yes. I'm afraid I cannot tell you my true reason.'

'Why not?'

'I cannot tell you that either.'

'Cannot or will not?'

She hesitated, then said, 'It would not be the right thing to do.'

'Perhaps you did not kill Frank and someone else did,' I said. 'Maybe Daisy did, and you have been protecting her all this time. As you say, Frank loved her more than the other Devonports. You might have known that he would want you to save her life no matter what she had done to him. And if you felt that life without him was not worth living . . . No wonder you're confused that Daisy has suddenly decided to make a mockery of your efforts by confessing.'

'Please tell us about the day that Frank Devonport died,' said Poirot. 'Exactly what happened?'

'It was horrible,' Helen said at once. 'Unbearable from start to finish. I knew I might find it difficult, in the circumstances, but nothing could have prepared me for how awful it was from the moment I arrived at Little Key.'

'Why did you expect it to be difficult?' I asked.

'Frank and his parents had been estranged for some time. I assume you have heard the story of how he stole from them in order to help Oliver Prowd and his invalid father?'

'I should very much like to hear your version,' I told her.

'My version, as you call it, is that I would *never* allow myself to be welcomed back by a family that had disowned me after a quite understandable action for which I had apologized over and over again. Frank paid back every penny of the money he took from his father. He admitted to his theft when an admission was quite unnecessary. Sidney and Lilian would never have noticed that things had been temporarily amiss. But Frank was honourable. He valued honesty and integrity above all else. It mattered deeply to him to tell the truth, and for that they banished him—a banishment that he not only understood but forgave. Frank . . .' Her face contorted in pain. 'He forgave people. Always. He—' She started to sob and buried her face in her hands.

There seemed to be nothing to do but wait.

When Helen finally recovered, she said, 'Frank would have disagreed, but I believe that Sidney and Lilian Devonport are evil, M. Poirot. They terrified Daisy and Richard into submission. Neither of them wanted to sever their ties with Frank but they obeyed their parents without question. Nobody wants to fall foul of two monsters who would stop at nothing, and that's exactly what Sidney and Lilian Devonport are: monsters.'

'And this is why you expected to find your first visit to Kingfisher Hill difficult?' said Poirot. 'Frank wished to be reconciled with these monsters while you wished that the *rapprochement* could be avoided?'

'Yes, I did. You will think me cold for wanting to deprive Frank of his family whom he loved, but I did not see how he could overlook the way they had treated him. In my opinion, such things should not be overlooked. Even

Richard and Daisy's behaviour . . . At the time, and it was not all that long ago, I thought cowardice of that sort was unforgivable. Blind obedience in the face of tyranny, it seemed to me.' A faraway look passed across her face. 'It's funny how one can be terribly brave in some respects and an utter coward in others, isn't it? In any case, it was Frank's family so I complied with his wishes as best I could, though in my opinion we would have been better off on our own.' She sighed. 'If only we had not gone to Kingfisher Hill that day, Frank would still be alive. I wish he had torn up their wretched letter!'

'Letter?' I said.

'Yes, the one asking him to come back. Everything about it was sickening. Sidney and Lilian offered no apology and took no share of the blame for their cruel treatment of Frank. They said neither that they loved him nor that they had missed him, only that he had betrayed the family inex-cusably and was lucky to be given this second chance. The letter also made it abundantly clear that everything that had happened in the past was never to be mentioned again. The condition of Frank being re-admitted to the family was that he was not allowed to refer to problems of the past because the whole situation was upsetting enough as it was. The words "We forgive you" were nowhere to be found. Instead they said Frank was lucky that illness had weakened their moral standards to the extent that they were now willing to tolerate the unforgivable. I said to him, "How dare they write in such terms and expect you to go running back to them?"'

'What did he say?' asked Poirot.

'He told me I didn't understand—assured me that they did love him and did forgive him and were simply too proud to admit they had made a mistake that they now regretted. Frank always saw the best in everybody. I'm afraid that is a talent I do not possess. I told him that he should go alone to Kingfisher Hill, but he was determined to introduce me to his family. "I want all the people I love to love each other," he said. Most of all, he wanted me to meet Daisy. I could not find it in my heart to refuse him. And I hoped that once I met his parents face to face I might be able to find some warmth or goodness in them. At the same time, I feared that I might soften towards them: I had no desire to think about them less harshly after the way they had treated Frank. That is why I was not looking forward to my first visit to Little Key.'

There was a loud knock at the door. All three of us jumped in our seats. A guard who we had not previously met appeared in the room and said, 'M. Hercule Poirot?'

'*Oui*, it is I,' said Poirot.

'Could you follow me please, sir? We have received an urgent message for you.' He lowered his voice. 'It's from the Home Office.'

'The Home Office?' Poirot rose to his feet. 'Catchpool, please continue to find out from Miss Acton the precise order of events on the day of Frank Devonport's death,' he said as he followed the guard out of the room. 'Who was where, and at what time, and for how long? I shall return!'

*

I did not wish to present myself as someone blindly obedient of orders, having so recently heard Helen Acton denounce that quality, so as soon as she and I were alone I started with a different question: 'Whose idea was it for you and Richard Devonport to become engaged?'

She had the grace to look ashamed. 'His. I told you, he proposed.'

'When?'

'When it became known that I had given my love for him as my reason for killing Frank. Evidently word reached him, as it would, I suppose. He came to see me.'

'Here?'

She nodded. 'We had the most peculiar exchange. I expected him to ask me if it was true, but he didn't. He merely asked if the police were right in saying that I had said so. I told him they were. Then he proposed and I accepted. Do you want to know what I think?'

I indicated that I did.

'Richard knew perfectly well that my sudden love for him was nonsense, but he didn't care. He leapt at the chance to have something that had belonged to Frank. I think he believed that, if only he had me, then he would not have entirely lost his beloved brother. Richard idolized Frank and believed him to be the golden one to whom all good things came. I'm well aware that I am not a great beauty, Inspector, if that's what you're thinking—'

'Not at all.'

'—but the very fact of my having been Frank's fiancée will have given me a value in Richard's eyes that bears no

181

relation to any of my attributes. Once I had agreed to become engaged to him, he announced his determination to prove my innocence, which was the very last thing I wanted him to do.'

'Did Richard give you a ring when the two of you got engaged?' I asked her.

'No.'

'But you had a ring from Frank?'

'Yes. A ruby. I told them to give it to Richard for safe-keeping. Obviously I can't wear it in here.'

'Are you aware that it is now being worn by Daisy Devonport instead of her own engagement ring—the one bought for her by Oliver Prowd?'

Helen nodded. 'I expect that seems strange to you. Daisy also worshipped Frank and no doubt wishes to feel as close to him as possible now that he's gone. If by some chance my life is spared . . .' She stopped and seemed to be considering something. Eventually she said, 'No, I could not bear to live without Frank, and with the knowledge of what I did to him. Even if I could, I would let Daisy keep the ring. I do not deserve it.'

'Oliver Prowd can't be too happy about Daisy discarding the ring he gave her,' I said.

Helen gave a hollow laugh. 'Oh, Daisy will have made it clear to Oliver that he has no choice in the matter and no right to complain. Frank used to say that Daisy could be a little tyrant. He said it affectionately, but having met her even only briefly, I can see that it's quite true. She is terrified of her father, yet she has learned from him how to terrify others into submission. Some of the stories Frank told me . . .' Helen shuddered. 'And from the way Daisy spoke to me about Oliver on the day that Frank died, it was absolutely clear that he does what he's told by her if he knows what's good for him. That afternoon was a case in point! She was furious with him. He wasn't there, at least not then, and she told me all about how she'd refused him entry to the house as a punishment for having crossed her.'

'Is that one of the things that made your day at Little Key so unpleasant?' I asked. Then I realized how crass I must have sounded and added quickly, 'Before Frank died, I mean. Obviously that was the worst part of the day.'

Helen Acton smiled. 'Inspector, you say that as if his death was something tragic that happened to me rather than something for which I was to blame.'

'Tell me about the unpleasant day, from the beginning,' I said.

'Everything was appalling from the moment Frank and I arrived at Kingfisher Hill. Far worse than I had foreseen. Lilian Devonport did not look at me, not once. She looked *near* me but never directly at me. No one else would have noticed, but she made sure her eyes never met mine from the second we got there until . . .' She could not bring herself to utter the words. 'Afterwards, she looked at me— screamed at me that I was a murderer, that they would hang me and she would dance on my grave. Those were the first words she spoke to me all day.'

'What about Sidney Devonport?'

'He stared at me all through the day with obvious disdain, as if trying to wish me out of his home by sheer force of will. It might have been partly my fault. I probably did not conceal my contempt for Frank's parents as effectively as I had hoped to. I'm not very good at hiding my feelings.'

'What about the others?' I asked her. 'Did they look at you and speak to you?'

'The person who was kindest to me was Verna Laviolette. She made a particular effort to include me. And, yes, Richard and Daisy both spoke to me. But that was horrible too. Daisy spoke *at* me more than to me—she sat beside me for about thirty minutes and fired words into my face like bullets, ranting about Oliver and all the things he had done wrong. I felt as if I was some kind of inanimate object whose only function was to be pelleted with her list of resentments. Richard seemed torn between wanting to please his mother and follow her lead by ignoring me, and at the same time wanting to be polite and please Frank by making me welcome. Each time he plucked up the courage to say a civil word to me, he looked at Sidney or Lilian afterwards to see if a reprimand was on its way. And he didn't dare speak to me too often.'

'Verna Laviolette was particularly kind to you?' My impression of the woman was that she was anything but kind.

'Yes. Verna was on my side. She made that clear. It must have enraged Sidney and Lilian to have their friend behave in that way when they were going to such pains to remain hostile and aloof. Oh, Verna didn't say anything explicitly but it was unmistakable and I appreciated it greatly. I have no idea what I did to make an ally of her—perhaps Sidney and Lilian's rudeness was so staggeringly obvious that she felt sorry for me.'

'How long had Daisy and Oliver been engaged?' I asked, thinking it odd that Sidney Devonport had allowed his daughter to agree to marry the beneficiary of Frank's theft of his money.

'Not long,' said Helen. 'Seven weeks, if you want to be exact about it. Frank had told me about Oliver's passion for Daisy. He had asked her to marry him twice before. She had said no. That was long before the theft. Then, on the day Frank died, very soon after I met her, Daisy told me the same story with great delight: Oliver had been sweet on her since forever, and she had always rebuffed him until, on the very same day that Sidney and Lilian wrote to Frank to propose a reconciliation, she sent a telegram to Oliver asking *him* to marry *her*. He accepted immediately, of course.'

'What made her change her mind about him?'

'I couldn't tell you. I had only just met Daisy on that day and only knew her from Frank's stories about her. I don't believe they're well suited to one another. Not at all.' She smiled faintly. 'Though nobody cares what a murderess thinks.'

'I should like to hear your opinion,' I told her.

'Daisy is too strong a character and Oliver too weak. It's a dangerous combination.' Helen's expression hardened. 'Did you know that Oliver cut Frank off, too, after they plotted together to steal the money? Oh, he didn't call it that, he didn't say, "I hereby rid myself of you," but that's what it amounted to. The two men did not set eyes on one another again until the day Frank died.'

'But I was told that Oliver and Frank made investments and then founded schools together after they stole Sidney Devonport's money,' I said.

'Yes, they were jointly involved in those ventures, but they were no longer friends,' said Helen. 'Everything was done via intermediaries. Oliver insisted. It was all his doing. When Frank was most in need of a loyal friend . . .' She blinked away tears. 'Oliver would not agree to meet Frank face to face or even speak to him. They went from being the closest of friends to being business partners at a distance. Frank was wounded to his core, but he would not condemn Oliver for his cowardice. "Not everyone has the courage to face their worst actions head-on, Helen," he told me. "If Oliver needs to blame me and shun me in order to be at peace with himself, then that is what he must do and I wish him well." Frank always found a way to take all the blame for himself and absolve others, and Oliver is the opposite sort of person. Quite the opposite!'

I could not wait to share all this new information with Poirot. I still wondered why Daisy had been seized by a sudden desire to marry Oliver Prowd, having twice rejected him, and on the very same day that her parents had written to Frank to suggest a reconciliation.

'What is on your mind?' Helen asked me. I saw no reason not to tell her. She listened without comment, then she smiled.

'Frank thought of the name Little Key,' she said. 'It's a quote from Charles Dickens: "A very little key will open a very heavy door".'

'The house used to be called Kingfisher's Rest, I believe.'

'Yes. Frank thought that was dreadfully dull. He persuaded Sidney to change it when they bought the house from the Laviolettes.'

'When was that?' I asked. 'How long before Frank died?'

'A long time. Two years at least.'

I cleared my throat and said, 'Returning to the sixth of December, the day you killed Frank . . . did Daisy tell you why she was angry with Oliver Prowd?'

'Oh, yes. She told me again and again, in as many different and colourful ways as she could think of. She and Richard and the Laviolettes had all spent the morning at another house on the Kingfisher Hill Estate while Oliver was attending to some business in London. Daisy had told him that when he returned to Kingfisher Hill he was to come to this other house and not go to Little Key as he normally would. He resented being made to wait in the home of a stranger for no good reason, and Daisy resented his resentment—all the more so because he was usually, to use her exact words, "as meek and obedient as a little lamb". But he could not see why Frank's return should mean that everyone else needed to be expelled from the house until further notice, and Daisy didn't understand why her normally docile acolyte should pick this day of all days to cut up rough. Daisy objected most strongly to his rebellion—with the result that he ended up staying much longer at the other house, the stranger's house, than anyone else. Daisy forbade him to come back to Little Key with her.'

'But Oliver was in the house when you pushed Frank off the balcony,' I said, remembering Marcus Capeling's account of the tragic events: according to him, Oliver Prowd had been accosted by Helen in her determination to confess. He was the one to whom she had first admitted her guilt.

'Yes, he was. He was kind to me, too, when I said that I had killed Frank—he was the one I told, you see, and he attended to me until the police arrived.' A tear escaped from her left eye and rolled down her face. She wiped it away. 'Everyone else was with Frank, but Oliver looked after *me*. He took me away from them all and sat with me, tried to calm me. He was kind.' She nodded and appeared soothed by the memory.

'But a moment ago you said that Daisy had forbidden him from returning to Little Key. Did she change her mind later and allow him to come back?'

'Yes. Exactly that. Daisy is unpredictable,' said Helen. 'Frank told me that she has always had that sort of temperament. At a certain point in the afternoon she decided that she liked Oliver again, so he was permitted to return. Then she was angry with him all over again because he brought someone with him without permission. Frank had told me all about the strict Devonport family policy: no guests or callers, ever, unless they have been invited or approved by Sidney himself. This man had not.'

'Who was he?' I asked. Marcus Capeling had said nothing about an uninvited guest on the day of Frank Devonport's death. By his account, the only people at Little Key on the sixth of December had been the Devonports, the Laviolettes and Winnie Lord.

'A man of around his own age who lived in that other house—the one Oliver had come from.'

'Kingfisher's View?'

'Yes. I think his name was Percy. Percy Semley, that was it. He was there when Frank died. Oliver came back to Little Key with Mr Semley in tow. Godfrey Laviolette was with them too—he had also stayed longer at the other house. The three of them were talking vigorously about fishing as they walked in. Frank and I could hear them from my room upstairs, where I had gone to pretend to sleep, to get away from Sidney's cold glare. Frank had joined me there a little later—he came up to check that I was all right. Daisy would also have heard the men arrive. She was upstairs by then too and her room was next to mine. She was waiting for Oliver's return and was all ready to forgive his earlier disobedience. She expected him to come back with only one intention: to kneel at her feet and beg forgiveness. Instead, he turned up in the middle of a jovial conversation about fishing with two other chaps, one of whom was not even an invited guest. She must have been furious.'

'Poirot and I have been told nothing about the presence of this Mr Semley,' I said.

'He was not at Little Key for long. Wait . . .' Helen frowned as she thought. Then her eyes widened. 'I am not certain that the police would have known he was there at all. I did not tell them about him, and I can easily imagine that nobody else might have mentioned him either. Sidney bundled him out of the front door a few minutes after Frank died, while Lilian was screaming and wailing like a creature being torn apart. I don't think . . . well, I should not say this because it might not be true, but I can well imagine that nobody at Little Key gave Mr Semley a single thought once he was no longer in front of them. It is hard to explain when you don't know them and haven't heard all the stories, but for all of the Devonports except Frank, it is very much as if no one else truly exists in the world apart from the Devonports. They treat everyone who isn't family as an inconvenience or a useful prop. And Mr Semley really had nothing to do with what happened. He is irrel-evant—hence Sidney's extreme displeasure at finding him there at such an upsetting moment. No one wants the worst moments of their life to be witnessed by strangers, do they?'

Poirot, I had no doubt, would agree with me: if Percy Semley was present when Frank Devonport died, that made him relevant. We were going to need to speak to him at his earliest convenience.

'Did you speak to Mr Semley at all?' I said.

Helen shook her head. 'He only arrived at the very last minute, before . . . before Frank died. With Godfrey Laviolette, Oliver and Winnie Lord.'

'Winnie Lord was with them?'

'Yes, she was the one Daisy sent to tell Oliver he could come back. She went to the other house twice that day: once to fetch Daisy, Richard and Verna, and the second time for Oliver, who brought Godfrey Laviolette and Percy Semley with him. But Winnie wasn't with the men for long after they returned. She must have gone off to do her work. There were only the three men in the hall when I . . . did what I did to Frank: Godfrey Laviolette, Oliver and Percy Semley.'

'How did Winnie strike you? Did you speak to her at all?'

'Not really. She was in the drawing room with us all for some of the afternoon—well, she was in and out with trays of food and drinks and things like that—and she gave me the occasional sympathetic smile. Even she could see that Sidney and Lilian were being uncommonly rude to me. And she showed me to my room when I said I was tired and wanted to rest before dinner. I did not sleep and could not have slept, as angry and desperate as I was, but that was what I said: that I wanted to sleep before dinner. In truth, I wanted only to get away from them all and be by myself.'

I made a mental note to find out why Godfrey Laviolette had not returned to Little Key at the same time that Verna, Richard and Daisy did.

The door opened and Poirot walked into the room. His face was flushed and his moustaches, in which he normally took such pride, were in a state of disarray. I only needed to glance at him to know that he had been greatly agitated by something.

'Many apologies, mademoiselle,' he said to Helen Acton. 'I am afraid that Inspector Catchpool and I must be on our way. It is likely that we will return soon. Catchpool, make haste, please.'

And with that, we left.

'What the devil is it, Poirot?' I said once we had moved a sufficient distance away from the guards.

'I have the most alarming news, *mon ami*. There has been another murder at Little Key. We must go at once. A car is on its way to collect us.'

'Another . . . who? Who has been killed?'

'This is what concerns me most.' Poirot gave a small shake of his head. 'There is a body in the house but it is not anyone known to the Devonport family or to their guests, all of whom are alive and well, I am told. Somebody has most certainly been murdered in the house . . . and yet *nobody knows who it is.*'

CHAPTER 11

A Body at Little Key

By the time we arrived at Kingfisher Hill, Sergeant Gidley from Scotland Yard was already there. He had evidently prepared Sidney Devonport for our imminent arrival and I was spared the ordeal of having to explain that I, who had last entered this house under false pretences, was now the person charged with getting to the bottom of not one but two murders that had taken place in his home.

I was aware of various members of the Devonport family standing about in the entrance hall as Sergeant Gidley ushered Poirot and me through to the drawing room, telling us that in there we would find both the body and the police doctor.

As he walked ahead of us towards the closed door and prepared to push it open, Poirot said softly to me, 'I am very afraid, Catchpool.'

'Of what?' I asked. 'We know what we are about to encounter, more or less.'

'Ah, but we do not yet know who has been killed. That

is to say . . . I fear that I know the identity of the victim and hope very much to be wrong. It is senseless, is it not? Whoever is dead, it is a tragedy. Yet when one feels that one might have prevented it—'

His musings were cut off by an enthusiastic 'Whenever you're ready, gentlemen!' from Sergeant Gidley, who was holding open the door to the drawing room. Poirot took a deep breath before walking in. I followed him.

In front of the fireplace, lying parallel to the edge of the hearthstone, was a woman's body. A short, stocky man with wire-rimmed spectacles and a pointed beard—the police doctor, I assumed—was kneeling on the floor beside her. She lay on her back, one arm by her side and another across her stomach. A fire poker with a bloodied tip lay at her stockinged feet. I could see no ladies' shoes anywhere in the room, yet she must have come in wearing a pair, and her emerald-green overcoat was fully buttoned up to her neck. Why would she remove her shoes but not her coat? I wondered.

A matching green hat covered her face completely and looked, from our vantage point near the door, as if it were afloat on a large sea of bright red.

'The cause of death was bludgeoning by the poker,' said Sergeant Gidley. 'And if her death was the only desired result . . . well, that could have been achieved with less effort.'

'Less bludgeoning?' I asked.

'Yes, sir,' said Gidley. 'Long after she was dead, the killer continued to assault her head and face until it was unrecognizable. Even more peculiar, though, is her clothing—or, rather, its absence. Underneath the coat she is wearing no dress, no blouse, no skirt. Only her undergarments.'

'Which means'—I formed the conclusion as I spoke—'that the killer must have removed her coat in order to remove her dress, or blouse and skirt, then put the coat back on her and buttoned it up. And taken away her shoes. That's interesting.'

'It is indeed,' Poirot agreed. 'Why not leave her in all her clothes? Why was the murderer happy to have her found in her coat, hat, stockings and underclothes, but not wearing her dress and shoes? Of course!' He nodded briskly. 'I know why.' He pointed to the fireplace. 'I assume that the dress and shoes were burned here? Is that not the heel of a shoe amidst the ashes?'

Sergeant Gidley leaned in closer and peered into the grate. 'I think you might be right, M. Poirot!' he said in a tone of wonderment. Poirot gave me a look that said: *is this the best that Scotland Yard has to offer?* I shrugged. I too had neglected to notice the contents of the fireplace. It was rather hard to focus on anything other than the horror on the floor, which brought something to mind—a memory that was both vague and insistent. Where had I seen that green hat and coat not so long ago? Wait . . . there went a memory, spinning past . . .

At the very moment that it came back to me with great certainty, Poirot said, 'It is as I feared.'

'Joan Blythe,' I said, though my mouth found it rather hard to form the words. *The woman with the unfinished face*. My lips were numb. I did not understand how this was possible. Fragments of questions struggled for prominence in my brain: what . . . ? How . . . ?

'It must be her,' I said. 'The coat and the hat—they're the same.' The strange thing was that, ten minutes earlier, if someone had asked me what colour of hat and coat Joan Blythe had worn on the day we first encountered her, I should not have been able to tell them.

'*Oui, oui*. It is undoubtedly her,' said Poirot. 'Our frightened friend from the motor-coach.'

'We cannot be certain it is her until we see her face,' I said.

'I am afraid that will not be possible,' said the police doctor, who had walked over to join us. He extended his hand. 'Dr Jens Niemietz. I am delighted to meet you. M. Poirot, I have heard so much about you. You have been described to me by many as a great man.' His accent was educated, soft, continental. I liked him immediately; his pleasure at being in Poirot's presence was contagious, and I reflected upon how lucky I was to be able to work with such a fine mind and good friend; it was too easy to take such benefits for granted.

'It is an honour to be able to help you,' said Niemietz. 'You too, Inspector Catchpool. Though if it is a face attached to our dead body that would be of most help, I regret that I cannot show you one. The poker that you see there was used with utmost savagery. Not only the face but the whole head has been . . . How can I put this delicately? Nothing recognizable survives, I am afraid. I know that you will have to lift the hat and look, and I would advise you to prepare yourselves for a shock, even if you believe there is no sight so terrible that you have not already seen it many times.'

'No one is to move the hat until I say so,' said Poirot.

'Sergeant Gidley,' I said, 'who is in this house at present apart from you, me, Poirot, Dr Niemietz and our murder victim?'

'The Devonports—all four of them. Apart from them, there's some friends of the family, Mr and Mrs Laviolette, and Daisy Devonport's fiancé, Oliver Prowd.'

'Anybody else?'

'No, that is everyone—all the same people who were here when the murderer struck at between ten and eleven o'clock this morning,' said Gidley. 'The body was found at eleven by Daisy Devonport.'

'Please find Mademoiselle Daisy and bring her here to this room,' said Poirot.

'Yes, sir..'

Daisy appeared less than a minute later. 'You asked for me, M. Poirot?' She was paler than when I had seen her before, and seemed tense.

'I did. I want you to look as this dead woman.'

She raised an eyebrow at him. 'I have already seen her. We all have, long before you turned up: *we* were the ones who found her.'

'And when you first informed the police of what you had found, you told them, did you not, that none of you knew who she was?'

'That's right. Her face and head are all smashed up.'

'How do you know that, Miss Devonport?' Sergeant Gidley asked. 'Did you disturb the crime scene?'

'Are you asking me if I lifted the hat to try to establish who it was that lay dead on my drawing room carpet?' Daisy followed her question with a mirthless laugh. 'Why, yes, I did. I then replaced the hat in its former position and no harm was done, apart from to my stomach. I was sick as a dog afterwards. It's . . . it's horrible, what's under there.' Her upper lip trembled a little. 'I was unable to identify her and so would anyone else have been. I advised none of them to look, for their own sakes. When I telephoned the police, I told them the truth: that an unidentifiable woman had been murdered in our home.'

'You did not, then, recognize her from her coat and hat?' said Poirot.

'From her . . . ?' Daisy laughed again, incredulously this time. 'No, I did not. Should I have?'

'Look carefully, mademoiselle. Have you not seen this coat and hat before, and not long ago?'

'I don't believe so, no. Why do you ask? You seem to think I *have* seen them and ought to know them.'

'The unhappy woman who sat beside you on the coach from London to Kingfisher Hill, before she leapt out of her seat and announced that she could sit there no longer . . . she wore a coat and hat of this same colour, *n'est-ce pas?*'

'Did she?' Daisy frowned. 'Well, you might be right but I did not notice if she did. The only thing I noticed about her was her infuriating behaviour. I might be a woman, M. Poirot, but where others of my sex see clothes, I see character. Hers was unsavoury and unbalanced, and so I turned away from her and tried to pretend she wasn't there—until, mercifully, she removed herself and you came and sat beside me instead.'

'I am not sure that someone who either murdered her own brother or is lying about having done so has any right to condemn others as being of unsavoury character,' I said pointedly.

'Don't be silly, Inspector.' Daisy seemed somewhat cheered to be under direct attack. 'No one has any *right* to do anything. Do you really still see the world in those terms: people deserving things or not deserving them? It is much simpler than that. Everyone can do and say precisely what they want, as long as they're prepared to take the consequences.'

'Mademoiselle,' Poirot said sternly. 'Whether you approve or disapprove of Joan Blythe—for that is her name, or at least it is the name she gave us—I am surprised that it does not interest you more to find her dead in your drawing room.'

'Do you mean to say . . . ? It's . . . it's not *her*, is it?' Daisy's mouth dropped open. 'I mean, even if the coat and hat are the same, it surely cannot be . . .' She turned and looked again at the body. 'It *can't* be,' she muttered. 'Though she is of the same build and . . .'

'It is she,' said Poirot.

Beside me, Sergeant Gidley made a note in his notebook:

'Joan Blythe.' Poirot's word was obviously good enough for him.

'Gidley, see if you can rustle up an aunt with a missing niece in or near Cobham,' I said. 'Miss Blythe told us she lived with her aunt.'

'This is quite ridiculous!' said Daisy, now red in the face and exercised. 'Why on earth would a complete stranger who happened to sit next to me for a few minutes turn up dead next to my fireplace? It makes no sense! Who would have let her in? Who would have killed her, when none of us knows her? Why did she come here in the first place? Unless she was carried in already dead!'

'That is not what happened,' said Dr Niemietz. 'The murder occurred here in this room. It must have been a frenzied attack. Look at the quantity of blood. And you saw her head yourself, Miss Devonport—what is left of it.'

'It still seems more likely to me that this is somebody else, *not* Joan Blythe,' Daisy insisted. 'Another woman who happens to have the same coat and hat.'

'M. Poirot, you mentioned something about this woman from the coach leaping out of her seat,' said Dr Niemietz.

'I did, yes.'

The police doctor directed a meaningful look at Sergeant Gidley, who nodded, produced a pair of gloves from his pocket and put them on. Having done so, he pulled a small piece of white paper out of his other pocket and held it up so that Poirot and I could read what was written on it.

I blinked several times as I stared at it, feeling as if a nightmare, too convincing to be imaginary, was slowly and tightly wrapping itself around me. The words had been written in black ink.

'Goodness only knows what it means,' said Sergeant Gidley. 'I can't make any sense of it. Dr Niemietz and I found it lying on top of the body—on her chest, tucked beneath the top button of her coat.'

I knew what the message meant. So did Poirot. Now, surely, the identity of our dead woman was beyond doubt.

The note read: '*You sat in a seat you should never have sat in, now here comes a poker to batter your hat in.*'

Two hours later, Dr Niemietz and Sergeant Gidley had left for London, taking Joan Blythe's body with them. Poirot and I were in the dining room at Little Key. Everybody had gathered there at our insistence, after our initial more polite request for them to join us had been declined. Around the table were seated Sidney and Lilian Devonport, Richard Devonport, Godfrey and Verna Laviolette, Daisy Devonport and Oliver Prowd.

Sidney's eyes glinted with anger. His fossilized, open-mouthed smile was still fixed in place, though today it appeared more like a grimace. Oliver Prowd seemed more confused than anything else. Lilian's expression was unteth-ered and absent, as if she did not know where she was or what she was doing there. Daisy was tense and alert, watching everybody keenly, while her brother Richard looked as if he might burst into tears at any moment. As for Verna Laviolette, she seemed as maliciously gleeful as ever, and I still found it nearly impossible to believe that she had been especially kind to Helen Acton, or could be to anyone. Her husband Godfrey kept fidgeting in his chair.

There was a newcomer, too—someone who had not been at Little Key when Joan Blythe was murdered, a man Poirot and I had not met before: Percy Semley from Kingfisher's View. As soon as I had mentioned that Semley had been at Little Key when Frank Devonport died, Poirot had insisted that we summon him forth.

'For what?' I had asked as Poirot had pushed me out of the house to go and find Semley.

'It is time to clear up some of the irritating little peculiarities blocking the way to the truth that is now almost within reach,' came the ambiguous answer.

Almost within reach: had Poirot really said that? For my part, I was further away from understanding why two people had been murdered at Little Key, and by whom, than I had ever been from any truth in my life. The words of the note found on Joan Blythe's body kept playing in my mind like a gramophone record that I could not switch off: *You sat in a seat you should never have sat in, now here comes a poker to batter your hat in.*

What could it mean? For one thing, Joan Blythe's green hat had not received any sort of battering from the poker. It was perfectly intact, which rendered the note inaccurate, unless whoever wrote it had used 'hat' as a metaphor for 'head' for the sake of making it rhyme properly.

A more pressing problem was the note's suggestion that Joan had been murdered as a punishment for sitting in that seat. If that was true, then for what was her killer punishing her? Ignoring his warning? That would make the warner and the killer one and the same person—and that made no sense at all.

Unable to make useful deductive progress in any direction, I turned my attention to Percy Semley who was sitting directly opposite me. He was chewing his bottom lip and staring down at the table. No doubt he was perplexed to find himself here. He resembled a sand-coloured and reasonably handsome giraffe. I decided that he was overwhelmingly unlikely to be of any use to us.

Poirot was our only hope. I knew that he intended to achieve great things before we left this room, so I placed all of my faith in him.

He rose to his feet. 'Ladies and gentlemen,' he said. 'In a matter of days—certainly in less than one week—we will gather once again around this table. On that occasion, we will be joined by one more person: Miss Helen Acton.'

Richard Devonport closed his eyes as his mother said, 'I will not allow that woman to enter this house.'

'Yes, you will, madame,' Poirot told her. 'I have obtained special permission for her to be brought here, and you will do exactly as Inspector Catchpool and I tell you to do, without complaint. All of you will do this. In return for your cooperation, when we are next gathered here with the addition of Mademoiselle Helen, I shall tell you who murdered Frank Devonport and also who murdered the woman whose body has today been removed from the drawing room. I will tell you who committed both of these heinous crimes and why they did so.'

'But we already know who killed Frank, Moysier Poy-row,' said Godfrey Laviolette. 'Helen Acton killed him.'

'No, she didn't,' said Daisy. 'I murdered Frank.'

'Silence!' her father bellowed at her. She shook in her chair, though her defiant glare did not waver. 'Helen killed Frank.' Sidney's voice trembled with rage. 'And if you have any care or respect for my family, M. Poirot, you will leave that monstrous woman exactly where she is, rotting in jail, until such time as she can be hanged!'

'This will be easier for us all if there is no shouting,' said Poirot. 'Monsieur Devonport, please sit down. We should all conserve our energy for what is to come.'

Sidney Devonport sat down heavily in his chair.

'It has not yet been established who killed Frank,' said Poirot, 'but one thing we do know is that Helen Acton cannot have committed this second murder. She was not here in the house at the time. Neither were you.' He looked at Percy Semley. 'Therefore, the woman in the drawing room must have been killed by one of the four Devonports, or by Godfrey or Verna Laviolette, or by Oliver Prowd.'

'But none of us had any reason to kill her,' said Verna.

'None of us knew her,' Lilian said.

'Of course we didn't,' Sidney growled. 'We had no reason to kill her, and we did *not* kill her. Nobody sitting at this table is a murderer!'

'Strangers must have entered the house,' said Godfrey Laviolette. 'Maybe the front door wasn't securely shut.'

'None of you can be sure if you knew her or not,' I said. 'Her face had been destroyed beyond all recognition.'

204

'It would be most helpful to hear from each of you where you were when *la pauvre mademoiselle* was killed,' said Poirot. 'Monsieur Devonport, may we start with you as the head of the household? Since you tell me so authoritatively that nobody here murdered this unfortunate woman, I can only assume that all of you were together in one room between ten and eleven and that none of you left the room?'

'I was with my wife,' Sidney said flatly.

'Yes, Sidney and I were together.'

'Where?' Poirot asked.

'In my bedroom,' said Lilian.

'From when until when, precisely?'

'I was there all morning from the moment I awoke. Sidney brought me my breakfast and the newspapers at . . . I'm not sure what time it was, but probably around nine o'clock.'

'It was thirty-five minutes after nine,' said Sidney. 'Godfrey and I were busy at Peepers HQ until then, and I'm afraid I forgot all about your breakfast, dear.'

'Well, I was unaware of the time,' said Lilian.

'So, you took up the breakfast at thirty-five minutes past nine—and then . . . ?' said Poirot.

'After that we both stayed in Lilian's bedroom drinking tea and reading the newspapers until we were disturbed by Daisy's screams.'

'Ungodly screams.' Lilian glanced disapprovingly at her daughter. 'There was no need to make quite so much noise. I nearly died of a heart attack.'

'What was I supposed to do upon finding a dead, faceless

woman sprawled across the carpet?' said Daisy smoothly. 'Say "Oh, how marvellous" and carry on with my day?'

'Mademoiselle Daisy, you found the woman's body at eleven?'

'Yes. The grandfather clock in the drawing room started to chime the hour while I was screaming. Before that, Oliver and I were walking around the garden. The weather has been so dreary and relentless recently, and this morning it was milder and even quite bright, so we thought we would make the most of it. We left here at . . . actually, I don't remember. Do you remember, Oliver?'

'Not precisely, no,' he muttered, looking down at his hands. The depth of his unhappiness struck me in that moment more forcefully than it had before. Did he still refuse to believe that Daisy had killed Frank as he had at first, I wondered. Or was he now convinced of her guilt and desolate at the prospect of losing her?

'Oh!' Verna Laviolette exclaimed. 'I think I might be able to help. Sidney, are you quite certain of when you took Lilian's breakfast up to her?'

'Certain,' he barked.

'In that case, M. Poirot, I can tell you that Daisy and Oliver set out on their walk very soon after that. You see, Sidney has a habit of—forgive me, Sidney, but one must be completely truthful when helping the police to solve a murder—he has a habit of closing doors much more deci-sively than he needs to.'

'*Slamming* is the word you want,' said Daisy.

'Well . . . yes.' Verna cast a nervous glance at Sidney as

she spoke. 'My bedroom, the guest room that I sleep in whenever I'm here, is next to Lilian's. I slept in rather late today, having been unable to fall asleep until three or four o'clock in the morning—quite usual for me, I'm afraid—and I was woken suddenly by a loud slamming sound. I thought, "Oh, boy, is there trouble brewing?" So I put on my dressing gown and went out onto the landing, and I saw Oliver and Daisy heading out for their walk. Then when I was back in my room I looked out of my window and saw them in the garden.'

'You heard the slam of the door and thought it might mean that there was trouble?' asked Poirot.

'Well . . . oh, darn it, M. Poirot, I'm going to be completely candid with you, even if you think the worse of me. Sometimes that sound can mean nothing, like today, when it only meant that Sidney had walked into a room and closed the door behind him. Other times, that same noise can mean Sidney's about to lose his temper with somebody and everyone else had better take cover if they know what's good for them.'

'Yet you did not take cover,' Poirot said. 'You went out onto the landing.'

'Yes, well . . .' Verna's cheeks had turned pink. 'I will admit that my curiosity is usually greater than my fear, irrespective of the occasion.'

'Verna, are you saying in front of all these people that you went out onto the landing to eavesdrop?' Godfrey Laviolette looked aghast.

'Yes, Godfrey, I am. Oh, come on, don't look at me like

that! It's basic human nature to want to know what's going on. Anyway, M. Poirot, none of that matters. I don't want to hog the limelight and talk about myself, inconsequential as I am. What I'm trying to tell you is this: once I'd satisfied myself that there weren't going to be any juicy tidbits for me to overhear, I went back to my room and through my window I saw Daisy and Oliver walking in the garden.'

'Thank you, madame,' said Poirot.

'You will not be invited to this house again,' Sidney told Verna.

'Oh, is that so?' She smiled. 'So how are you and Godfrey going to be able to work on Peepers together, if I'm no longer welcome? You don't think my husband's going to come here without me, do you? Godfrey won't stand for that, will you, Godfrey?'

'Monsieur Prowd,' interrupted Poirot. 'Does the account of Madame Laviolette match your memory of what happened this morning?'

'Yes,' Daisy answered for him.

Prowd nodded. 'Yes. Forty minutes after nine, that sounds correct. Daisy and I walked around the garden, then around the estate. We walked up to the swimming pool and then we strolled in the wooded area beside it. Then at around fifteen minutes before eleven Daisy said that she was tired and wanted to go home, so we did. She walked into the drawing room, found the body and started to scream.'

'Where were you when she found the body?' I asked him.

'In the entrance hall, about ten steps behind her. I wish

I could have got to the drawing room first and spared her the ordeal.'

Daisy gave him a sharp look, from which I gathered that in her opinion she was far better equipped to handle ordeals than her fiancé.

Godfrey Laviolette said, 'Can I take my turn now? When Sidney left me to go to Lilian, I went to the library to read. There I found Richard.'

'That's right. I was in the library writing letters and reading from nine o'clock,' said Richard.

'What about you, Mr Semley?' I asked. Since he was here, it seemed rude to exclude him.

'I was at home,' said Semley. 'This mess has nothing to do with me.'

'You were alone at Kingfisher's View?' Poirot asked him.

'No, I was with my aunt.'

'What is her name?'

'Hester Semley. I was with her for most of the morning. Certainly between ten and eleven.'

'And she will confirm that the two of you were together?'

'Yes, of course,' said Semley.

'*Eh bien,*' said Poirot. 'Then it seems that the only person in this house who was alone at the time of the young woman's brutal murder, and therefore without the convenient alibi, is you, Madame Laviolette.'

'Golly.' Verna's eyes widened. 'You're right, M. Poirot. I was alone all morning, until I heard Daisy screaming and came downstairs. I swear to you, I didn't touch that girl. Why would I do such a thing?'

Ignoring her question, Poirot said, 'Those of you who were in the house at any time during the morning—did you hear anyone knock at the door? Between ten and eleven o'clock or even before then?'

'I did,' said Richard Devonport. 'I'm afraid that is all I can tell you, though. I was engrossed in my book and only dimly aware of somebody needing to answer the door. I decided, rather selfishly, that it could be left to someone who was not busy reading. Oh! If I was reading, that must mean I had finished writing my letters, which means the visitor must have arrived shortly before ten. Godfrey was already in the library with me—'

'I heard no one at the door,' Godfrey cut in.

'There was definitely a knock,' said Richard. 'I would place it at about ten minutes before ten.'

'But you heard nothing more than this?' Poirot asked him. 'No conversation or introductions?'

'I did not,' said Richard. 'As I say, I was thoroughly immersed in my book, and the door knocker is much louder than voices speaking at an ordinary level.'

'I heard . . . something, now that I come to think of it,' said Verna. 'How funny that I didn't think of it before. Not the front door, but I heard Lilian's bedroom door close softly, a while *after* I heard Sidney slam it. I remember thinking, "Well, it can't be Sidney who closed the door that time. He's never closed a door so quietly in his life." I went out onto the landing again—'

'For goodness sake, Verna, will you stop spying on our friends?' Godfrey exclaimed. The cheeks of his smooth, ageless face had turned bright red. He looked like a wooden doll onto whom somebody had painted red spots for colour.

'Stop bullying me, Godfrey,' Verna retaliated. 'I imagine that M. Poirot and Inspector Catchpool are delighted that I'm able to tell them all the things I observed.'

'Delighted,' I said coolly. I did not like her at all.

'What did you see when you ventured out onto the landing?' Poirot asked her.

'I saw Lilian,' she said simply. 'She was about to walk down the stairs. I assume she did, but I didn't see her go all the way to the bottom. I went back to my room.'

Lilian Devonport frowned. 'Verna, you cannot have seen me. I was in my bedroom the whole time.' She sounded more puzzled than angry.

Verna looked confused now too. 'It's peculiar,' she admitted. 'I didn't hear the door close or slam a third time, you see, and yet when Daisy started screaming we all ran out of our rooms and Sidney and Lilian both came out of Lilian's room at the same time that I came out of mine. So why didn't I hear Lilian going back to her room after going downstairs?'

The question was directed at Poirot, but it was Lilian who answered it: 'For the simple reason that *I never left my room in the first place*,' she said. 'You cannot have seen my face, Verna.'

'No. You're right, I did not. I saw your long hair, from the back. It was loose. And you were wearing your night-gown. And it was definitely your bedroom door that I heard opening and then closing again.'

'It was not me, Verna,' said Lilian quietly.

'Wait,' said Oliver Prowd. 'Daisy and I were outside, Richard and Godfrey were in the library, Sidney was in Lilian's room with Lilian. There were no servants here this morning—darling, you told me at breakfast that Sidney had let the little scarecrow go, the girl who had briefly replaced Winnie?'

'What of it?' said Daisy. 'She was worse than no help at all.'

'I simply mean that . . . well, if it was not Lilian that Verna saw going down the stairs dressed in Lilian's night-gown, and the rest of us are all accounted for, then who was it?'

'There is no one else it could have been,' said Richard.

'What if there is?' said Oliver, looking around the table. 'What if there is someone else in the house—someone who has been hiding for goodness knows how long and who is still here now?'

CHAPTER 12

Irritating Little Questions

Silence descended on the room. After a few seconds, Poirot said, 'Tell us, Monsieur Prowd. You have a theory, do you not?'

'I wouldn't call it a theory, but what if the woman Verna saw on the stairs was the same one who ended up dead in the drawing room? She might have arrived yesterday and spent the night here in one of the many empty bedrooms.' Seeming to warm to his theory, Oliver went on: 'No one apart from Richard heard a knock at the front door this morning—not even Godfrey who was in the library with Richard at the time. So perhaps Richard never heard the door. He might have imagined it.'

'Is that possible, Mr Devonport?' I asked him.

'I don't know,' said Richard. 'I . . . goodness me, I'm not sure. Until it was called into question, I would have said I was certain that I had heard the door, but maybe I . . . No. I'm sorry, Inspector. I could not swear to it. Oliver might be right.'

'I have heard that many of the houses at Kingfisher Hill are haunted,' said Percy Semley. 'By spirits,' he added, in case any of us had imagined a less conventional sort of haunting.

Poirot turned to him. 'Monsieur Semley, in a moment, Inspector Catchpool and I will accompany you to your home where we will speak with your aunt. Until then, please say nothing unless I ask you a question. The same instruction applies to you all. I have several things I wish to ask before I leave for Kingfisher's View. Some of my questions might seem trivial but they are not, so please answer as fully as you can and with complete honesty. It is only once these little matters have been cleared up that I will be able to proceed towards solving the larger, more important puzzles. Madame Devonport, is it customary for you to open and close doors very quietly? Are you the opposite of your husband in this respect?'

'She is,' said Daisy. 'Mother creeps around the house silently, like a little mouse.'

'Then, Madame Laviolette, is it not possible that it was indeed Lilian Devonport whom you saw at the top of the stairs, and that you did not hear her return to her bedroom subsequently because she did so very quietly?'

'I suppose . . .' Verna considered the matter. 'I mean, I would say it was kind of unlikely but I suppose it is just about possible.'

'I never left my bedroom,' Lilian Devonport said indignantly. 'Are you accusing me of lying, M. Poirot?'

'His sort have no shame,' growled her husband.

214

'Monsieur Devonport, on the day of your son Frank's murder, you compelled Oliver Prowd, the Laviolettes and your other two children to leave this house and spend the morning at a different house—that of Percy Semley—while you and your wife privately welcomed home your estranged son and his fiancée, Helen. What I wish to know is this: why did you choose Kingfisher's View?'

'I don't have to explain myself to you,' Sidney said.

'There are many houses on this estate that are nearer to Little Key than is Monsieur Semley's house. Are you, perhaps, a dear friend of Hester Semley? Dear enough that she would not object to you asking her to accommodate your family members and guests for the morning?'

'No,' Sidney snapped. 'The woman is a tiresome windbag and no friend of mine.'

'I say, old boy!' Percy Semley looked wounded. 'What has Aunt Hester ever done to upset you? She's a harmless old thing.'

'I did not say that she had harmed me, I said that I found her tiresome. We are supposed to tell the truth, are we not? I *do* find her tiresome—very—and that is after minimal acquaintance. If I knew her any better than I do, I should no doubt detest her.'

'Oh, now, steady on!' Percy objected.

Sidney addressed his next remark to me. 'We nearly bought Kingfisher's View, which was up for sale. That is how we first made Miss Semley's acquaintance. Then Godfrey and Verna decided to sell this house, and we bought it in preference to Kingfisher's View. Being our good friends,

Godfrey and Verna offered us a competitive deal that it would have made no sense to refuse. Hester Semley, instead of accepting our decision and minding her own affairs, hounded us relentlessly.'

'You are being horribly unfair, Mr Devonport.' Percy protested.

'Please, *mesdames et messieurs*, may I have quiet, unless I am asking a question or you are answering one. Monsieur Devonport, can you explain to me why, in spite of your aversion to Hester Semley, hers was the house to which you sent everybody on the morning of your son Frank's return to—'

'That was my doing,' Godfrey Laviolette interrupted. 'Verna and I *are* good friends of Hester Semley, who, I should like to say, is a generous-spirited and warm-hearted lady without a bad bone in her body. We often play golf with her at the club here. When I heard Lilian talking one morning about the need to get everyone out of the way so that she and Sidney could spend some time alone with Frank, I suggested that we might all stroll over to Hester's place. I knew we would receive a warm welcome there, and we did.'

'And, despite your dislike of Miss Semley, you agreed to this suggestion?' Poirot asked Sidney.

'Why wouldn't I? It seemed a sensible solution.'

'Why was this privacy so important?' Poirot asked. 'Later in the day, everybody else met and spoke to Frank, *n'est-ce pas?*'

'Yes,' said Daisy emphatically. 'I for one have never

understood why Mother and Father needed to see Frank first, without the rest of us here—and for so long, too. Mother, why was it? Tell us.'

Daisy was lying and she wanted us all to know it. It was the sort of ostentatious, proud lying that is better described as a form of acting. Her theatrical manner revealed that she knew the answer to her question only too well and wanted to force Lilian to state it, knowing this was the last thing her mother wished to do.

'There was no particular reason for it,' said Lilian. She might have been acting too—much more subtly and convincingly than her daughter.

'No reason at all,' Sidney agreed. 'We simply wanted to see Frank alone.'

'He was not alone,' I reminded them. 'He was with Helen Acton.'

'That was unfortunate,' said Lilian.

'You disliked her even before Frank's death?' I said.

'No, I simply wished to be reunited with my son without a stranger being present.'

Sidney nodded his agreement.

'I see,' said Poirot. 'I have now several questions for you, Monsieur Laviolette.'

'Oh, lucky you, Godfrey!' Verna laughed.

'Why did you ask me to say nothing about the name of this house having been changed from Kingfisher's Rest to Little Key? You told us—did he not, Catchpool?—that we should not mention this in the presence of Monsieur or Madame Devonport.'

Godfrey looked caught out. Then he shrugged and said, 'I didn't want to upset anybody. Frank was the one who suggested a new name for the house when they bought it from us. He dreamed up Little Key. I knew that any talk about the name would upset Sidney and Lilian. It would have made them think of Frank.'

Daisy laughed. 'What Godfrey is too polite to tell you is that, since Frank's death and Helen's arrest, there has been an unspoken rule in this house—one of so many. Nobody must mention Frank or Helen. We must all gaily go about our lives as if neither of them ever existed. Anything that my parents do not wholeheartedly approve of is banned from conversation and thought—not only their own, but mine and Richard's too, and Oliver's. Even their friends and equals, Godfrey and Verna. Anyone who sets foot in this house gets to know about the unspoken, unwritten rules very quickly.'

I could see from the faces around the table that this was true. Everyone apart from Sidney and Lilian recognized Daisy's account of life at Little Key.

Poirot said to Sidney Devonport, 'Is this, then, also the explanation for why Winnie could not be mentioned in your wife's hearing? When Catchpool and I first arrived here as your guests, you gave a signal for your son Richard to distract your wife before explaining that there had been a problem with Winnie. Why did you do that?'

'Would you have me neglect to shield Lilian from things I know will upset her?' Sidney said coldly. 'Is making people suffer now thought to be a virtue?'

'If it is, you're the most virtuous man in the world, Father,' said Daisy.

Ignoring her, he said to Poirot, 'Winnie was and is nothing but an aggravation. Trying and failing to manage her had already caused Lilian considerable distress. Yes, it is true: I did not wish her to be bothered by further talk of that little wretch.'

'I see,' Poirot said in a neutral tone. 'Monsieur Devonport, I understand that when you and your wife banished Frank, after he stole from you—'

'Must we talk about that?' said Lilian.

'We must, madame. When Frank was sent away from this family in disgrace, Daisy and Richard were not permitted by you, I believe, to continue their relationship with their brother?'

'I refuse to answer questions about this!' Sidney Devonport roared, banging his fist down on the table. A few people gasped. Others hastily swallowed exclamations of surprise.

'It is true,' said Verna Laviolette. Her husband gave her a sharp look, and Daisy nodded avidly.

Poirot said, 'Although they were reluctant to do so, both Daisy and Richard severed all ties with Frank at the request of their parents. Monsieur Richard, am I correct?'

After a few seconds of agonized silence, Richard made a noise that was unambiguously affirmative: a sort of coward's yes.

'This is marvellous!' Daisy clapped her hands together. 'Richard and I have both been so terrified of Father for so

219

long, you cannot possibly imagine, M. Poirot—and now, thanks to this murder and the official importance of us all telling the truth, even Richard is speaking up. As for me, Father, I am no longer afraid of you or Mother at all! It's wonderful. Though it makes me angry too. Knowing that I can now say whatever I want to say and do whatever I want to do does rather make me loathe my former slavish self. Were you really ever so terrifying, or was I simply the silliest little mouse for taking you seriously in the first place? I suppose, in my defence, I did need your money. Not any more, though—not now that I'm engaged to Oliver.'

'What about you, Monsieur Prowd?' Poirot asked him. 'Did you, do you, share your fiancée's fear of Sidney and Lilian Devonport?'

'I . . . I . . .'

'He did,' said Daisy authoritatively. 'You did, darling. You were as scared as any of us, and every bit as observant of the required silences.'

'Daisy's right,' said Richard after clearing his throat. 'The honesty that you demand of us now that there has been a murder—a second murder—has changed things. It's strange how different they have been, the two tragedies. After Frank's murder, the silences multiplied and intensified. We all became more fearful, I think. But now . . .' He left the sentence incomplete.

'Now Inspector Catchpool and I are here to show you that telling the truth with discernment and yet ruthlessness is the only way to resolve all problems,' Poirot said.

'I suppose that's why you first turned up here in disguise,

as two men who just couldn't get enough of Peepers?' Daisy said with a smirk.

'Ah!' He smiled back at her. 'There you have the point. I have plenty of questions for you, mademoiselle. First, however, I wish to ask your father: why did you allow these two engagements? Both Richard and Daisy cut their ties with Frank when you demanded it of them. I assume, therefore, that you could have forbidden the engagement of Daisy to Oliver Prowd, the man who colluded with Frank in the theft of your money, and that of Richard to Helen Acton. Yet you did not. Why? It makes no sense to me.'

'You are an impudent, pompous blackguard and I have no intention of answering any more of your questions,' said Sidney Devonport.

'He perhaps cannot explain it to you,' said Daisy. 'I'm not sure he understands it himself. I do, very well. Richard does too. That's because, for us, the thoughts and feelings of other people are real. Father cares only about himself and Mother. Nobody else counts. And, like all who behave as tyrannically as he does, he has almost no understanding of his own behaviour. If tyrants understood what they did and why they did it, they would surely behave differently—don't you think so, M. Poirot?'

Poirot turned to Richard Devonport. 'Why did you ask Helen Acton to marry you—a woman you had only just met and who had confessed to killing your brother?'

'I wondered if you might ask me that,' said Richard. 'I did it to call her bluff.'

'Please elaborate,' said Poirot.

'I did not believe she had killed Frank. I still don't believe it. She loved him. That was clear in the short time I spent with them. I had no idea why she was lying, and I thought that if I tested her by proposing marriage . . .' He broke off with a shrug.

'You thought she would say, "Golly, you've put me in a bind now—I had better come clean and reveal all"?' Daisy laughed. 'No determined liar would admit defeat so easily. My brother is naïve, M. Poirot. Why on earth *wouldn't* she agree to marry you, Richard? It makes her lie look all the more plausible, doesn't it? Love at first sight at Little Key, how unbearably romantic. You love her, she loves you!'

'When she agreed to marry you, you could have told her that you had been merely conducting the experiment,' Poirot said to Richard. 'Instead you allowed the engagement to continue.'

'I . . . yes, I did.'

'He enjoyed imagining that a woman who had loved Frank might love him too,' said Daisy.

'Darling, don't be cruel,' Oliver Prowd muttered.

'She's right,' said Richard quietly. 'I cannot pretend that that sort of consideration played no part in my decisions. And when I became certain that Helen had not killed Frank, that she was lying, I felt I had to do something. Perhaps I had come to care for her in a very short time, I don't know. All I know is that I could not bear the thought of her hanging for a crime she had not committed.'

Looking at Sidney, he added, 'That is why I wrote to you, M. Poirot, and asked for your help, suggesting that you feign an interest in Peepers in order to be invited here by my father.'

Sidney's lip curled in anger. It was the first time I had seen his mouth make a different shape.

Poirot turned to Verna Laviolette and said, 'I have a question for you, madame. Why did you decide to sell this house?'

A flash of something that looked very much like fear passed across her face.

Poirot proceeded as if he had not noticed, though I knew he had. 'Paradise had been ruined—that is what your husband told me. What had happened to ruin the paradise of Kingfisher Hill for the two of you?'

'Godfrey, I'm going to tell him the truth whether you like it or not,' said Verna. 'Everyone else has been spilling the beans all over the place and now it's my turn. The fact is, M. Poirot, Godfrey and I could not afford to keep this house and a big house in London, too.'

'What nonsense,' said Sidney. 'Godfrey, you're as wealthy as I am! We made our money together.'

'And then, more recently, Godfrey lost plenty of ours in a series of bad investments that you know nothing about,' said Verna bitterly. 'Did I say bad? I should have said catastrophic.'

Her husband's face was bright red. 'Stop it,' he hissed at her. 'Stop it right now or I won't be held responsible for what I do to you later!'

'Did you hear that, Inspector Catchpool?' said Daisy. 'It sounds as if another murder might be on the way. How thrilling to have three!'

'There is nothing thrilling about murder,' Poirot declared with force. 'It is tragic and devastating and continues to cause suffering many years after it has happened—to the innocent and to the surviving loved ones of the guilty. It is and will always be an abomination—a stain on the face of the earth.'

Daisy scowled at him and said savagely, 'Do you think I don't know that? I know it better than you do.'

'Then perhaps you will help to ameliorate all of our suffering by answering my questions as truthfully as possible,' said Poirot.

'I expect you're going to ask me why I killed Frank,' she said. 'Very well—I shall tell you.'

Daisy stood up. 'I loved Frank very much,' she said. 'He was my hero. I am a person who needs heroes, M. Poirot. Some people have no use for them—have you noticed that? I have to have them, and Frank . . . well, he was not like anyone else. No one else would have suggested changing the house's name to Little Key because of something in a Charles Dickens story. Frank always wanted everything to be so much better than it was. He believed that any obstacle could be overcome if one tried hard enough. When Father cut him off without a penny, he did not tell himself that he was down on his luck or unfortunate in any way. Instead, he made his own money, created the most wonderful schools, and became a teacher who inspired dozens of young people to learn and achieve.

'Maybe he was right to believe that anything was possible, or maybe he was only right about himself: *he* could achieve great things because he always believed that he could, and never gave up. Richard and I were not so brave. We could not overcome our fear of our parents when they ordered us to shut Frank out of our hearts and lives as if he had never existed. We did as we were told. Of course we did—that is what we had been trained from birth to do. To defy my parents felt impossible to me at the time, entirely impossible. So I was resourceful. I designed for myself a way to avoid suffering. I cannot *bear* to suffer in the way that most people seem willing to when the occasion arises. Can you guess what I did, M. Poirot? Inspector Catchpool?'

I could not. Neither could Poirot.

'I'm disappointed in you both,' said Daisy. 'It's rather obvious. I set out to convince myself that Frank was a thief and a scoundrel, that I was better off without him, no longer loved him, and would not miss him. You did too, didn't you, Richard?'

'I tried, but I failed,' he said. 'No matter what Father and Mother said, I could not agree with them. What Frank did was wrong, but . . . one does not stop loving a brother when he makes an error of judgement.'

'Especially when he does so to help his friend,' said Oliver Prowd quietly.

Daisy smiled at me. She said, 'I am stronger and more

225

determined than Richard. I tried and I succeeded. At first it was hard. Then with practice it grew easier. You see, Father and Mother had doted on Frank before he stole from them. He was easily their favourite of the three of us. That they had turned against him so decisively had to mean something—I convinced myself of it. It had to mean that Frank was evil and immoral, a danger to our family and not at all the person I had believed him to be. Before too long, I believed it as zealously as Mother and Father did. And happiness was regained!' Daisy threw up her hands in a mockery of joy. 'No more suffering for me.'

'And then?' said Poirot.

'Well, then, Mother discovered that she was suffering from an incurable illness, didn't you, Mother? And suddenly she wanted her lost, favourite son back. She asked Father if he would be willing to welcome Frank back to the fold so that she could be reunited with him before she died. Father capitulated. And there you have it. That is why I had to kill Frank.' Daisy sat down.

I was exceedingly relieved to hear Poirot say, 'I do not understand this at all, mademoiselle.' I too was more confused than before she had commenced her explanation.

'It's perfectly straightforward,' said Daisy. 'Father had drummed it into me that Frank was a menace and a danger, and I ended up believing it more passionately than he or Mother did—it was the only way to avoid abject misery. Please, do not make me repeat the whole story. I was indoctrinated, partly by my parents and partly by my own efforts. And how much more of a danger would Frank be, I asked myself, with Mother in her sickly, enfeebled state and Father morally cowed by his shame at having abandoned his principles and welcomed a thief back into his home? What if Frank took this opportunity to steal even more money from us or revenge himself in some other way? I decided that, since everyone around me was weakening, I would have to be the strong one and save the family.'

Without speaking a word, Sidney Devonport got up and left the room, slamming the door behind him.

Lilian was crying. 'Oh, Daisy, oh, my child,' she said. 'Please say that it isn't true.'

'It is quite true, Mother,' Daisy replied evenly. 'And . . . you believe me.' She smiled. 'I can see that you do, and Father does too. That is a relief.'

'Why can't I die now?' Lilian asked of no one in particular. 'Must I live to see my daughter hanged for the murder of my son?' She looked up to the ceiling. 'Why can't I be taken *now*?'

'Perhaps you have not yet suffered enough, Mother,' said Daisy in a hard voice. I remembered what I had first called her: Diamond Voice.

'I should like to say . . .' Godfrey Laviolette cleared his throat.

'*Oui*, monsieur?' said Poirot.

'I am presently in as secure and prosperous a financial position as any fellow could ever hope to be.'

We all turned and stared at him, thinking it odd that he should choose this moment to change the subject.

'I have been in this same enviable position for as long as I can remember,' he went on. 'What's more, Verna knows it. What she said before about our finances—it was a lie. Many of our friends had their fortunes wiped out by the crash—obliterated!—but not us.' He looked at Poirot. 'So don't listen to my wife: we didn't sell this house because we were short of money.'

'Then what was the reason?' I asked him.

'I'd prefer not to say, Inspector Catchpool. However, I will do you the courtesy of explaining, as sincerely as I can, why I do not wish to answer.' He had the strangest expression on his face. It was half of a smile—as if, by his estimation, I had not yet earned the other half. 'Verna and I had our reasons for wanting to leave Kingfisher Hill. They were good, sound reasons. Like I told you before: the way we saw it, this place was a ruined paradise.' With a heavy sigh, Godfrey went on, 'We also knew that our good friends Sidney and Lilian would disagree with us if we drew their attention to the conditions that had caused us to wish to leave. Sometimes, folks disagree about whether a particular event or change is a good thing or a bad thing. Happens all the time.' Godfrey laughed nervously.

'What do you mean, Godfrey?' asked Lilian. 'What have you not told us about Kingfisher Hill?'

'Lilian, I swear to you—on my own life and the lives of all my children and grandchildren—if I were to tell you, you would not think it was a problem at all.'

'Then why haven't you told us?' she retorted.

'Because I didn't want to spoil your enjoyment of buying this place.'

'But if I would not have thought it was a problem . . . ?'

Godfrey made an exasperated noise. 'There's nothing wrong with this house, Lilian. Nothing at all. You and Sidney love it here. Just forget about it, okay?'

'For someone who thinks Kingfisher Hill is a ruined paradise, you spend an awful lot of time here,' Daisy said to Godfrey.

'Only because of that tedious game,' said Verna.

'Oh, tedious, is it?' said Godfrey. 'Now it's all coming out.'

'Yes, it is, dear. It's the dullest thing in the world. By the time one gets to the forty-third rule on the list, one is quite ready to scratch out one's eyes. I yearn never to have to play it again—and never to come to Kingfisher Hill again.'

'You may leave at your earliest convenience, Verna,' said Lilian.

'Not quite yet,' said Poirot. 'For the time being everybody will stay where they are, please.'

'What about me?' asked Percy Semley. 'May I leave? The master of the house has taken himself off somewhere, so I don't see why—'

'You will stay where you are and you will keep quiet,' Poirot told him. 'Mademoiselle Daisy, thank you for explaining why you murdered your brother. There are a few other matters that you can perhaps clear up for us, also.'

She looked at him expectantly.

'You were the first to enter the drawing room this morning after the dead woman had been murdered. You found her body, yes?'

'Have we not covered this ground already?' Oliver Prowd asked.

'Yes, I found her,' said Daisy.

'And in spite of the green coat and hat, it did not occur to you that she was the woman who had sat beside you on a coach a few days ago. You were shocked to discover that, in my opinion, it was she—the same woman.'

'Yes,' said Daisy. 'As I said . . . I did not notice what she was wearing.'

'But mademoiselle, there was a note that had been laid upon the body: "You sat in a seat you should never have sat in, now here comes a poker to batter your hat in." Do you seriously expect us to believe, mademoiselle, that you read that note and *still* it did not occur to you that this might be the same woman from the coach, a woman who had said in your hearing that she was afraid to sit in that seat because she had been warned that she would be murdered if she did?'

Daisy looked at Poirot as if he had lost his mind. 'Why would those words make me think of her? I had quite forgotten her existence until you mentioned her.'

'I do not believe you,' said Poirot. 'I find it not at all credible that you did not know *at once* that these two women—on the coach and in your drawing room—were the same person.'

Daisy nodded. 'I understand why you don't believe me, but it did not cross my mind and that's the truth. Shall I tell you why I didn't think of it? Because the idea that a stranger who knew neither my name nor my address should turn up dead in my drawing room a few days later . . . why, that is such a preposterous proposition that it seems to me to be beyond impossible. And one does not consider the impossible as a possibility.'

'A skilful answer,' said Poirot. 'I congratulate you. Shall we see if this next question requires from you the same level of imaginative skill?'

'How many more?' said Daisy in a bored voice. 'Are we to remain stuck in this room forever?'

'*Non, pas du tout.* You will soon be released from captivity.'

'Very well, then, get it over with.'

'Before the stealing of the money, Monsieur Prowd had asked you twice to be his wife, as I understand it. Both times you refused him. Then on the day that your parents wrote to Frank to suggest a *rapprochement*, you sent a telegram to Monsieur Prowd in which you proposed marriage to him. Was there a connection between these two things? And why had you changed your mind and decided that you wanted to marry him after all?'

'Oh, I always knew that I would marry Oliver one day. I simply could not do it too quickly if I wanted him to desire me madly. You wouldn't understand, M. Poirot— you're not a woman. But after the theft and Frank and all of that, well, I was far too afraid of Father and Mother to

231

go anywhere near Oliver. I thought that was that, but I was wrong. When I heard that Father had written to Frank and was intending to forgive him for everything . . .' She shrugged. 'My parents could hardly object to my marrying Oliver after that, could they?'

'May I ask you . . . ?' Poirot began.

'You may,' said Daisy with a grin. No doubt she was pleased by her answers so far and was looking forward to the next question.

'When Helen Acton confessed to the murder of Frank, why did you say nothing? Why not tell everybody then that it was you who had pushed him?'

'What an absurd question.' She laughed, though I heard a certain amount of strain in her words. 'There was Helen, rushing down the stairs crying, "Oliver, I killed him, I killed him." It was perfect. Helen, for some baffling reason, seemed keen to be thought guilty, so I saved my own neck and allowed her to have her way. If you're going to ask me why I later confessed, M. Poirot, the answer ought to be quite plain: I had foolishly told you the truth already, on the coach. Then there you were in my house when I arrived home . . . It seemed like a good time to come clean.'

'*Non.*' Poirot said quietly. '*C'est incroyable.* If you wished to save your neck, as you put it, why kill your brother in this way and that moment—when Oliver Prowd, Percy Semley and Godfrey Laviolette were standing in the entrance hall below the balcony?'

This, I thought, was a good question—for Daisy, Helen

or whoever had in fact murdered Frank Devonport. Why had they done so in such a public way, with witnesses all over the shop?

'Helen Acton also must have been present to witness what you did,' Poirot went on, 'or else she would not have been able to run down the stairs *immediatement* and tell Monsieur Prowd that *she* had pushed Frank to his death. Mademoiselle, if you did indeed kill your brother as you would have us believe, then it seems to Poirot that you must have planned for the murder to happen in front of all of these people. Now, why would you do that?'

'I shall leave that to you to work out,' Daisy replied sullenly. Her good mood had evaporated.

Poirot nodded. 'And work it out I shall,' he said. 'Do not fear. I will soon know what happened and why it happened. Now, it is time for me to go with Percy Semley to Kingfisher's View. Catchpool, you will stay here in this room. Everybody else is free to leave—the dining room, not the house.'

I waited, hoping for an explanation of why these new instructions did not constitute a raw deal for me. After being cooped up for so long, I craved fresh air.

'One by one, each of you will come in here and describe to Catchpool your exact movements on the day that Frank Devonport died,' said Poirot. 'Is that clear? It is of vital importance that we have a full and true account of the sixth of December last year from each of you. Sidney Devonport must also give his account. If he tries to exempt himself, do not stand for it, Catchpool.'

This was getting worse by the second. When it came to not standing for things, my level of aptitude was flimsy at best. Poirot knew this perfectly well, and I would have reminded him of the fact if he and Percy Semley had not already departed for Kingfisher's View.

CHAPTER 13

Aunt Hester

I did not accompany Poirot to Kingfisher's View, and so did not witness first hand any of the events that I am about to describe. I feel exactly as if I did, however, because Poirot brought the scene to life for me later in vivid detail, and I hope that my account captures everything with the same vitality here.

The first thing my friend noticed about Hester and Percy Semley's house was that it was superior to Little Key in every possible respect. It was more attractive from the outside, had more impressive gardens and was positioned in a more secluded part of the Kingfisher Hill Estate. It had a better sense of balance and proportion inside. Poirot could not help noting also that there was no point of perilous altitude in the entrance hall of Kingfisher's View from which a person might be pushed to his death.

As Poirot arrived with Percy Semley, an English Setter bounded forward to greet them. The dog was white with orange ears and a smattering of orange freckles (although that is probably not strictly how one should describe them), and he made several attempts to bite Poirot's gloved hand in a genial sort of way. It was not an attack, more a case of him wanting to have a friendly chew on this exciting new visitor.

A second dog lolloped forward as Percy Semley was trying to persuade the more energetic one to leave Poirot in peace. This dog was taller and heavier than the bouncier one, and also an English Setter: white with dark grey patches that according to Poirot made him look like a Dalmatian designed by someone with no sense of discipline.

Hester Semley, who appeared next, was a small, bony, bespectacled woman with thick coiled springs of white hair all over her head. Poirot estimated her age at around sixty. She spoke and moved very quickly. Once introductions had been made, she held forth at length: 'I am delighted to meet you, M. Poirot. I am aware of your work, of course. What brings you to Kingfisher Hill? Oh, well, no doubt you will tell me all about it in a moment. Percy, take his coat. Take his hat. Sterling, *do be patient*! I see you've met the boys, M. Poirot—Sterling is the one pestering you. Don't worry, he won't hurt you. I don't think he likes the taste of your glove. They are leather, are they not? Sterling doesn't like the smell of leather. Never mind, you weren't to know. Just *wait*, Sterling! Percy, take his gloves. Put them in the pocket of his coat. Sterling only wants to nibble on your hand a little, M. Poirot. It's his way of saying hello and showing you that he wants to be your friend. As soon as you sit down he'll forget about your hands and give your face a good lick instead! He's not shy like his older brother. Pound! Pound, come here and say hello to our guest. He is a most eminent detective and solver of many murders—isn't that right, M. Poirot? Who knows when someone so distinguished will next visit us? If I were you, Pound, I would follow your little brother's example and make the most of this opportunity.'

Pound the Setter did not think an illustrious guest was anything to get excited about. He settled down on the floor and started to lick his front paw.

'You have named your dogs Pound and Sterling?' said Poirot. 'After your Great British currency?'

'I have,' said Hester Semley ferociously as if she were not merely answering a question but also renewing a commitment. 'Those fools in charge of us all will see us taken out of the Gold Standard if someone does not stop them. It's a terrible thing. They say the pound cannot retain its value and no doubt it will not, thanks to their idiocy, but the way I see it is perfectly simple, M. Poirot: if you have no ability when it comes to fiscal matters, then do not involve yourself in fiscal matters! But I'm sure you have not come here to be told how I would organize the affairs of this great country if I were the government.'

'I am sure you would do an excellent job,' Poirot told her.

'Oh, I would,' she agreed as she ushered him into her drawing room. 'I most certainly would. If I undertake to do any job, I make sure to do it well, which is why I shall endeavour to answer your questions to the best of my ability. No doubt you wish to ask me all about the murder of the young woman at Little Key?'

The dogs had followed them into the drawing room. Sterling sat panting enthusiastically beside Poirot's chair but mercifully did not try to lick his face.

'M. Poirot wishes to know my whereabouts when the crime was committed, Aunt Het,' said Percy. 'I told him I was with you.'

'He *was* with me, M. Poirot. And you might think I would say that even if it were untrue, but I would not. People need to face the consequences of their actions, whether one is related to them by blood or not. Percy Semley, if you ever break the law, I shall report you straight to the police, nephew or no nephew!'

'I know, Aunt Het.' It sounded to Poirot as if Percy had responded to this assertion in these precise terms many times before.

'So, is that all you wish to know?' Hester Semley asked. 'Surely not, since this young woman was killed at Little Key and is hardly the first to suffer that fate in that house. Percy, go and make tea or coffee. Which would you prefer, M. Poirot?'

'I will take coffee, thank you. You are right. I would also like to ask you about the murder of Frank Devonport.'

He had been about to say more but Hester Semley had already begun to answer and continued to answer for some time thereafter.

'I know nothing about the murder of Frank Devonport apart from what everybody knows: that his fiancée Helen Acton confessed and is to be hanged, and that she told the police that the reason she did it was because she had fallen in love with Richard Devonport. Balderdash! Now, if a woman engaged to Richard claimed to have fallen for Frank, that I would have no trouble believing, but it simply would not happen in reverse. So, what was Helen Acton's true motive? That is what you must find out, M. Poirot. Mustn't he, Sterling? That's right! Oh, are you one of those people who doesn't like to be licked? He will only do it for a few moments. It's easier if you don't make a fuss.

'Now, what you might not know is that on the day that Frank was killed, there was something of an exodus early in the morning from Little Key to here. Richard, Daisy, Godfrey and Verna all came here at about half past nine in the morning. Sidney and Lilian insisted on having the house to themselves for Frank's grand welcome ceremony— well, they could have saved themselves the bother if they had simply not expelled him from the family in the first place. Some people are nothing but fools! Your son steals from you and you fail to report him to the police—you protect him from the law—at the same time as disowning him? I ask you, what sense does that make? No sense! I would have done the precise opposite.'

She paused for breath and Poirot took his chance. 'Please tell me everything that happened that day. You say that Richard and Daisy Devonport and the Laviolettes arrived half an hour after nine. Monsieur Oliver Prowd was not with them?'

'No, he was in London. He arrived shortly before two o'clock and expressed a certain dissatisfaction with the situation. Mildly, mind you. He wasn't threatening a revolution or anything like that. He wouldn't dare—Daisy has him wrapped around her little finger. It was only that he did not see why they should all have to wait here until invited back to Little Key by Sidney or Lilian. He was tactful about it, but it was clear that he found the whole production to be overly dramatic and irrational, and when he said so, Daisy went wild and started to scream at him that he had no right to criticize her family, of which he was not yet a member even by marriage and would never become one if he continued to say such things. Her tirade was vicious and relentless—you were most upset by it, weren't you, Pound? Of course, it makes perfect sense when you think about it.'

'What—?'

'Daisy and Oliver had both missed Frank dreadfully. The torment of knowing that he was back at Little Key and yet *still* they were not permitted to see him. Not that anyone had ever told Oliver that he couldn't see Frank, but their friendship had ended, that's for sure . . .' She broke off. 'I've forgotten what I was talking about.'

'You—'

'Oh, yes—I was saying that Daisy and Oliver can hardly be blamed for venting their ill temper on one another. They must both have been in a state of nervous agitation at the imminent prospect of seeing Frank again and yet also being made to wait by that bully Sidney Devonport. Dreadful man. Daisy takes after him. She can be rather dreadful herself. She likes to be in charge of everything and is afraid of almost nothing, but she *is* afraid of Sidney.'

'You should have heard her earlier, Aunt Het,' Percy cut in. 'She told Sidney exactly what she thinks of him. She really seemed to want to crush him.'

'Do not speak while I am speaking, Percy.'

'But you're always speaking, Aunt Het.'

'Perhaps Daisy has finally conquered her fear of her father,' continued Hester. 'It will be good for her if she has. Certainly, on the day of Frank's murder she was still scared of him. That is why she set about poor Oliver with such savagery. She knew he was quite right to find the situation ridiculous—all of them waiting here like fools for no good reason—and her pride couldn't bear it. She's far too proud and vain to say, "I know Father's demands are objectionable but I'm afraid to stand up to him," so instead she took it out on Oliver, who had inadvertently drawn her attention to her own weakness and subservience. Many people are not at all ashamed of their own fears, M. Poirot, but Daisy is. Her subjugation to Sidney ate away at her. I could see it.'

Poirot opened his mouth, which Hester Semley took as an opportunity to accelerate her own disquisition. 'Most people are endlessly willing to be frightened of one thing or another. Oh, that's not how they would see it. They would say they were respectful of social conventions or concerned with sparing the feelings of others. Balderdash! They are cowards who know nothing of freedom. Still, I don't know why we're talking about those people because we're supposed to be talking about Daisy, who is the opposite. She wishes, and has always wished, to live free and unafraid. Yet in a cruel irony, she is the daughter of Sidney Devonport. Percy, you should have been a Devonport child. You would have made a good one. Why aren't you fetching the coffee?'

'Oh, I forgot about that,' said Percy. He hurried away to do her bidding, closing the door behind him.

'He is not very bright,' Hester told Poirot. 'What was I . . . ? Oh, yes, you wanted to know what happened on the day that Frank was killed. I can only tell you about what happened here. Daisy was still berating Oliver when Winnie arrived—Winnie is the Devonports' servant. Remind me to tell you something important about her. Sidney had sent her over here to tell everybody that at last they could return to Little Key, which is what most of them did, but not Oliver. Daisy was so angry with him that she told him he was not welcome to accompany her. Poor chap! I don't think I was the only one who felt sorry for him. Godfrey Laviolette immediately suggested a round of golf to cheer Oliver up, and the three of them went off to play: Godfrey, Oliver and Percy. Pound, Sterling and I stayed here—didn't we, boys? We had a little nap. Then the golfers returned after about an hour and a half. Percy took the boys out for a run in the woods.'

Seeing the question forming on Poirot's face, Hester said, 'Not Godfrey and Oliver. I should hardly describe Godfrey Laviolette as a boy, even if he does have that strange, smooth skin that seems never to wrinkle. I meant the dogs. *My boys.*' She reached over and stroked Pound, who rolled onto his back and stuck his legs in the air. Sterling, as if noticing the unequal distribution of attention, sat up and prodded Poirot with his front paw. Poirot calculated that he could not risk stroking him unless he wished to be licked again, which he decidedly did not.

'Now, something you will certainly want to know about if you're interested in the Devonport family is the conversation that took place between Godfrey and Oliver that afternoon while Percy was out and after they had all played golf. You must remind me to tell you all about *that,* as well as Winnie Lord. And after that . . . well, I'm not sure I am able to offer any further assistance. You evidently don't believe that Frank was murdered by his fiancée Helen Acton—no, you don't, or else you would not have asked about everybody's movements on that day—but if you're thinking that someone else killed Frank, I can only say that I'm sure you're right and it could have been anyone. Anyone at all. I mean, obviously it was neither of the Laviolettes. But—'

'Why is this obvious?' Poirot asked.

'*Please*, I am speaking!' Hester Semley sighed. 'Now I must interrupt the flow of my thoughts in order to answer you. It is obvious because Godfrey and Verna are decent, kind-hearted people. I am very fond of them both. They would never kill anybody. Whereas any of the Devonports might, because they are either a tyrant, in the case of Sidney, or else they have had their personalities so disfigured by living with a tyrant that all kinds of destructive seeds have very likely been sown. I see that you have another question for me. You may ask it.'

Poirot was reluctant to fill the blissful and unexpected silence with words. He said, 'My friend Inspector Catchpool . . . he was surprised when Helen Acton described Verna Laviolette to us as kind. I will admit, I too was a little surprised.'

'Then you're both fools,' said Hester. 'Verna is one of my favourite people. You could not hope to meet a kinder, more thoughtful woman. Do you know how we met? No, how could you? I'll tell you. Godfrey and Verna used to own Little Key, though it was called Kingfisher's Rest in those days—a much more suitable name, and the Estate Committee really should have forbidden Sidney to change it. I don't give a fig about it coming from the pen of Charles Dickens! So does Uncle Pumblechook. How would you feel if one of your neighbours named his house Uncle Pumblechook?'

She seemed to be waiting for an answer. As solemnly as he could, Poirot said, 'I understand that the Devonports' original plan was to buy this house?'

'It was. Everything had been agreed. Then they discovered that the Laviolettes wished to sell Kingfisher's Rest, and Godfrey offered them a very good price. I can't help thinking he must have been desperate for money in fact, because, really, why else would he have sold the house for so much less than it was worth? It was a deal that only a fool would refuse, even if this house *is* a great deal more aesthetically pleasing than Uncle Pumblechook, which is what I shall call the Devonports' house from now on.

'In any case, that is how Verna and I became friends. We had been neighbours in the estate for some time, but I did not know her well. After Sidney decided to buy her house instead of mine, she came to see me. To apologize and to make sure I was going to be all right. She was incredibly charming and gracious about the whole affair and offered to help me find a new buyer for this house. I told her, "No, thank you." You see, M. Poirot, something strange had happened: as soon as Sidney Devonport told me that he no longer wished to buy my house—the very second the words left that unsightly gargoyle mouth of his—I knew that I did not want to sell my house, not to him and not to anybody. Hearing him say so casually that he didn't want to live here made me realize that, in fact, *I* did.'

There then followed several more minutes during which Hester Semley explained why Kingfisher's View was more advantageous than any other house she had ever encountered. (Poirot spared me these particular details.)

As soon as he was able to make himself heard, Poirot said, 'Could there have been another reason for the Laviolettes wanting to sell their house? One that had nothing to do with money?'

'I suppose so, though I cannot think what it might have been.'

'Immediately before they decided to sell, had anything changed on the estate?'

'Nothing at all. Things rarely change here at Kingfisher Hill, and thank goodness for that!'

'What about Monsieur Alfred Bixby and the Kingfisher Coach Company?' asked Poirot.

'What about them?'

'Do not some residents disapprove of Monsieur Bixby and his business? The vulgarity of the blue and orange char-a-bancs and his use of the name "Kingfisher"?'

'Oh, yes, but that was true long before Godfrey and Verna bought a house here. The tawdriness of Mr Bixby predates us all. Wait.' Hester Semley sat up straight and pushed her spectacles higher up her nose. 'Something *had* changed at Kingfisher Hill, and just before Godfrey and Verna decided to sell their house, too: the gate porter had changed. I objected most strongly, but I was alone in my objection and eventually I had to concede defeat. No one was on my side apart from Lavinia Stent and she is worse than useless. Even Percy thought I was being unreasonable.'

'The gate porter?' said Poirot.

'Yes, at the entrance to the estate. The old one retired and a new one was put in his place—a man of distinctly unsuitable appearance. Did you not notice him as you arrived? Covered in hair! Almost no forehead to speak of. His hairline starts no more than an inch above his eyebrows.

246

As it happens, his predecessor, the old gate porter, was at the opposite end of the scale—he was as bald as a golf ball and had no eyebrows to speak of—but he always looked smart, unlike this new fellow. And who could object to a golf ball? It's not this new chap's fault, I can see that, and I am not opposed to hairiness in and of itself. And I'm sure the new porter is a reliable and polite employee—in fact I know he is—but was there any need to position him at the entrance gates so that everybody sees him the moment they arrive? Could he not have been put somewhere less public? Less visible? What are you grinning about, M. Poirot? Are you thinking that I am a ridiculous old woman to care about such things?'

'I am thinking,' said Poirot, 'that, thanks to you, the pieces of a small puzzle begin to fall into place. This story about the new porter and the old porter who was the golf ball—it has provided me with an answer. Hopefully more will follow.'

Hester Semley leaned forward with interest. 'Are you suggesting that the old gate porter and the new gate porter are connected to these killings at Kingfisher Hill?'

'*Pas du tout*—'

Poirot was unable to say more because, at that moment, Percy stumbled inelegantly back into the room with coffee, cream and sugar precariously balanced on a wobbling tray. Both dogs got up and started to bark.

Normally the noise would have disturbed Poirot, but his personal triumph of deduction had rendered him temporarily immune to irritation. Lavinia Stent—a woman whose name he had never heard before and whom he would almost certainly never meet—might have been worse than useless to Hester Semley but she had been extremely useful to Hercule Poirot.

Once refreshments had been taken, and once Percy had left with instructions to make several telephone calls on his aunt's behalf, Poirot reminded her that she had something to tell him about Winnie Lord.

'Ah, yes,' she said. 'Nobody has seen her at Kingfisher Hill for some time. Is it true that she is no longer in the Devonports' employ?'

Poirot confirmed that, as far as he was aware, this was true. 'She was not there when Inspector Catchpool and I first visited Little Key, and Sidney Devonport said that her return was out of the question.'

'I see. Well, I don't know what she did finally to make herself so unwelcome but I *do* know that it could have been anything from the most serious dereliction of duty to something quite inconsequential. Sidney and Lilian took against her long ago, not on account of anything Winnie herself had done but because of Daisy.'

'Please explain,' said Poirot.

'Well, of course I'm going to explain!' Hester Semley glared at him. 'How could you begin to understand what I'm talking about if I didn't explain? Really, M. Poirot, I don't know if you're in the habit of conversing with people who lack the power of speech and comprehension or only tell you half of a story—'

'I am in the habit of trying to obtain as much information as possible from those who are determined to tell me as little as possible.'

'I see. Well, I am trying to tell you as *much* as possible so please do not interrupt me again. After Frank was sent packing by Sidney and Lilian, Daisy grew close to Winnie. They very quickly became inseparable. Sidney and Lilian were horrified—their daughter, a Devonport, suddenly all chummy with a servant? They could not abide it! Daisy knew this and it only made her more determined to flaunt her friendship with Winnie. She might not have had the courage to stand up to her parents over the matter of Frank, but she has never been afraid to drive them to fury in more subtle ways, as long as it could not be proved that it was her intention to do so.

'I think she must have decided to turn Winnie into her new little sister, since Sidney and Lilian had decreed that she must lose a brother. There was much giggling in each other's bedrooms at night, and Daisy sometimes helped Winnie with her tasks in the kitchen. Then there were trips to the theatre, presents, shared confidences—even secret words and codes, according to Verna. In case you're wondering, I only know about all of this because Verna has told me. And the thing is, Daisy is extremely clever. She will have known that Sidney and Lilian depended on Winnie and would have been reluctant to let her go.'

'But they did—they have—let her go,' said Poirot.

'That was later,' Hester said. 'When Daisy decided to take Winnie under her wing, she was correct in her assessment: at that time, Winnie was viewed as absolutely essential to the smooth running of the Devonport household. Lilian described her as a servant in a thousand. She and Sidney would have been extremely reluctant to have to start from scratch and train up a new girl. So they tried to go on as usual with Winnie, but privately, with Daisy, they stamped their feet and screamed at her about how she must on no account fraternize with the help. Verna overheard many such tirades. It was not difficult for her to do so— Sidney does not care to keep his voice down when he's angry. Each time, Daisy would say, "Of course, Father, you're quite right. I shall try to do better in future," and then she would continue to behave towards Winnie in exactly the same way.

'Now, let me tell you, M. Poirot: it is possible that Daisy was lonely and pining for Frank and this led to her developing a genuine affection for Winnie as a sort of substitute for her brother, but in my opinion—and Verna agrees—her main aim in pursuing this behaviour was to make her parents suffer. I think she wanted to say to them without actually saying it, "Look what you've done. You sent Frank away and now I've made a sister out of your trusty servant, and you hate it, don't you? Well, you should have thought about that, shouldn't you?" Do you understand what I mean?'

Poirot gave a nod of confirmation, feeling like a pupil being prepared by his teacher for an important test.

'All of this had an adverse effect upon Winnie,' Hester went on. 'I am not sure why—the tense atmosphere at Little

Key, I imagine, and knowing she was partly the cause of it—but the standard of her work declined. Having always been supremely efficient, cheerful and able to perform her duties to the highest standards, she became morose, unreliable and a positive hindrance in every way. Though there was an intermediate stage.'

Poirot opened his mouth to ask what she meant, then thought better of it.

'At first, it seems, Winnie was so delighted to have found favour with Daisy that she neglected certain of her duties simply because her attention was no longer wholly focused upon her work. She was thrilled to have acquired a new sister in the form of Daisy, and she lost interest in everything else. Then, after Frank died, her work deteriorated still further and this time the slide in standards was accompanied by withdrawal and an unhappy aspect. She went missing once or twice too—wandered off when the family was relying on her to cook and serve breakfast or dinner—then reappeared a while later without apology or explanation. Of course, she might have been badly affected by the tragedy, but I happen to believe that she was more unhappy about Daisy's reaction to Frank's murder than about the murder itself.'

'How did—?'

'M. Poirot, if you ask me how Daisy reacted to Frank's death, I shall set Pound and Sterling on you. That was the very next thing I was going to tell you. You really must learn the virtue of patience.'

Hester Semley glared at Poirot in silence for a full five

seconds. Then she said, 'Daisy was distraught after Frank died. Oh, everybody was terribly upset, but Verna said that three people took it much harder than the rest: Helen Acton, Daisy and Lilian. Daisy's profound unhappiness brought out her cruel streak. And who had the worst of it? Winnie, of course—the adoring disciple. My theory is that Winnie realized only then that she meant nothing to Daisy and never had. She saw that, for Daisy, she had never been more than an entertaining way to aggravate her parents. Now, I should tell you that Verna disagrees. She thinks that Daisy grew genuinely fond of Winnie after Frank was banished, whereas I think the desire to do something—anything—to make Sidney and Lilian suffer was paramount. I believe Daisy used poor Winnie with that sole aim in mind.' Hester sighed. 'Then, devastated by the loss of Frank, which came so soon after the hope of being reunited with him, Daisy began to persecute Winnie in various subtle ways: constantly criticizing her, mocking her . . . So, of course, Winnie's work in the house deteriorated even further. It comes as no surprise to me to learn that she slipped up once too often and was given her marching orders. I doubt Daisy will have cared too much about that.'

Poirot thought of the next question he wished to ask, did not ask it, and was unsurprised when Hester answered it anyway.

'Which brings me to Oliver Prowd and the conversation he had with Godfrey, here in this room on the day that Frank was killed. Once Daisy, Richard and Verna had set

252

off with Winnie for Little Key, Oliver was inconsolable. Godfrey told him to buck up or something of the sort, and it all came pouring out. I made myself scarce so that the two of them could talk man to man, though of course I heard every word. No, I will not apologize for that, M. Poirot. This is my house and I like to hear what people say in it.'

'Monsieur Prowd was unhappy about his altercation with Mademoiselle Daisy?' Poirot asked.

'That, certainly, but it was not only that. He felt terribly guilty about the way he had treated Frank, you see. At one time the two men had been inseparable. Like brothers. Frank had stolen money from Sidney only to save Oliver and his ailing father from penury, and Oliver had accepted the money and Frank's advice about how precisely to invest it. Oliver had willingly entered into a business arrangement with Frank—the schools. Do you know about the schools?'

Poirot indicated that he did.

'Oliver had been happy to benefit from Frank's criminal activity and from his good head for money and business,' Hester Semley went on. 'But as a friend? He had shunned Frank. As he told Godfrey that day, Frank had come to remind him of everything he wished to forget: his terrible fear of financial ruin and that his father would die in poverty, his tacit participation in a criminal act. Most of all, his inability to rescue himself. He felt indebted to Frank and inferior to him, and his feeling of worthlessness together with everything else . . . well, suffice to say that from Oliver's

253

point of view the friendship could not go on. He and Frank continued to communicate from a distance when they needed to, but they did not see each other again. Oliver told Godfrey that he could not have borne a face-to-face meeting with Frank, so it was no wonder that he dreaded the impending encounter at Little Key. He could hardly avoid Frank now, could he? He was engaged to Daisy and now Frank had apparently been welcomed back to the family—'

'Pardon me.' Poirot was determined to speak and was prepared to be chided for interrupting if necessary. 'Some minutes ago, you said that Mademoiselle Daisy *and Oliver Prowd* had missed Frank inordinately. That is why Monsieur Prowd was eager to go to Little Key as soon as possible once he returned from London, *n'est-ce pas*, instead of being detained here? Yet you say also that he dreaded encountering Frank Devonport.'

'Are you a fool?' said Hester bluntly. 'You think both things cannot at the same time be true? Of course Oliver had missed Frank. He had missed him desperately. If you had only heard him speaking to Godfrey, you would understand completely. It was his low opinion of *himself* that had prevented Oliver from pursuing his friendship with Frank, not any lack of affection for Frank. All those months that he could not bear to see or speak to him, he wished things were different and felt the lack of his lifelong friend most keenly. But he could not overcome his shame.'

'I see.' Poirot nodded. 'And so once it became clear to

him that he now had no choice but to meet Frank face to face . . .'

'He knew it would be a deeply uncomfortable encounter, and also that it was unavoidable, so he wished to get it over and done with as soon as possible,' said Hester.

'The worst thing of all, he told Godfrey, was that he knew Frank would forgive him without hesitation. That would make him feel even more ashamed. And then there was his anguish over Daisy. She was so excited about Frank's return, it made Oliver feel a little unloved. It reinforced his sense of inferiority. "She loves him more than she loves me," he said to Godfrey. "She always will." I'm sure I have no need to tell you this, M. Poirot, but I would advise you to question both Winnie Lord and Oliver Prowd very closely.'

'An interesting suggestion,' Poirot said evasively.

'You'd be a fool to disregard my advice,' said Hester. 'On the day of Frank's grand return to the family home, both Winnie and Oliver would have been keenly aware that Daisy's feelings for them were *nothing* compared with the strength of her love for her older brother. How on earth could either of them hope to hold her attention even for a moment with Frank around? Jealousy is a powerful motive for murder, M. Poirot. I'm sure I don't need to tell you that.'

'Did Monsieur Prowd say anything else to Monsieur Laviolette that struck you as important?' asked Poirot.

'Not really. Only more in the same vein: self-pity, shame. He seemed to want to confess everything, every past mistake, as if Godfrey were a priest or something! Oh, and he begged Godfrey not to say a word about any of it to Daisy.'

'What past mistakes?' said Poirot.

'All the women who had mistreated him, all those he had mistreated. There was one girl who deceived him for months, claiming to be destitute and without family, and then Oliver discovered that she was a member of the Danish Royal Family. He felt like a prize idiot for having believed her.'

'The . . . the Danish—'

'Then there was the one with whom he had behaved in an unprincipled and unchristian fashion—that was how he put it. He meant sex, of course. Young people are prudishly reluctant to utter the word, I find. I cannot think why. It's only a word. In any event, Oliver had blamed the girl for the unprincipled activity when the fault had belonged as much to him and he felt terribly guilty and ashamed.'

'The same pattern as with Frank,' said Poirot.

'Quite,' Hester agreed. 'Oliver was aware of it too. He recognized and loathed his own hypocrisy. Poor Godfrey, I don't think he knew quite what to say to any of this. Oliver would have been *far* better off confiding in me, of course, but what man of his age wants to unburden himself to an old woman? Especially about something as shameful as putting a young woman in the family way and then blaming her for it and abandoning her.'

'There was a baby?' said Poirot, immediately alert. This was interesting, he thought.

'It did not, I think, go that far.' Hester shot Poirot a knowing look. 'Oliver's narrative became rather oblique at that point, but he did say that the Harley Street doctor who was attending to his dying father would not help them, though he easily could have. Oliver called him a hateful man in one breath, then with the next he was denouncing his own appalling behaviour and praising the doctor's wisdom and judgement. Good old doctor, say I, if he would not help Oliver and his lady-friend to get rid of a baby! Doctors are supposed to save lives, not end them when they've barely begun.'

'What became of the woman and the baby?' asked Poirot.

'Oliver did not say, not precisely. Let me be clear: he did not even say in so many words that there *was* a baby. Nor did he say that they did away with it, but it was quite apparent that they did. One can always find a questionable doctor to do one's bidding if one has the resources. In any case, Oliver treated the girl cruelly afterwards and had nothing more to do with her—and unless he was lying to Godfrey, which I don't think he was, he felt terrible about it all, just as he felt terrible about his treatment of Frank. My theory, M. Poirot, is that all of the poor man's past mistakes were replaying themselves in his mind in a rather frenzied way as a result of his anxiety at the prospect of seeing Frank again. His self-loathing had become tem-porarily uncontrollable. It was evident that Godfrey was quite unequal to the task of making him feel any better. The best he could come up with was to suggest a game of golf. I don't know—perhaps that works for men, but it

257

certainly wouldn't make me feel any better. Knocking a little ball around with a funny stick for hours on end! It's the most ludicrous waste of time.'

'Did Oliver Prowd happen to mention the name of his father's doctor?' Poirot asked. 'The one who would not assist with the . . . the solving of the problem?'

He expected Hester Semley to answer in the negative and was pleasantly surprised when she said, 'Yes, he did. I remembered it because at first I thought Oliver kept referring to him as F. Grave—the initial F. and the surname Grave. But the emphasis was wrong each time he said it and I soon realized my mistake. It was Ephgrave—a strange name. Come to think of it, I have a copy of the London telephone directory. Shall we look it up? I don't know if the spelling is E-f-f or E-p-h, and I'm not sure how you think Oliver Prowd's father's old doctor might help you to solve either of your two murders.'

'Please, let us consult the directory.'

More slowly than Poirot would have believed possible, Hester Semley rose to her feet. 'Follow me. No quick movements, please, or you'll wake the boys. They need their afternoon nap or else they'll be grumpy all evening.'

It took Poirot several minutes to tiptoe as far as the drawing room door. As he approached it, the sight of something on a nearby shelf stopped him as surely as if he had hit a wall. It was a book that had caught his eye, or rather the title of a book: *Midnight Gathering*. The coincidence of finding it here was surprising enough, but far more surprising to Poirot was the name of the author. '*Sacre tonerre!*' he muttered. Then he smiled. 'Now, at last, I can make the fast progress,' he thought to himself. 'I must find Catchpool. There is much to be done.' And he cast a guilty eye in the direction of Pound and Sterling in case somehow his thoughts of movement and speed might drift across to the dogs and wake them from their nap.

CHAPTER 14

Poirot Makes a Task List

'Well?' I spluttered, trying to avoid swallowing a mouthful of water. 'Did you ask Hester Semley how a book belonging to Daisy Devonport came to be in her house?' I was swimming in Kingfisher Hill's famous Victor Marklew swimming pool. Poirot walked on the grass beside me—65 feet up and 65 feet down again—and we talked as I swam. Poirot had suggested this 'so that time is not wasted by your aqueous pursuits, Catchpool.'

I had tried to persuade him to join me but he had refused, insisting that the water would be icy cold. It was not. The pool was heated to a temperature that was eminently bearable as long as one never stood still in it. Remarkably, I had it all to myself. I was not able to swim as fast as I would have liked, however; I had to slow down to match Poirot's walking pace. Still, it was wonderfully invigorating at any speed. There is nothing like a swim in the outdoors, with fresh air and water on your face. 'You really should try it, Poirot,' I had told him a few moments ago. 'It's invaluable for clearing the head.'

'My head is in no need of clearing,' he had replied. 'And if you cannot say the same of yours, you should devote yourself not to frolicking in water like a dog but to arranging your thoughts more carefully in future, with the order and the method. Have I not always told you this?'

Now he said, 'Of course I asked about the book. Why do you assume that it was Daisy Devonport's copy of *Midnight Gathering* that ended up at Kingfisher's View? It was not. It was a copy that had been given by Daisy to Verna Laviolette as a gift. Verna had read and enjoyed it, then passed it on to Hester Semley.'

'So Daisy has both received it as a gift and given it as a gift,' I said, trying as we spoke to keep track of the number of lengths of the pool I had swum. It was hard to count and talk at the same time.

'She has given it not only to Verna Laviolette,' said Poirot. 'According to Hester Semley, she also gave a copy to Oliver Prowd after he accepted her proposal of marriage. When she gave it to Verna, she apparently told her that it was her favourite book in the world. She said, "I give this book to all the most important people in my life." I have now read parts of it myself: it seems to be an interesting tale of a most unsympathetic and enervating family.'

'No wonder Daisy Devonport likes it so much!' I said.

'Tell me, Catchpool, why do you say that Mademoiselle Daisy, as well as giving *Midnight Gathering* as a gift, has also received it as one?'

I stopped swimming and looked at him. Surely he could not have forgotten. 'She told you on the coach when you sat next to her. She said the copy of the book that she had with her, the one I had angered her by looking at, had originally been a gift *from* . . . And then she stopped before telling you from whom it had been a gift.'

'You are right in every detail. This is fascinating, is it not?'

'What, that she was first given it and then, presumably, liked it so much that she gave it to others? I can't see anything remarkable about that. What interests me far more is the name of the author. How could I have failed to notice it? It must have been right there on the cover, beneath the title.'

It was the first thing Poirot had said to me when we met after his visit to Hester Semley. 'You will not believe me, Catchpool, when I tell you the name of the author of *Midnight Gathering*. That book was written by a woman called Joan Blythe! Yes, I assure you, I am in earnest.'

Now I said, 'I wonder if that's why *our* Joan Blythe was so scared when she heard me say "Midnight Gathering" on the coach. She had not mentioned having written or published a book, and suddenly I came out with the title. She might have thought . . . well, I don't know what she might have thought, but I can see how it might shake her a little.'

'You told me that she was terrified, not merely shaken,' Poirot reminded me. 'Also you are assuming that Joan Blythe from the motor-coach is the same Joan Blythe who wrote the book. There is no reason to suppose this.'

'Either way, a coincidence of this magnitude . . . it's

impossible! Either we have Daisy travelling with a copy of *Midnight Gathering* and then happening to sit next to a woman who is the author of that very book, or—even less likely—Daisy sits next to a woman who is *not* the writer of the book she is reading but who has exactly the same name as the book's author.'

'Catchpool, Catchpool.' Poirot sighed. 'You still do not see what is so clear?'

Suddenly I did, or I thought I did. 'Joan Blythe might not have been the real name of the woman on the coach,' I said. 'She didn't want to tell us her real name. Having seen Daisy's book and noted the name of its author, she gave Joan Blythe as her false name.'

'Sometimes, my friend, I despair of you,' said Poirot. 'Yes, she might very well have picked Joan Blythe as her assumed name having seen it on Mademoiselle Daisy's book, but . . . how can you see this and not see the rest of the picture?'

I put my head under the water and swam as fast as I could to the far edge of the pool, then back again to where Poirot was standing still, waiting for me. Surfacing, I said, 'The woman in the Devonports' drawing room with her head smashed to smithereens—was that Joan-Blythe-from-the-coach, as I suppose I must call her from now on to distinguish her from Joan-Blythe-the-author? Or was it not?'

'Officially she has not yet—'

'—been identified. I know. Nevertheless, you have an opinion. You think you know who she is.'

'You wish to be included in my provisional thoughts?' said Poirot. 'Very well. Yes, the dead woman is, as you call her, Joan-Blythe-from-the-coach. Her real name is not Joan Blythe and she was most decidedly not the author of *Midnight Gathering.*'

'Then who was she?

Poirot smiled. 'Soon, my friend, I will be able to tell you everything you desire to know. I am very close now to piecing together all the different parts of this puzzle. There are, however, certain things I must do—and things, also, that you must do.'

'I thought there might be,' I muttered, thinking not for the first time how lucky it was that my boss at Scotland Yard held Poirot in such high esteem. My other cases would quietly be reassigned to colleagues, enabling me to devote myself entirely to helping Poirot for as long as he needed me.

'Tell me first about the day of Frank Devonport's murder,' he said. 'You have spoken to everybody, I hope, and taken down their accounts?'

'Yes, and it all seems straightforward. Nobody's version of the sixth of December contradicts anybody else's. Oliver Prowd left for London very early in the morning. Shortly after nine, Daisy and Richard Devonport and the Laviolettes set off for Kingfisher's View, the Semleys' house, where they arrived at half past nine. Frank arrived at Little Key at ten o'clock with Helen Acton. They spent the morning there with Lilian and Sidney Devonport.

'A little before two, Oliver returned from London and

went to Kingfisher's View as instructed. Then at two Winnie Lord arrived to tell the exiles that they could now return. Daisy, Richard and Verna Laviolette *did* return then, but Oliver and Godfrey did not—they set off at five o'clock from Kingfisher's View, with Percy Semley in tow. Semley invited himself along, apparently. He had heard wonderful stories about Frank from various Kingfisher Hill people and wanted to meet him. Neither Godfrey Laviolette nor Oliver Prowd had the courage to tell him that his presence would not be welcome.

'Meanwhile, back at Little Key everyone had congregated in the drawing room at around twenty minutes after two, when Daisy, Richard and Verna returned from Kingfisher's View. Present for this drawing room gathering, therefore, were all five Devonports—Frank, Richard, Daisy, Sidney and Lilian—as well as Helen Acton and Verna Laviolette. Winnie Lord came in and out to serve refreshments and clear away afterwards.'

'Excellent. All is as I expected,' said Poirot. 'Continue.'

I shivered. Speaking at length made even slow swimming impossible, and I was getting cold. 'Everyone agrees that Helen Acton left the drawing room at around four o'clock. She was tired, she said, and needed to rest before dinner. She went upstairs. Around ten to fifteen minutes later, other people started to leave the drawing room. Verna Laviolette, Sidney, Lilian and Daisy all went upstairs to their bedrooms. Frank also went upstairs, but to Helen's room, not his own.

'At around half past four, before going up to her room,

Daisy sent Winnie Lord to Kingfisher's View to retrieve Oliver. Richard Devonport, who did not go upstairs after everyone left the drawing room—he went to the library— says that Winnie arrived back from Kingfisher's View at half an hour after five o'clock. With her were the three men: Oliver Prowd, Godfrey Laviolette and Percy Semley. Richard heard their voices from the library.'

'Then, according to Richard Devonport, he was alone in the library for some time?'

'Yes. He claims to have heard Winnie say that she had to get on with preparing dinner, and after that he heard only the voices of the three men, until . . . well, until Frank fell from the balcony and Helen came running down the stairs crying, "Oliver, I did it, I killed him." As to the precise wording of her confession there is some disagreement, but all versions have Helen Acton freely admitting that she pushed Frank from the balcony. Poirot, if I'm not swimming, I must get out and wrap myself in those towels.' I pointed at them. 'Better still, let's go back to Little Key and continue the conversation there.'

'Your account so far has been most informative,' he said. 'I wish now to hear in more detail about these ten minutes between half past five and twenty minutes to six. The interruption of returning to the house will not be helpful to my train of thought.'

'Poirot, the blood in my veins is almost blue from the cold.' I pointed at my arm.

'So I see. Alas, it will prove impossible to make me responsible for this turn of events, however hard you try,

Catchpool. It was not Poirot who persuaded you to plunge into an expanse of cold water. Please continue.'

'I shall remember this,' I told him. With a sigh, I sank back into the water up to my neck and made a series of vigorous movements with my arms and legs to stimulate the circulation.

'After half past five is where the accounts start to differ. Daisy says that she heard Oliver's voice and knew that he had returned. When she went out onto the landing, she saw that he had brought Percy Semley with him, and she was angry. Semley was not invited and it was inappropriate for Oliver to have brought him. At that point, according to Daisy, Helen's bedroom door opened. Frank emerged. Not Helen, says Daisy: Helen was still inside her bedroom. From the balconied landing, Frank saw Semley, Godfrey Laviolette and Oliver Prowd downstairs in the entrance hall, and moved towards the stairs, clearly intending to join them. Daisy claims that this was the moment when she resolved to take action to protect her family from the danger presented by Frank's return. She pushed him violently over the balcony, he fell and . . . well, we know what happened to him after that.

'Daisy doesn't understand what happened next, she told me. Suddenly Helen was at her side—she had not heard Helen come out of her bedroom—and then, to Daisy's astonishment, something happened that made no sense: Helen hurried down the stairs and confessed to Frank's murder. By now, having heard the great crash and the exclamations of the men downstairs, everybody who was not standing in the entrance hall was on the landing—not only Daisy but also Verna Laviolette and Sidney and Lilian Devonport. Richard Devonport came out of the library and ran over to where his brother's body lay. The only person who did not appear was Winnie Lord—she must still have been busy in the kitchen and not heard the commotion. As to the people on the landing, watching from the balcony . . . well, here we encounter a problem. The accounts given by Verna, Sidney and Lilian are all different, from each other and also from what Daisy told me.'

'How are they different?' asked Poirot.

I had established a good rhythm for my arm and leg movements and was warming up somewhat. 'Verna's version is the most interesting. She says Helen Acton cannot have pushed Frank and neither can Daisy have done it, because Frank was already falling, in mid-air, when Helen and Daisy stepped out of their bedrooms. She says she would swear to that. When I asked her who might have pushed Frank, she said without hesitation, "Lilian. She was standing close enough to have done it." Sidney Devonport was there too, Verna said, though he was further away—but she conceded that he might also have pushed Frank while Lilian stood by and watched. I don't know about you, but I scarcely find it credible that, having finally decided to forgive Frank his trespasses—'

'Ah, but if Sidney and Lilian murdered him, then the performance of forgiveness and reconciliation would have been a sham, *n'est-ce pas?*'

'I suppose so,' I said doubtfully. 'All the same, what Verna told me was very different from what I was told by Sidney, Lilian and Daisy. Sidney and Lilian said that, when they emerged from their rooms, Helen was standing on the landing and Frank was already falling. They both say that Daisy appeared a moment or two later, as Frank was about to hit the ground. Meanwhile, Daisy says that her parents were not on the landing at all—neither of them—or, if they were, she did not notice them there. She says that she pushed Frank and was aware of Verna's presence and, a few seconds later, Helen's, but claims she did not see either Sidney or Lilian up on the balcony until she had followed Helen down the stairs. As for the assembled hordes downstairs in the entrance hall, none of them looked up before Frank . . . landed, as it were, so they were of no use in determining who appeared on the balcony when and in what order.'

'You have made the excellent report, my friend,' said Poirot with satisfaction. 'You may now get out of the water if you wish. We must waste no time, for there is much to do. And I am afraid that I must leave you alone at Kingfisher Hill for a short while.'

'Why?' I asked as I wrapped the two towels around me. They weren't much use on the warming front; I was colder out of the water than in it.

'Our dead woman from the coach,' said Poirot. 'I must visit her next of kin.'

'Joan Blythe? But . . . do you mean her aunt in Cobham?'

'She has no such relation. It is her mother that I intend to visit in order to ask her about her daughter's green coat and hat. Your Sergeant Gidley has been most helpful in providing me with an address. After that, my next appointment will be with the doctor of the late Otto Prowd: Dr Alexander Ephgrave of Harley Street. I shall speak to him, and then I shall visit Coutts bank to discuss the financial affairs of Godfrey Laviolette with his banker. Finally, I shall visit the offices of the publisher of a certain book.'

'*Midnight Gathering*,' I guessed.

Poirot smiled. 'Well done, Catchpool. Your swim appears to have improved the functioning of your little grey cells. It is a happy day indeed—for I am nearly certain of what will result from all of the enquiries I am about to make. I am unlikely to be wrong.'

Seeing my expression of helpless frustration, he said, 'You too could be in a similarly fortuitous position if you would only apply your mind to the problem at hand. Here, I will give you the hand of the helper. Think, my friend: *Midnight Gathering*, the book. Where it was when you first saw it? Think of what Daisy Devonport told me on the coach about it being a gift—you repeated her very words to me only minutes ago, so I know that you remember them. Then recall Helen Acton's confession, seconds after Frank fell to his death. What did she say to Oliver Prowd when she ran down the stairs?'

'Yes, but what do all of these things have to do with each other?' I shivered in my towels, envying Poirot his thick coat, hat and gloves.

'That is the question we must answer.' His tone was one of cheerful anticipation, not dread. 'Think of Oliver Prowd's confessions to Godfrey Laviolette, as described to me by Hester Semley. Think of Helen Acton pretending to be tired in order to escape from the Devonports' unwelcoming company. She went to her bedroom, did she not? Then we have the two houses: Kingfisher's View and Little Key. Why did the Devonports buy the Laviolettes' house and not Hester Semley's? And a more vital question still: why did the Laviolettes want to sell their home at Kingfisher Hill? Only one thing changed on the estate immediately before they decided they wished to sell their property here, one detail that could hardly be significant: the replacing of the gate porter. And do not forget Lavinia Stent!'

'I suspect you of toying with me, Poirot. Are you deliberately filling my head with useless trivialities?'

'*Non. Pas du tout.*'

'I fail to see how Lavinia Stent, a woman who agreed with Hester Semley, though ineffectively, about the unsuitability of the new gate porter, might be involved in either the murder of Frank Devonport or the murder of Joan Blythe.'

Poirot nodded briskly. 'Do not worry, my friend. I anticipated that you would not be able or willing to do the necessary thinking, so I have prepared for you a list of important tasks. Work your way through these items and you will help to move our investigation further forward, even if you understand only minimally. Simply do as I ask, following my instructions to the letter, and record accurately and in detail what results from your actions. This, surely, you are able to do?'

*

Poirot refused to hand over the list until I was dry and dressed. Once I was in a state of readiness that I hoped he would deem acceptable, I followed his first instruction and knocked on the door of his room at Little Key, which, I had learned yesterday from Verna Laviolette, was the one that Helen Acton had been assigned on the one unhappy occasion that she had come here. Verna told me that I had been allocated Frank Devonport's room, and I had so far searched it twice in the hope of finding something helpful. Alas, I had found nothing.

Poirot and I had been given this temporary accommodation at Little Key in order that we could pursue our investigation, though it was clear we were not welcome. Sidney Devonport growled whenever he came upon either of us by chance, then turned and walked in the opposite direction. Daisy, depending on her mood, either glared at us or smirked as if she knew something we did not. Lilian and Richard Devonport both avoided our eye and Godfrey Laviolette had been very little in evidence. He had taken to locking himself into the room known as Peepers HQ for hours on end. Sidney, by contrast, had not been near that room and appeared to have lost all interest in his once-cherished board game. Oliver Prowd had at first been at our heels all the time, asking to be let in on the details of what we were doing and what was our current thinking about both murders. Then his manner had changed to one of frosty resentment as soon as he saw that Poirot and I were not going to include him in our deliberations.

The only person who seemed pleased to have us around was Verna Laviolette, who was happy to converse with us at length without demanding anything in return. It was strange: when I had first heard her described as 'kind', I had been unable to imagine it. She had seemed to me then to be acerbic and too sharp-edged to be capable of much kindness. More recently, though, I was noticing a softer side to her. With no servants in the house now that both Winnie and her scrawny replacement had gone, Verna, assisted by Daisy, was preparing all the food, and it was Verna who served every meal to Poirot and me. We had eaten on our own in the morning room since our return to Little Key—partly because it was our preference but mainly because Sidney Devonport had made it clear that he did not wish to share his dining room with us. Quite often, Verna opted to keep us company and eat with us instead of with her husband and the Devonports. On these occasions her manner was markedly less spiky than it had once been. Tragedy and disaster are said to bring out the best in some people—perhaps she was one of them.

Poirot did not respond to my first knock at his door, so I tried again. This time he answered immediately. 'Ah, Catchpool! Come in, come in.'

'Let me see this list of tasks, then,' I said with a strong sense of foreboding. I was not afraid of expending effort or energy, but, knowing Poirot well by now, I had no doubt that he was capable of asking me to do absolutely anything: the possible and the impossible. Since meeting him I have felt much less in command of my own life and am always poised for some new surprise or adventure. It is exciting and often stimulating, but also rather hard on the nerves.

Poirot handed me a piece of paper and I cast my eye over the list he had made for me. It read as follows:

Tasks for Catchpool

1. Find out who gave the book *Midnight Gathering* to Daisy Devonport as a gift.
2. Also ask Daisy: why did her father allow Richard to propose marriage to Helen Acton, and to remain engaged to her, when she had murdered his son?
3. Also: if Frank was so evil and dangerous that Daisy needed to kill him to protect her family from further betrayals, why then did she agree to marry his collaborator in the theft, Oliver Prowd? This is a contradiction that makes no sense.
4. Why did Sidney and Lilian Devonport want to see Frank and Helen alone for several hours on the morning of Frank's murder?
5. Did anybody hear any arguments or raised voices in the hour before Frank was pushed to his death?
6. Was suicide ever considered by anybody as an explanation for Frank's death?
7. Make a list of all who were present at Little Key at the time of Frank's death. For each of the ten, write down a possible motive for murder.

I read the seven items on the list three times. Then I said to Poirot, 'Ten people?' I did a quick calculation in my mind. 'You're including Percy Semley?'

'*Mais oui*. He was present.'

'But he was downstairs. He, Oliver, Godfrey Laviolette, Richard, Winnie Lord—they were all downstairs and cannot possibly have pushed Frank from the balcony.'

'That is true,' Poirot agreed. Then he said, 'Unless some of the information we have been given is false.'

'Which brings me to the next problem,' I said. 'I shall do my best to get the answers you want, but you realize, I hope, that I can only ask questions. I have no way of making anybody answer, or answer truthfully.'

'Of course you have the way! Are you not the Scotland Yard inspector in charge of both murder investigations?'

'Theoretically, yes.' I sighed. 'You know I'm hardly the most authoritative chap at the best of times, Poirot, and it's so much harder in this house, of all places. Every time I think about my first visit here, the ridiculous story you told Sidney Devonport about our deep interest in Peepers, I shudder with embarrassment. It's a uniquely uncomfortable position to be in: to demand utmost veracity from those you have shamelessly deceived.'

'Ah, you English with your excessively developed sense of shame!' said Poirot. 'Do not worry that people may lie to you. That will be as useful as if they tell the truth. Now, there is one more thing that I have not added to the list. It is something that I want you to tell Daisy Devonport—but not at the same time that you ask her these other questions. This is vitally important, Catchpool. It is why I have not put the final item on the list. Only once you have already done everything on the list should you proceed to this last instruction.'

'What is it?' I asked.

'You are to tell Mademoiselle Daisy that you have received a telegram from Sergeant Gidley.'

'That says what?'

'That Helen Acton has retracted her confession. She now admits, finally, that she did not murder Frank Devonport. What is more, she agrees that Daisy did and that she saw Daisy push Frank in a most violent fashion.'

'None of this is true, is it?'

'It is wholly untrue,' Poirot announced with pride. 'It is my little invention. Please be as meticulous as possible when recording its effects.'

Shortly after issuing this order, Poirot set off for London with the help of our old friend Mr Alfred Bixby and the Kingfisher Coach Company. Tempted as I was to retreat to my quarters and avoid the rest of the household, I steeled myself and worked my way through the list of tasks that Poirot had assigned to me.

On several fronts, I was unlucky, or at least unsuccessful. (Poirot would no doubt have reminded me that mental attitude, order and method were more closely linked to success than was luck.) No one offered me any sort of answer to questions 2, 3 and 4 on Poirot's list. Daisy scowled at me as if I were a rat that had appeared on her dinner plate when I asked her to explain the discrepancy of her being willing to marry Oliver Prowd at the same time as wanting to kill

Frank for his betrayal. One look at her face was enough to make me give up all hope of getting an answer out of her.

In answer to the question of why Sidney and Lilian had wanted Frank and Helen all to themselves for the morning, everyone I asked said the same thing (apart from Sidney, who turned and marched off without a word): there was no particular reason. They had simply wanted it because they wanted it.

Asked on a separate occasion why he had allowed the two engagements—Daisy's to Oliver and Richard's to Helen—Sidney Devonport had barked at me, 'Mind your own damn business!'

Daisy had said, 'I suspect you are too stupid and lacking in experience to understand, even if I were willing to explain it to you, which I am not.'

Richard had mumbled something to the effect that it was not his place to try to understand his father. 'The truth is, I cannot make sense of my own behaviour most of the time,' he said.

The suggestion that Frank Devonport might have taken his own life by choice was met with voluble derision from all quarters. No one had loved life more than Frank, I was told by all.

I had more success in relation to items 1 and 5 on Poirot's list. Everybody apart from Sidney was happy to inform me that they had not heard any arguments, raised voices or anything untoward in the house in the hour before Frank's death or at any time during the day. I had the impression that they were all telling the truth on this point.

As for *Midnight Gathering*, nobody could tell me who had given Daisy her copy of the book, though Oliver Prowd and Verna Laviolette both volunteered that Daisy had given them a copy as a gift. Oliver's, he said, was presently in his house in London, and Verna told me hers was at Hester Semley's house, which of course I already knew.

Daisy, when asked, took the opportunity to tease me. 'A man called Humphrey gave it to me.' Then she laughed and said, 'I am talking nonsense, Inspector Catchpool. Nobody gave it to me. I gave it to myself. There is no such person as Humphrey.' I reminded her that she had told Poirot the book had been a gift. She merely shrugged and said, 'I must have been lying. I probably decided it was none of his business and made something up.'

Throughout all of my exchanges with Daisy Devonport, she made it abundantly clear that she was not afraid of me or of anything much. Her manner seemed to say, 'I have confessed to the murder of my brother already, so there is really nothing else for me to be afraid of.'

When I attempted item 7, the list of motives, I found some people easier than others to invent motives for.

Frank Devonport's murder—possible motives for those present

Sidney Devonport (on balcony at time of Frank's death)—revenge for the theft. Frank was thriving, and Sidney decided after some time that mere banishment from the family was not sufficient punishment. He lured Frank back home with talk of a second chance, but his intention was always to murder him.

Lilian Devonport (on balcony at time of Frank's death)—exactly the same motive as above. Possibly shared with Sidney, if they acted together. Or (highly unlikely but just about possible given the madness into which some people descend) Lilian could not bear to 'abandon' her most beloved child, and she knew she had not long to live. She wanted to 'take Frank with her', as it were.

Helen Acton (on balcony at time of Frank's death)—cannot think of a motive. Unless her 'lie' about falling in love with Richard Devonport was a double bluff. Perhaps, unbeknownst to the rest of the family, the two of them had been acquainted for some time and grown to love one another. Why this would require Helen to kill Frank rather than simply end her engagement to him, I cannot imagine.

Daisy Devonport (on balcony at time of Frank's death)—her stated motive. She had convinced herself that Frank presented a grave danger to the family. Perhaps also revenge for the theft, if she saw her parents' money as also hers.

Richard Devonport (in library at time of Frank's death)—as the less stellar Devonport brother, did he perhaps fear that Frank's return would eclipse him altogether? That Frank would once again run Sidney's business affairs and he, Richard, would be ousted? Also maybe revenge for theft of family money.

Oliver Prowd (in entrance hall below balcony at time of Frank's death)—jealousy of Daisy's affection for Frank, as Hester Semley described to Poirot. Fear that Daisy would lose interest in him now that Frank had returned.

Winnie Lord (in kitchen at time of Frank's death)—exactly the same motive as Oliver Prowd, according to Hester Semley.

Godfrey Laviolette (in entrance hall below balcony at time of Frank's death)—cannot think of any possible reason, unless related to the Laviolettes' secret reason for wishing to leave Kingfisher Hill.

Verna Laviolette (on balcony at time of Frank's death)—same as for Godfrey above.

Percy Semley (in entrance hall below balcony at time of Frank's death)—cannot think of any motive Percy might have had.

I reread what I had written for each person. 'Whoever it was, why did they do it in front of a large audience?' I said aloud to myself. 'People on the balconied landing, people in the hall below. It could hardly have been more public. *Why?*'

As for Joan-Blythe-from-the-coach, I could think of no reason why any Devonport, Laviolette, Lord, Prowd or Semley should want to bludgeon her to death so violently.

I waited until the following morning to tackle the final task that Poirot had assigned to me—the one he deemed so important that he had not put it on the list at all. After breakfast I set off in search of Daisy. I found her in the Peepers room, sitting in a chair by the window, staring out at the garden.

'Not you again,' she said flatly. 'More questions, I suppose.'

'No. There is news that I thought you would want to hear immediately. From Sergeant Gidley. It arrived by telegram a few minutes ago.'

'What news?' She stood up. My expression must have alarmed her; it had occurred to me as I was speaking, and therefore too late, that she might demand to see the telegram. What would I do in that eventuality?

The answer came to me: I would refuse, of course. If Gidley had sent me a telegram, I would be under no obligation to show it to anybody.

'Helen Acton has admitted to lying,' I said.

'Lying?' Daisy walked slowly towards me. 'Lying about what?'

'She has retracted her confession. She now admits that she did not murder Frank, and has given a new statement in which she says that . . .' I cleared my throat. Poirot would have been able to pull off this act with far more aplomb. Still, that was no use to me; he was in London. I was the one staring into the avid, relentless eyes of Daisy Devonport. 'Helen Acton has confirmed that you are telling the truth: you were the one who pushed Frank, and she saw you do it,' I said. There, it was done.

Daisy gasped. Her hands started to shake.

'I appreciate that it must be rather a shock,' I said.

'Where is Poirot?' she said in a new, ragged voice that I had not heard before. 'I need to speak to him as a matter of urgency.'

'He has gone to take care of some business in London. Anything you wish you tell him, you can tell me. He and I are—'

'Bring him back,' said Daisy. "I need to speak to him *now. Right now.*'

CHAPTER 15

A New Confession

At eleven the following morning, a driver dropped Poirot off at the gates of Little Key. He had telephoned at eight to alert me to his likely arrival time, and I was waiting for him.

'All is as I expected it to be, *mon ami*,' he said. 'My investigations have been fruitful. Every one of my suspicions has been confirmed. Godfrey Laviolette's financial situation is more than satisfactory. His banker tells me that it has always been so. As for our Joan Blythe from the Kingfisher coach, I had a most enlightening conversation with her mother. The green hat and coat were brand new, as I knew they would be. They had not been worn before the day that you and I first saw her wearing them. Ah—I see you wonder why this is important. Soon you will see!' Poirot handed me his suitcase and started to walk towards the house. I hurried after him.

'I spent a delightful hour with the publisher of *Midnight Gathering*,' he went on. 'He was able to furnish me with essential information about the other Joan Blythe, the writer of the book. Most helpful of all was the former doctor to the deceased Otto Prowd, Dr Ephgrave, to whom I spoke at length. What he told me was the ice upon the cake. *Alors*, all is in hand. Tomorrow, Sergeant Gidley will arrive, and he will bring with him Helen Acton. Then we will clear up once and for all the perplexing affair of the killings at Kingfisher Hill. Now, tell me, Catchpool, how have you fared in my absence? Wait! Not now. Anyone might overhear us.' This was true. We were by now standing in the entrance hall of Little Key. 'I shall unpack my things and then we will talk.'

An hour later we were seated in the library, awaiting Daisy Devonport. I had given Poirot the fine detail of all the conversations I had conducted in his absence, ending with the most dramatic one and Daisy's insistence that she must speak to him immediately.

'Ah, *c'est parfait*!' he cried. 'You will see, my friend: the conversation that we are about to have with Mademoiselle Daisy—this too will unfold exactly as I predict. If I had a pen and paper, I could write it down like the lines of a play. It is almost as if I am able to observe the future.'

He really was pleased with himself today!

When Daisy entered the library, it was clear that she had been crying, and recently. Her eyes were red and swollen. 'Thank goodness you're back,' she said to Poirot, lowering herself into the nearest chair to his.

'How may I help you?' he asked her.

'I pray that you can. I have been so awfully foolish, M. Poirot.'

'Mademoiselle . . . I wonder, will you permit me to tell you, and Catchpool here, the story that you wish to tell me?'

Daisy looked confused. 'You do not know the story. Only I know it.'

'Do not be so sure,' said Poirot. 'You may stop me if I get something wrong. Do you agree?'

Still looking nonplussed, she nodded.

'You are here, are you not, to make a new confession? Not to the crime of murder this time, however. This morning you wish to confess to a lesser sin, the sin of lying. You have told a very serious lie, have you not?'

'Yes.' Tears spilled over and ran down Daisy's face.

'And—as if that were not enough—you have heinously contrived to conceal from me and from Inspector Catchpool many important things. Is this not so?'

She nodded.

'You did not murder your brother Frank, did you?'

'No, I did not.'

'What about the lady in the green hat and coat? Did you kill her?'

'No,' said Daisy. 'I have killed nobody. But . . .'

'Silence, please. Allow me to tell you what you did. You took the poker from the fireplace and destroyed the head and face of the dead woman. You bludgeoned her until you were certain that she would not be recognized. Yes?'

'Yes,' Daisy whispered.

'And the note written in black ink? "You sat in a seat you should never have sat in, now here comes a poker to batter your hat in". . .'

'I wrote the note and placed it on her body,' said Daisy.

'Indeed.' Poirot's eyes moved around the room as he deliberated. 'This is fascinating. Fascinating! You wrote the note because *at the same time you did and did not wish to reveal the dead woman's identity.*'

Daisy looked at him. 'You are extremely clever, M. Poirot. I am no match for you.'

Poirot paused, apparently savouring her words. 'Tell me, if you did not kill the woman in the green hat and coat, then who did?'

'I don't know. Truly, I don't. It might have been anyone. Anyone apart from Oliver or me. We were out walking together between ten and eleven. But everyone else, even those who were supposed to be with somebody at the time . . . I mean, it's not impossible for two people to have done it together, is it?'

'No, it is not,' Poirot agreed. 'Let us talk about the dead woman, the woman from the coach. She gave her name as Joan Blythe. Does that name sound familiar to you?'

'Yes,' said Daisy. 'That is one of the things I wanted to tell you. M. Poirot. I have withheld so much and told so many lies, I wish I could say that I am sorry. It feels true—I *am* sorry now—but if I were not in a state of mortal fear, would I be sorry? I doubt it. Which means that you should scorn my apparent contrition. It means that I regret my dishonesty for my own sake, not for any other, nobler reason.' She looked very young and afraid and I tried hard not to feel sorry for her. For all I knew, this was just another act.

Poirot said, 'All I seek is the truth of what happened, mademoiselle. The rest is a matter for your conscience.'

She nodded. Gathering herself a little, she said, 'Joan Blythe is the name of the author of a book that is very dear to me: *Midnight Gathering*. I had it with me on the coach. You saw it, Inspector Catchpool, do you remember? I'd put it down on the seat beside me, and I turned and found you staring at it rather oddly. Then later you accused me of having stolen it, M. Poirot, when I had done no such thing. For some reason, the book caused you both to behave in a most peculiar way. In any case, Joan Blythe—the real Joan Blythe, whoever she might be—is that novel's author. It was given to me by a friend of mine, a man called Humphrey. I subsequently gave it as a gift to many other people.'

'Why did you not tell me the truth on the coach, when I asked how the book came into your possession?' said Poirot.

'And why did you tell me that you had invented Humphrey?' I asked her.

'I did tell you the truth,' Daisy said to Poirot. 'I told you it was a present someone had given me. I was about to say that it was from a friend called Humphrey when I realized that you had just accused me of theft and did not deserve to know any more than I had already told you. It hardly mattered to you—it could have been Humphrey, Cedric or

James for all you would care.' She turned to me. 'I told you the truth at first too. Then I decided to have some fun and take it back, pretend it was a lie. I quite enjoy lying sometimes. It's good sport.'

'This I have no difficultly in believing,' Poirot said with a small sigh. 'Did you enjoy pretending to have murdered your brother Frank?'

'That provided me with a darker sort of satisfaction,' said Daisy. 'I would not describe it as enjoyment.'

'And you believed you were safe from punishment for this crime to which you had confessed? For as long as Helen Acton adhered to her story that she killed Frank, you were safe. She was already in prison and condemned to die. You were at no risk of being hanged for a crime of which another woman had already been convicted.'

'So I thought,' Daisy said quietly.

'Then when Catchpool told you that Helen Acton had retracted her confession, you panicked. You could not allow your own confession to be the only one. Here, suddenly, was a tangible danger that you might be the one to hang.'

'You are very clever, M. Poirot. You understand why I am now willing to tell you the truth.'

'Allow me to return the favour, mademoiselle.'

'What do you mean?'

'I, also, will now tell *you* the truth: Helen Acton has not retracted her confession. That was our little lie that we devised for you.'

Daisy's mouth fell open. She stared at me hard.

'Do not blame Inspector Catchpool,' Poirot told her. 'The idea was mine. Now, tell me, do you wish to confess once more to the murder of Frank? If not, that leaves Helen Acton as the only one claiming to be guilty. Her execution will no doubt be expedited if you are no longer offering a rival confession for consideration.'

'But . . . I don't want Helen to die.' Daisy's voice shook. 'Frank loved her and she loved him. I know she did. I saw it. Not for long, but I saw it. It was real. You could feel it in the room. But I do not want to tell any more lies, not to save Helen, not for any reason. I am tired of lying, so tired.'

I knew what she meant. I rarely lied, but when I did— usually at Poirot's instigation or to pacify my mother—I found it exhausting.

'I will ask you again to make sure,' said Poirot. 'Did you kill your brother Frank? Did you push him over the balcony to his death?'

'No, I did not. I swear it. I have never murdered anyone! I only wanted you to think that I could, and that I had. I see now how stupid and vain and petty I have been. There is nothing I can say that will make up for what I've done, I know that. My behaviour has been inexcusable.' She shut her eyes and closed her hands into fists. 'If you only knew how I have dreamed of committing murder and getting away with it. I have spent nearly a year wishing I could do it—ever since Father sent Frank away—but I am incapable. I am no better than a frightened child. So instead I boasted of doing the thing I was afraid to do. It might not make sense to you, but I only wanted to pretend to be someone who possessed the courage I lacked!'

'You wished to kill Frank?' I asked her.

'No. Not at all.' Daisy stood up and walked over to the window. 'I adored Frank, but having lost him forever . . . it won't make sense to you, I'm sure, but after his death, I fantasized endlessly that it was I who had killed him to punish Father. And Mother. If they thought they could have him back after they had deprived *me* of him . . .' Her face contorted in pain. 'And then sometimes it was my parents I dreamed of murdering—the people who cared so little for my feelings that they disowned my brother even though I begged them not to. Oh, we all knew the hierarchy of importance: Father at the top, above everybody, then Mother, then Frank. Richard and I were irrelevant. Mother could have made Father see sense if she had only been brave enough to stand up to him. Look what happened when she fell ill and asked if Frank could be forgiven—he granted her wish!'

'Mademoiselle, if you did not push Frank to his death, then who did?'

Daisy shook her head. 'I wish I knew. When I came out of my room, he was already falling.'

'And you saw people standing on the landing near where he had fallen, did you not? Whom did you see?'

'Helen. Verna. Mother and Father.' Daisy turned to me. 'May I answer your other questions now, Inspector, the ones I would not answer when you asked me yesterday? I should like to atone for my dishonesty by being as truthful as I can from now on. I did tell you the truth about one thing: you asked me why Father and Mother sent us all over to Kingfisher's View on the day Frank was killed. I gave you an honest answer: they simply wanted it. In their estimation, in the ordinary course of things, only they and their wishes matter. On that particular day Frank mattered too, but none of the rest of us ever had—so why on earth would they want us cluttering up the house? There was nothing more to it than that.'

This was a fuller answer than she had given me the first time. I believed her.

'You also asked why Father tolerated Richard's engagement to Helen. It's quite simple: after Frank's murder, my parents decided to pretend that neither Frank nor Helen had ever existed. Not straight away, mind you. They screamed and wailed over Frank's lifeless body for about thirty minutes, after which they closeted themselves away in Mother's bedroom. When they eventually emerged from that room, we all saw at once that a . . . a sort of wall had gone up around them. From that moment until the two of you arrived and started asking uncomfortable questions, they behaved as if they'd never had a son called Frank and as if there was no such person as Helen.'

'And so when Richard proposed marriage to her and she accepted . . . ?' Poirot prompted.

'Richard saw that in this particular matter, Father was powerless. News of the engagement reached him, of course, but he has never acknowledged it. We all knew that he wouldn't. In order to protest about it, he would have had to utter Helen's name, which might have led to a conversation that would have been impossible for his pride to withstand. Richard could have said, "Who are you to tell me what to do, Father? You said Frank was to be banished forever, then changed your mind on a whim to please Mother." Obviously Richard would never be so bold, but the possibility was there and that was enough to ensure Father's silence on the subject. He knew only too well that changing his mind about Frank had diminished his moral authority beyond repair. And he and Mother were very quickly unwilling to think about Frank *at all*. They did not want to be bereaved, or to have had a son who had stolen from them, a son who was then murdered. They created a new reality that they could stand to live in—one in which *nothing had happened*, none of the unbearable, shameful things. How could they then object to Richard's engagement without stepping out of their invented world and into our real one?'

'What about your engagement to Oliver Prowd?' I asked her. 'Did you think along the same lines as Richard: that Sidney would disapprove of your marriage to Oliver yet be unable to object?'

'Yes, I did. What could he have said? "I forbid you to marry the man who conspired with Frank to steal from me"? I would have feigned innocence and said, "But, Father, I don't understand. If Frank can be given another chance then why not Oliver? You said that we must never weaken and allow Frank to worm his way back in." Don't you see? Father had succumbed to persuasion from Mother to make her last days more bearable, but he *loathed* himself for doing so. He saw it as unpardonable weakness on his part and took pains to ensure that Richard and I would have no occasion to raise the subject for discussion.'

'Do you love Oliver Prowd?' Poirot asked her.

'Of course I do. Not as much as he loves me, but I would never wish to love a husband *that* much. One would feel rather powerless.'

'I have another question for you, mademoiselle. When you came into the drawing room and found me there with Inspector Catchpool, Sergeant Gidley and the police doctor—do you recall the scene?'

'Yes. That woman's dead body was there, lying on the floor, and I was about to have to pretend that I had not recently smashed up her head with a poker. Of course I recall it. I shall never forget it.'

'Then you may also recall that Catchpool and I discussed her identity. The name Joan Blythe was mentioned. Why did you not immediately say, "This is a coincidence, for Joan Blythe is also the author of my favourite book"?'

Daisy smiled sadly. 'Because *Midnight Gathering*, at that point, was the very furthest thing from my mind. I knew Joan Blythe wasn't the dead woman's name, and I knew why she had told you it was.'

Poirot was nodding as she spoke. 'You knew, did you not, that her real name was—'

'Winnie Lord,' said Daisy.

I wished I could see through the skin of his forehead to the fine mind beneath. *How* had he known that Joan Blythe and Winnie Lord were one and the same person? It was unfathomable to me!

'Let us play a little game,' Poirot said to Daisy Devonport. 'I will tell you parts of a story—the parts that I know. It will be like the jigsaw puzzle. You will fill in the missing pieces. Do you agree?'

She nodded.

'I have known for certain only since yesterday that Joan Blythe from the motor-coach was Winnie Lord, though I guessed it much earlier. But there was something I knew almost from the start, something that helped me greatly. *I knew that you and Joan-Blythe-from-the-coach were travelling together.* You were not two passengers who happened to be seated for some minutes side by side; you were travelling companions.

'Knowing as I did that the two of you had embarked upon this journey by motor-coach together and yet ended up pretending, for my benefit, to be strangers to one another—this has made the solving of all of the puzzles seem possible to me from the very beginning, when it did not seem possible to Catchpool. For him there were only the many strands that made no sense when each was viewed as unconnected to the others. He remarked upon the impossible coincidence of them all happening at once: first, a woman warned by a stranger that she would be murdered if she sat in a particular seat. Then, that seat being next to one occupied by a woman who tells Hercule Poirot that she has committed murder herself.

'How can it happen, Catchpool asked me, that *two*

women speak to us so candidly of murder during the same journey, two unconnected women—or so he believed! *Eh bien*, then there was the apparent coincidence *le plus incroyable*: that these two revelations should occur when we are *en route* to Kingfisher Hill to investigate yet another murder, for which an innocent woman might be about to hang. Of course, mademoiselle, there was nothing coincidental about any of it, as you know—you, the inspired inventor who orchestrated the entire scene!

'You and Winnie Lord were travelling to Kingfisher Hill. It was where you both lived. You had been to London and now you were returning. You did not know that your brother, Richard, had asked for my help in proving Helen Acton's innocence. He had told no one. When you became aware that here was Hercule Poirot, the famous detective, within easy reach, it did not strike you as anything but a coincidence. An opportunity. You had no notion that I was *en route* to Little Key to solve the murder of Frank Devonport. According to the law that crime was already solved and justice was soon to be done. You, meanwhile, had spent many months indulging in the morbid fantasy that *you* had committed the murder of Frank in order to punish your parents—to deprive them of him in the very same way that they had deprived you. *Alors*, you decided to play a little game with Poirot. The part of you that likes to tell lies in order to create certain effects . . . it could not resist.'

'It did not try,' Daisy admitted. 'I was certain I could confess to you without letting slip any details that would identify me. I was excited to hear what you might have to say on the matter. I yearned for you to solve the mystery and guess why I did it—which you failed to do. I didn't kill Frank but if I had . . . well, I would have had a very interesting and clever motive, wouldn't I? I thought to myself, let's see if the great Hercule Poirot can work it out.'

'Ah, but you faced an obstacle,' said Poirot. 'How could you make this confession to me? I was sitting next to Catchpool, several rows behind you, and you were sitting in the seventh row with Winnie Lord. You could hardly stand and shout about murder over the heads of all the other passengers.'

'How did you know that Winnie and I were travelling together?' said Daisy.

'It was obvious,' said Poirot. 'Catchpool had seen a book on the seat beside you: *Midnight Gathering*. When you saw him looking at it, you picked it up and held it for a moment. Then when Catchpool started to move along down the aisle, you put the book back on that seat, the one that was later taken by Winnie Lord. But the coach was full—completely full—and you knew that, mademoiselle, because Alfred Bixby, owner of the Kingfisher Coach Company, had boasted most volubly and made sure we passengers all knew that every ticket was sold and every seat taken.'

'You notice everything, don't you?' said Daisy.

'But Catchpool does not yet comprehend,' said Poirot. 'When I finally sat beside you, mademoiselle, you told me that you would not have been surprised if Monsieur Bixby had employed actors to give a false impression of the coach being full. When you said that, I knew at once: you were as aware as I of the fullness of the coach. You knew that every seat would be taken by somebody eventually. There was no chance that the one next to you would remain unoccupied. Why, then, I asked myself, would you leave your book on it so that no one could sit down, when there were people boarding the vehicle at this exact moment? Sooner or later you would have had to move the book and accept a neighbour for the journey, so why would you not do so immediately? There seemed only one possible answer: you were saving that seat for a particular person. Winnie Lord.'

'But the two of them were not together,' I said, confused. 'Joan . . . Winnie . . . was standing alone. You, Miss Devonport, were standing some distance away and making loud, unpleasant remarks about her for all to hear. As if she were a stranger for whom you had nothing but disdain.'

'I was angry,' said Daisy. 'Winnie and I had been together until she behaved in a way that disappointed me greatly. That was when she ran away from me and started to behave like a gibbering fool. I hoped that by speaking so harshly, I might bring her to her senses—remind her that she and I were friends and that she owed me a certain loyalty. I had always been good to her. The green hat and coat she was wearing were gifts from me and they were not inexpensive.'

'What made her run away from you?' said Poirot. 'Wait—I think I know the answer. Remember, Catchpool, that when you first spoke to Winnie Lord and introduced yourself as an inspector from Scotland Yard, she replied that you *could not be* a police inspector, that it was impossible. She demanded to know your true identity. This provides the clue to what must have taken place between her and Mademoiselle Daisy only minutes before, leaving her so shocked and afraid—and making you, mademoiselle, so angry. You frequently find yourself feeling disproportionately angry, do you not? You experience the wild rage that can barely be contained when there has been only the mildest provocations.'

Daisy closed her eyes.

Poirot said, 'On the coach, when Catchpool here merely glanced at your book, you reacted with disproportionate aggression, as you did when you spoke so savagely of Winnie Lord in front of the other passengers. When I first sat next to you, you expressed hostility towards me. Generally, mademoiselle, you were full of the rage that had no obvious cause. This is how a person behaves when they have suppressed their natural anger—caused by an oppressive parent, in this instance, and the forced disavowal of a beloved brother—for far too long.'

'M. Poirot, may I tell you something?' Daisy leaned forward.

'Please.'

'When I saw that I would have to smash up Winnie's head and face so that no one would recognize her, I . . . I rather relished the prospect. She was dead already, with the poker lying beside her and some blood under her head, and . . . well, I worked up a considerable sweat while doing it.

I felt calm and peaceful afterwards, as if the anger that had been boiling in me for so long had drained away.'

'You must also have been angry with Frank,' said Poirot. 'Your parents had caused you the greatest unhappiness by forcing the two of you apart . . . yet Frank was ready to forgive them and seemed to return with no bitterness in his heart. Did you not feel betrayed by him?'

Daisy smiled. 'Goodness me, you really are as clever as people say you are.'

'And you are a highly imaginative young woman.'

'When I first met you, I accused you of making too much of a fuss about murder,' said Daisy. 'That is not my true opinion. Murder is a terrible thing. The most terrible of all. I wish . . .' She gasped suddenly. 'I wish that Frank were still alive. I wish it with all my heart.'

'Yes, I see that it is so,' Poirot said gently. 'When he was killed, you were grief-stricken—more full of rage than ever. You wanted to make others suffer as you suffered. You asked yourself: what would be the cruellest possible punishment that you could inflict upon Sidney and Lilian Devonport? A clever and devious plan occurred to you. When did you think of it? Long before you first encountered Hercule Poirot by the side of a motor-coach, I think.'

'It was very soon after Frank died,' said Daisy. 'I heard Helen tell the police that she had already pushed him over the balcony by the time anybody else appeared on the landing. And I . . . I saw with my own eyes that all Mother and Father saw was Frank falling to his death. They did not notice me at all, though I was there too, standing between them and Helen. They couldn't have been sure that it was not I who pushed Frank.'

'*Eh bien*, you had the idea that was at once outrageous and all too easy to put into action,' said Poirot. 'What if you were to pretend that *you* were the killer and that your motive for murdering your brother was the belief, instilled in you by your parents' determined indoctrination, that Frank was a danger to the family? Why, then Sidney and Lilian Devonport would be forced to confront an intolerable realization: that they had lost the son they had only just regained *and that it was entirely their own fault*, and a direct result of their unwillingness to allow you to have your own thoughts and feelings about Frank. Such effort had they put into making you believe he was a danger—and now, when they have relented and want only to reclaim their banished, lost son . . . *now* they must pay the price for having so brainwashed you against him!'

'Yes. It was the perfect reversal,' said Daisy. 'When I wanted to keep Frank, they wouldn't allow it. Then, when *they* wanted to keep him, *I* wouldn't allow it—and for the very same reason: because now I was the one to believe him to be a terrible danger, and I only believed that because they had made me believe it. It makes for a marvellous story, don't you think, M. Poirot?'

'How much of this "perfect reversal" story did you tell to Winnie Lord?' said Poirot.

'That is why she was in such a state of distress, yes? You

300

saw Poirot and decided that you must play your game with him—confess to this murder you had not committed—and so why not practise by first telling the tale to Winnie?'

'I needed something to keep me entertained,' said Daisy. 'Alfred Bixby was taking an age to open the doors of the coach and I was freezing to death.'

'That must be why Winnie responded so strangely when I introduced myself as a police inspector,' I said.

'Indeed,' said Poirot. 'Winnie Lord was at that very moment considering whether to go to the police with this new information she had just received. Then suddenly, a representative of Scotland Yard appeared beside her! It must all have seemed so *incroyable* to her as to make her wonder: could all of this be a joke played by her friend Daisy Devonport? First the confession, and so soon afterwards, the policeman?'

'Winnie turned out to be no friend of mine,' Daisy said bitterly. 'I thought she would stand by me no matter what, but she proved to be a disloyal piece of work if ever there was one. She threatened to tell the police—even though I had just taken her up to London and bought her a beautiful new hat and coat. I had to offer her a sizeable amount of money to secure her silence. I knew she and her mother were in desperate need of it.'

'Mademoiselle, tell me . . . what precisely did you say to Winnie Lord about why you had killed Frank?'

'Before we boarded the coach? Nothing at all. Only that I had done it and Helen was innocent. Afterwards, when I found her weeping by the side of a road near the Tartar

Inn at Cobham, I told her a lot more. I said that . . . Well, first I told her everything that I had told you.'

'And then?'

'She was by turns sullen and hysterical,' Daisy said impatiently. 'She kept asking how I could let Helen Acton hang for a crime I had committed. Had I not just told her that I had *confessed*, and to none other than Hercule Poirot? Silly fool. She really was tedious about it. At that point I couldn't resist telling her the whole story of why I had murdered Frank, though of course I had done no such thing—but anything to relieve the boredom of having to deal with her.'

'So you told Winnie Lord only then—at Cobham—that your true reason for killing Frank was *not* that you believed him to be evil and dangerous, but instead that you wished your parents to think you had done it for this reason and to believe that their earlier indoctrination of you against your brother had caused the tragedy?'

'Exactly, yes,' said Daisy with a slight smile. 'So that they would have to live with the knowledge of their own culpability. I told Winnie that I was only going to admit to my *false* motive, you see: saving my family from the evil and dangerous Frank. My perfect revenge only worked if they thought I had done it because of *what they had made me believe* about Frank.'

'I see,' said Poirot. 'So if that was your false motive, then your other one, your "perfect revenge" motive, as you call it—would you describe that as your *true* motive, even though you did not commit the murder?'

Daisy nodded. 'It *was* true. A motive can be true even if one has not acted upon it.'

'Fascinating,' Poirot murmured.

'I had hoped that Winnie would be interested in discussing everything that was brilliant about my plan—the structural exquisiteness of it—but instead she only whined about how unpardonable it was that I had allowed the police to believe a different story for so long and risked Helen Acton's life. Ugh, she was a fool! Do I sound despicable, M. Poirot? Perhaps I am. But Winnie knew as well as I did that Helen *wanted* to take the blame, or else she would not have done so! She could easily have said that Frank fell. Who would have thought of murder if she had only said it was an accident? Helen wanted to die. She still does. But Winnie was too stupid to see that.'

Poirot nodded. He said, 'Let us hear now about the other story you invented. The one that had not been created in your mind months in advance but was, rather, an improvisation on the day of our journey by coach.'

'What do you mean?' Daisy looked puzzled.

'The mysterious stranger with his warning of murder,' said Poirot. 'The seat in the seventh row beside the aisle, on the right.'

'Oh, that.'

'*Oui*, mademoiselle. That.'

'As you say, it was an on-the-spot improvisation.'

'Hold on a minute,' I said. 'Are you suggesting that—'

'Yes, Catchpool,' said Poirot. 'The story told to us by Winnie Lord was preposterous, sensational nonsense from start to finish. There was not a grain of truth in it. It was invented by Mademoiselle Daisy with the sole aim of arranging for me to sit next to her so that she could make to me her murder confession.'

My face must have made for a gruesome picture at this point in the proceedings. To think that I had listened so carefully to Winnie's lies and wasted hours since that day trying to make sense of the large helping of codswallop she had fed us!

'And Winnie agreed to tell this ridiculous tale at your behest, when she believed you to be a murderer?' I asked Daisy. 'No wonder she could barely bring herself to board the coach and sit beside you after what you had told her.'

'I have already told you: I offered her a large sum of money to do as I asked. I bought her unquestioning compliance just as Father had always bought Mother's and mine and Richard's.' Daisy frowned. 'But I'm not a tyrant like Father. I was always good to Winnie. I cared for her. When I told her I had killed Frank, I expected her to be shocked, naturally, but there was no need for her to walk away from me as if I had a contagious disease. If she had made a similar confession to me, I would have asked her *why* first of all. I'd have done my best to understand her predicament. And . . . well I *hadn't* committed a murder, so it felt rather unfair to be ostracized when I knew I was innocent.' Seeing my expression, Daisy said sharply, 'You do not need to point out to me the flaw in my reasoning, Inspector Catchpool. I'm well aware of it. Do you want the whole truth or do you not? Our true thoughts are often profoundly irrational.'

'Did you tell Winnie Lord to pretend that her name was Joan Blythe?' asked Poirot.

'No. That was the one thing I didn't think of: a name for her. She must have thought of the book and decided that the name of its author would do. *Midnight Gathering* would have been at the forefront of her mind because—'

'Please, allow me,' Poirot interrupted. 'May I tell this part of the story?'

'Very well.' Daisy eyed him doubtfully.

'Catchpool.' He turned to me. 'Remind us of what Mademoiselle Daisy told me when I asked her where she had obtained the book?'

'She said, "It was originally a gift from . . ." then stopped and would not say the rest.'

'The word "originally" is most informative,' said Poirot. 'When one is given a gift that one keeps—and we know that you still had the book in your possession, mademoiselle—one has no need to say the word "originally". One would use that word only if the book, at the time of asking, was no longer the gift that it once was, that it had *originally* been. Do you see, Catchpool?'

'No, I don't see at all,' I said.

'Think about it, *mon ami*. If the book was given to Daisy Devonport by her friend Humphrey and she still had it, as we know she did, then it remained a gift from Humphrey. There would be no need to use the word "originally". If, however, it had at one time been a gift from Mademoiselle Daisy to Winnie Lord, a gift that Winnie had very recently returned as a gesture of disgust and defiance after

Mademoiselle Daisy confessed to the murder of Frank Devonport . . .'

'Are you saying that the book was a present from Daisy to Winnie Lord, and then Winnie gave it back to her?' I said.

'I believe this is so, yes.'

'He is quite right,' said Daisy. 'Winnie loved that book. Carried it with her wherever she went. I had written a special message inside it for her, and it meant the world to her. Soon after I told her that I had killed Frank, the driver of the coach came to take our suitcases and bags to stow them away. Winnie made him wait while she removed *Midnight Gathering* from her case. She handed it back to me and said, "I don't want this any more. You can have it back." So, yes: it was *originally* a gift from me to Winnie— one she later rejected. That is why I had it with me on the coach. I would hardly have . . .' Daisy stopped abruptly. A red hue crept across her face.

'You would hardly have wanted or needed to read *Midnight Gathering* yourself,' Poirot finished her sentence for her. 'You knew every word in its pages and every episode in its narrative almost by heart—*because you, Daisy Devonport, under the name Joan Blythe, are the book's author.*'

'Please, you mustn't tell a soul.' Daisy's face had turned white. 'I know I have no right to ask it of you, but I beg of you—'

'How did you know, Poirot?' I said incredulously.

'A little guesswork, followed by the calculation of

306

probabilities.' He looked at Daisy. 'Why, I wondered, was this one novel of particular importance to you—you who have such a vivid imagination, such a skill for making up sensational and irresistible stories—and you who also, if you will pardon me, care so much more for your own inventions and what goes on in your own mind than for the truth or what might matter to anybody else? Why would you give this book to everyone who matters to you? My suspicion was confirmed when I visited a publisher in London yesterday—a Mr Humphrey Pluckrose of Pluckrose & Prince. You were not altogether lying, mademoiselle, when you said that Humphrey Pluckrose had given you the book. It was not a gift, however; you had signed a contract with his firm that obliged him to furnish you with copies of your own novel.'

'Please keep this knowledge to yourself,' begged Daisy. 'My writing is the only part of my life that my family knows nothing about and has no involvement in. It is my freedom.'

I thought of Winnie Lord's fear when I uttered the words 'Midnight Gathering'. When she heard me say it, she must have thought that the jig was up: that I had seen her take the book out of her suitcase and hand it to Daisy. If I had, I would have known that they were not strangers to one another. When I explained that the woman who had been sitting beside her in the seventh row had a book with that title, her fear dissolved: it was then clear to her that I knew nothing of her personal connection to *Midnight Gathering* or to Daisy Devonport.

'Will you keep my secret?' said Daisy. 'Please, M. Poirot, Inspector Catchpool. It is of paramount importance to me that this should remain unknown. Nobody apart from the employees of Pluckrose & Prince knows that I am Joan Blythe.'

'Do you know what is of paramount importance to me?' Poirot said softly. 'The truth about the two murders at Little Key. You have told me so much of it, mademoiselle, but still not all of it. Never mind. I shall tell the rest to you—as soon as Sergeant Gidley can fetch Helen Acton from Holloway prison and bring her here.'

CHAPTER 16

Little Key, Heavy Door

The next day at noon, the drawing room at Little Key was full of people. Every seat, including those borrowed from Peepers HQ, was occupied. Poirot, Sergeant Gidley, Inspector Marcus Capeling and I sat on straight-backed chairs in a row closest to the door. Helen Acton, with an unreadable expression on her face, sat on the piano stool with her back to the piano. I imagined her turning, lifting the instrument's lid and starting to play, though it was hard to fathom what sort of music would be appropriate for an occasion of this type.

Also present, and seated on the more comfortable armchairs and sofas, were Sidney, Lilian, Daisy and Richard Devonport, Oliver Prowd and Godfrey and Verna Laviolette.

'Ladies and gentlemen,' Poirot began.

He was at once interrupted by Oliver Prowd, who said, 'What about Percy Semley? Should he not be here too?'

'No,' said Poirot. 'I will speak of him later, for he is important, but his presence is not required. Let us start,

309

then, with the facts. We have two murders to discuss today: the murder of Frank Devonport and the murder of Winnie Lord.'

'Winnie?' said Lilian. 'Then are we to assume—'

'It is not an assumption, madame.' Poirot cut short her enquiry. 'It is a fact: the body found in this room was the body of Winnie Lord.'

'Good gracious,' said Richard Devonport. 'Who would want to murder Winnie?'

'The killer's identity will soon be known to you all,' said Poirot. 'For now, I will say this: it was very important to Winnie's attacker that she should not be identified as Winnie. That is why her dress, handbag and shoes were stripped from her body and burned in the fire.' He pointed at the grate. 'Any of you might have recognized these items as belonging to her, for they were not new. By removing the recognizable items and leaving only the brand new green hat and coat that she had never before worn in this house, somebody—not necessarily her killer—ensured that Winnie could not be identified.'

'Who killed her?' asked Lilian. 'I should like to be told straight away.' This was met with a general murmur of agreement.

'Madame, there is an order I have decided upon, and I should like to adhere to it.' Poirot looked around the room. 'Whoever burned the clothes of Winnie Lord so that no one would know who she was also destroyed her face for the same reason. Now, let us think who the killer of Winnie might have been. Not Helen Acton, who was in Holloway

Prison at the time. And if we believe all of the accounts that we have been given, then most of you were with at least one other person when Winnie was murdered. Only one of you was not. You, Madame Laviolette.'

'I didn't kill her,' said Verna. 'Godfrey, I didn't. I wouldn't. What could I possibly have against poor old Winnie?'

Her husband reached over and patted her hand. 'I know you didn't, Verna. Be quiet. Let Moysier Poy-row say his piece.'

'Verna Laviolette, also, might have pushed Frank Devonport to his death,' Poirot went on. 'She was upstairs when he fell from the balcony. So were Daisy, Sidney and Lilian Devonport, and so was Helen Acton, who confessed almost immediately to the murder of Frank. Everyone agrees that Richard Devonport, Oliver Prowd, Godfrey Laviolette and Percy Semley were downstairs when Frank fell, so they cannot have killed him,' said Poirot. 'Winnie Lord, also, was downstairs, preparing dinner. She too is eliminated from suspicion.'

'Is the answer not immediately obvious?' said Lilian. 'There cannot be two killers roaming around Little Key. It is quite impossible. Surely that means both murders must have been committed by Verna.'

'Your loyalty is touching, dear.' Verna regarded her old friend with cold eyes.

'Helen Acton killed Frank,' said Sidney gruffly, staring down at his feet.

'Yes, I did,' said Helen. 'Mr Devonport speaks the truth. You should listen to him, M. Poirot.'

'The same person did not commit both murders,' Poirot announced. 'Madame Laviolette, in fact, committed neither murder. And . . . regrettably, Madame Devonport, what you decree to be impossible is true: there *are* two killers at Little Key. Both are in this room now.'

'How horrible,' said Richard.

'Madame Laviolette, you might not be a killer but, like Helen Acton and Daisy Devonport, you are a liar. You and your husband did not decide to sell this house because you were in financial difficulty. I spoke two days ago to your banker in London. He told me that you have been extremely wealthy for as long as he has known you. Why, then, did you suddenly decide to sell your home at Kingfisher Hill, and why did you lie about your reason for doing so?'

'Fascinating though it might be to hear the answer, what has this to do with the murder of my brother?' Daisy asked.

Poirot smiled. 'You think that I waste time on trivialities, mademoiselle? *Non.* These little details, apparently unconnected to the two killings, are vital to know. They are the little key that will open the heavy door.'

'Financial difficulties,' Godfrey Laviolette muttered. 'What a stupid lie.'

'Monsieur Laviolette—you felt no obligation to tell your good friend Sidney Devonport what it was about the Kingfisher Hill Estate that had made you want to leave it as soon as possible, selling your house for much less than it was worth. You said, did you not, that it was not something that would have disturbed the Devonport family at all? *Eh bien*, you did not believe you were concealing from them something that might have put them off.

'What could this mysterious feature of the estate have been?' Poirot wondered theatrically, rising from his chair to walk around the room. 'I asked Percy Semley's Aunt Hester, who is a keen and meticulous observer of life at Kingfisher Hill. She told me that, immediately before the Laviolettes decided to sell Kingfisher's Rest, as this house used to be known, only one thing changed on the estate: the gate porter. Hester Semley objected to the appointment of the new gate porter and she happened to mention that only one other resident supported her in her objection: a Lavinia Stent. This assisted me greatly, for if Lavinia Stent and Hester Semley were the only two who disapproved of the new man, that meant that Godfrey and Verna Laviolette had no reservations about his appointment.'

'He's a thoroughly decent and amiable fellow,' Godfrey said.

Poirot gave him a look of warning. Then he said, 'There was, of course, another significant change at Kingfisher Hill at the same time that the Laviolettes decided to sell this house—or a short while before they made their decision, I should say: *the Devonports announced that they intended to buy a house on the estate*. They planned to buy Hester Semley's house. That, ladies and gentlemen, is what made Godfrey and Verna Laviolette so eager to leave. If it was not the new gate porter and nothing else about the estate had changed, why, then it can have been nothing else. Madame Laviolette, I am right, am I not?'

'Aren't you always?' said Verna drily, eyes downcast.

Poirot went on, 'Most people who buy houses here seek an idyllic rural retreat from their busy London life. The Laviolettes were no exception. Godfrey Laviolette and Sidney Devonport were firm friends. Their families spent considerable amounts of time in each other's company. The two men had made their fortunes together, worked together on the game Peepers . . .'

I winced at the mention of it.

'. . . which is perhaps why it was so important to the Laviolettes to think of this idyllic country estate as theirs alone, not something to be shared with the Devonports. To have them visit was one thing, but the idea that their friends were about to buy a piece of their private paradise . . . *non, c'etait insupportable*. Yet what could they do? They owned only one house, not the whole estate. They could not prevent Sidney Devonport from buying a home here. So they solved the problem in the only way they could. Rather than share their private retreat, they would leave it—and quickly. I imagine, Madame Laviolette, that you did not wish to share ownership of Kingfisher Hill with the Devonports even for one week if you could avoid it. And the only way to avoid it was to sell them your house before they could buy Hester Semley's.'

'This makes little sense to me,' said Richard Devonport. 'Everyone with a country home at Kingfisher Hill shares the land and the facilities with many other families. That is rather the point of country park estates of this sort, and everyone knows what they're getting when they buy in.'

'Sharing with strangers is one thing,' said Verna Laviolette. 'Having your private little getaway ruined by invasion from your London friends—people who belong to another part of your life—that's quite another.'

'Do you mean to say that M. Poirot is right about your reason for selling?' Richard sounded astonished.

Verna shrugged. 'As I said before: isn't he always right?'

'But, Verna, you and Godfrey are always here,' said Oliver Prowd, who seemed to share Richard's bewilderment.

'My word, are you boys as cloth-headed as you seem?' Verna replied. 'Do you know what prevents you from understanding? It's a characteristic of men: you focus only on the intellectual side of things. You never stop to imagine how a person might *feel*. M. Poirot, now, he's different. He understands the human heart, don't you, M. Poirot?' Verna let out a long sigh. 'Selling this house meant that Kingfisher Hill was no longer ours. It was the Devonports'. I was willing to visit them at *their* home, once it was no longer mine. Sure—why not?'

'You were willing, yes,' said Poirot, 'but were you happy to do so?'

'I had no choice,' she said in a flat voice. 'Godfrey and Sidney were obsessed with Peepers, which meant they wanted to be together all the time. I could have stayed home on my own, but where's the fun in that?'

'Tell me, madame, where was the fun for you in coming here to stay with the Devonports?'

'There was none. I've just told you: Godfrey was here constantly, so I had no choice.'

'You did not, then, find it enjoyable to come here and indulge your hatred of Sidney and Lilian Devonport?'

A sly smile crept across Verna Laviolette's face. 'Now that you put it like that . . .' she said.

'Catchpool and I could not understand it at first,' said Poirot. 'You were described to us as kind and thoughtful, first by Helen Acton and then by Hester Semley. Yet in our presence, you always seemed to be . . . something else. There was the cruelty, always, below the surface of your words and your *comportement*. Only later did I realize: Catchpool and I had only ever seen you in the company of the Devonports—the people who, as you saw it, had driven you out of Kingfisher Hill. And you find it impossible, in Sidney and Lilian Devonports' presence, to feel kindness and sympathy towards them, *n'est-ce pas?*'

Verna looked at Daisy, then at Richard. 'I don't bear either of you two any ill will,' she said. 'I hope you know that.'

'I know it,' said Daisy at once. I remembered that Verna Laviolette was one of the people to whom she had given a copy of *Midnight Gathering*. Was Daisy fond of Verna, I wondered, precisely because she sensed the older woman's resentment of Sidney and Lilian?

'Lilian didn't even ask me how I'd feel if they bought a house here,' said Verna. 'Can you imagine? Not even asking?'

'Madame Laviolette, you did not only lie about why you sold this house,' said Poirot. 'You also lied about seeing Lilian Devonport walking down the stairs on the morning of Winnie Lord's murder. You saw no such thing. You merely wished to implicate Lilian, hoping, for purely malicious reasons, to see her accused of this murder. Both she and Sidney contradicted your account. They both swore they were together in Lilian's bedroom between ten and eleven and that neither of them left the room. So, you needed to do two things in order for your spiteful plan to work: cast doubt upon Lilian's alibi, and invent an alibi for the two people who did not have one: Daisy Devonport and Oliver Prowd. They did not walk together in the garden that morning—you lied about that, Madame Laviolette. You knew at once, did you not, that it must have been either Daisy or Oliver who had killed Winnie Lord?'

Verna said sullenly, 'I did not know it was Winnie, but . . . yes. Something was going on in the drawing room. I was watching through my half-open door. Oliver came out, Daisy ran in . . . Then I saw Daisy a little later wearing different clothes.'

'Mine had blood on them after I smashed up Winnie's head,' Daisy told Poirot. Her father made a growling noise. 'I put clean clothes on and burned the bloody ones along with Winnie's.'

'You are contemptible, Verna,' said Lilian quietly.

'Well, it takes one to know one, sister.' Verna looked wildly around the room. 'Will you all quit looking at me like that? Lilian's nearly dead anyway. What difference does it make? I like Daisy and Oliver, and I didn't want either of them to get into trouble.'

'They must have been surprised and delighted to hear

you invent for them this walk in the gardens that did not take place,' said Poirot. 'Eagerly they rushed to confirm the story and be cleared of suspicion. Mademoiselle Daisy, perhaps you would like to explain the note that you wrote and left on the body of Winnie Lord for the police to find. May we all hear what was written in the note, please?'

Sergeant Gidley recited its contents: '"You sat in a seat you should never have sat in, now here comes a poker to batter your hat in."'

We all listened as Daisy told us about the day of the journey by coach, provoking much exclamation and the occasional gasp. What a talented storyteller she was. She made it sound twenty times more exciting than I could have. She omitted no detail and sounded rather proud as she recounted the story she had invented for Winnie to tell us: the mysterious stranger, the warning about the seat.

When she had finished, Poirot took over the narrative once more. 'Daisy Devonport knew that the warning from the nameless stranger was an alluring mystery that Catchpool and I would find irresistible. She was free to make it as tempting and outlandish as she wanted, knowing it would never be resolved. The precise opposite, in fact, was true: it needed *never* to be resolved in order to maintain its grip on our imaginations. She used the exact same logic when she wrote the note and placed it on Winnie Lord's body. It was a deliberate attempt to occupy my thoughts with deductions that had no possibility of ever leading to an answer. But the note was a trick—there was no true answer! And for as long as Catchpool and I were busy wondering why somebody would kill this poor woman merely for sitting in the wrong seat, and how this came to happen at Little Key when Joan-Blythe-from-the-coach had no connection to this house, we would be unable to make progress towards solving any of the real mysteries.

'This was the thinking of Mademoiselle Daisy, who both did and did not want the body to be accurately identified. She wanted me to identify the murder victim as the woman from the coach, a complete stranger to this household—that is why the green hat and coat were left on the body. At the same time, she wanted no one to know that the dead woman was Winnie Lord, or that Winnie and Joan-from-the-coach were one and the same person.'

'But Winnie was your friend,' said Verna Laviolette to Daisy. 'Why on earth would you want to kill her?'

'I did not,' Daisy said sadly.

'No, mademoiselle, you did not,' Poirot agreed. He looked around the room. 'What most of you do not know is that Daisy Devonport confessed to Winnie Lord that she had murdered her brother Frank. She did not kill Frank—somebody else did—but Daisy entertained a fantasy of confessing publicly to the crime. The first person to hear her false account was Winnie Lord. She told Winnie that she, not Helen Acton, had killed Frank and that she planned to confess this to the great Hercule Poirot, who was waiting nearby to board the same coach. Furthermore, she offered Winnie a significant amount of money in exchange for her silence about the true motive for this murder she had not committed. However, Winnie Lord, despite at first being willing to lie, had a conscience that promises of money could not suppress. She decided she must tell the police what she knew, so she went to Scotland Yard and asked to speak to Inspector Edward Catchpool. Now, here is a point worthy of note . . .'

Poirot smiled at me. 'Pay close attention, Catchpool. Sergeant Gidley, please tell me: when Winnie Lord first asked for Catchpool, had you already told her that he was the man leading a new investigation into the murder of Frank Devonport?'

'No, M. Poirot, I had not,' said Gidley. 'She came in and asked for Inspector Catchpool before I had a chance to say anything much at all.'

'Indeed so!' Poirot pronounced triumphantly. 'This, Catchpool, was the important item you failed to add to your list. You had spoken to Sergeant Gidley after hearing from your landlady that he had news for you about a visit from Winnie Lord—but you failed to ask him this vital question: did Winnie ask for you *before or after* being told that you were the one in charge of the Frank Devonport case? If it was before, how ever would Winnie Lord even know your name? Joan-Blythe-from-the-coach, on the other hand . . . *she* might have wished to tell Inspector Edward Catchpool *in particular* that she had lied to him and now needed to tell him the truth about a murder of which an innocent woman had been convicted.'

'You're right,' I said. 'None of that occurred to me, not even for a second. Well deduced, Poirot. So that's what Winnie meant when she said, "I know who disposed of

Frank Devonport, and I know why, and it's not the reason you all think."'

'*Précisément*,' said Poirot. 'She was referring to Daisy Devonport's false motive and her alleged true motive, both of which had been told to her by Daisy. She believed that the false motive would by then be known also to the police. Sergeant Gidley explained to her that Inspector Catchpool was not at Scotland Yard but at Little Key. It was *then* that Winnie Lord learned of the new investigation into the murder of Frank Devonport.

'Determined to speak to Catchpool as soon as she could, Winnie set off for Kingfisher Hill without telling her mother where she was going or why. Her mother was frantic with worry. When Winnie arrived at Little Key—this was the knock heard by Richard Devonport from the library—the door was opened to her by Oliver Prowd. Naïve fool that she was, Winnie confided in him the reason for her visit. She told him she knew that Daisy had killed Frank and confessed to it, but that it was important for the police to know the true reason for Frank's death; Daisy had confessed her true motive to her, and Winnie planned to tell Inspector Catchpool about it as soon as he arrived. Catchpool and I were not yet at the house. We were at Holloway Prison questioning Helen Acton. Monsieur Prowd, you invited Winnie Lord into the empty drawing room and closed the door. Then you took a poker from the fireplace and struck her on the head with it. You killed her, did you not?'

Oliver Prowd did not deny it. He remained silent, his face unreadable.

'Why, Oliver?' Richard Devonport was pale with shock. 'Why would you do such a thing? Daisy, how could you . . . ? You knew he did this and you . . . you . . .'

Daisy shot him an impatient look. 'What did you expect me to do? Faint and weep? I was shocked, of course, but one cannot indulge in shock and self-pity when there's a practical problem to be solved. Oliver only did what he did to Winnie to protect me. In return, I . . . I did what I could to protect him.'

'How touched you must have been that he had killed for your sake,' said Poirot. 'You judge the morality based only on the benefit to you personally, mademoiselle. This I see very clearly.' To the others, he said, 'Monsieur Prowd knew that Daisy had already confessed to the murder of Frank, and he had seen that her confession had been believed by nobody, apart from Sidney and Lilian Devonport, perhaps. And Helen Acton had confessed to the same crime *and been convicted of it*. At that point, Monsieur Prowd believed that his beloved Daisy was not in especial danger of being hanged for murder. He himself did not think she was a murderer—he must have thought she was playing some complicated game of the mind. I imagine that he hoped to persuade her to retract her confession. However, when Winnie Lord arrived with her story of the false motive and the true one—a tale that sounded so much more psychologically credible—Oliver Prowd's fears increased substantially. He decided that Winnie must at all costs be stopped from giving her account to Inspector Catchpool.'

'Oliver meant only to keep me safe,' Daisy said shakily. 'This is all my fault, not his.'

'And now,' said Poirot gravely, 'let us finally solve the murder of Frank Devonport . . .'

'When I visited Hester Semley, she told me of a conversation between Oliver Prowd and Godfrey Laviolette that she had overheard, a conversation that took place at her house on the day of Frank Devonport's death,' said Poirot. 'Monsieur Prowd spoke of a woman with whom he had behaved in an unprincipled and unchristian fashion. He admitted to having treated this woman poorly. He also mentioned that the two of them had sought the help of a doctor—the same doctor who was attending to Monsieur Prowd's dying father, Otto Prowd. This doctor had refused to help and was no doubt shocked to be asked. Ladies and gentleman, Hester Semley leapt to a most understandable conclusion.'

'A baby?' said Daisy breathlessly. 'No, that cannot be. Oliver would have told me—'

'*Attendez-vous*, mademoiselle. There was no baby. Hester Semley was incorrect to assume that a pregnancy was involved. I have spoken to the doctor in question, Dr Ephgrave of Harley Street. From him I heard the true story. The young woman was a teacher at a school owned by Frank Devonport and Oliver Prowd. When Monsieur Prowd's father grew so ill that he could not leave his sick bed, he expressed a wish to his son. He knew he had little time left and he wanted to learn a new skill—to use his mind for something stimulating, for as long as he had a

323

mind left to use. *Alors*, Monsieur Prowd asked this young woman, this teacher, to come to the house and teach the French language—that was her subject—to his dying father.

'This arrangement worked well. Otto Prowd was happier for a while, until his health deteriorated to the point where he could no longer proceed with the lessons. He was close to death . . . and yet, at the same time, not so close.'

'What do you mean?' asked Richard Devonport.

'By now the young teacher had grown fond of the old man, who had been such a keen and good pupil. When Oliver Prowd told her that in the opinion of Dr Ephgrave it might be another month before Otto Prowd died, the young woman decided that this was intolerable. Oliver Prowd agreed: he did not wish his father to spend the next month in agony with no hope of recovery. Together, the two of them went to Dr Ephgrave and begged him to end the suffering of the old man, to give him a drug that would enable him to pass out of life immediately and peacefully. Alas, the doctor would not agree to the suggestion.'

'He was a dreadful prig,' said Oliver.

'Two hours after Dr Ephgrave had refused to help with this plan, Otto Prowd was dead,' Poirot told the assembled group. 'Who was it that held down the pillow over his face, Monsieur Prowd? Surely you will tell us now. Dr Ephgrave said nothing to the police because he saw no way to prove it, but he suspected that either you or the French teacher smothered your father to death. He is correct, is he not? This was the unchristian thing that you did, together with a young woman?'

Oliver nodded. 'We couldn't bear to see him suffer like that. He wanted us to do it. We did it with his full agreement—both of us, together. We agreed: it had to be done that way or not at all, so that we would share the responsibility. We both pressed down on the pillow. It was horrible, but it was necessary. It felt right. Father was spared any further suffering.'

'You, however, were not,' said Poirot. '*Pas du tout*. Your conscience troubled you excessively—as it should have done. We humans have no right to play God, Monsieur Prowd. Yes, there is sickness and there is suffering—but it is not our place to decide when life should end. Your conscience knew this even if you did not. It troubled you so gravely that you decided, shortly after the deed was done, that you did not wish to share the blame. You decided that the smothering to death of Otto Prowd was mainly the fault of the young woman who had been your collaborator.'

'Yes. I was vicious and unkind to her. She was the stronger of the two of us. Oh, not physically, but her will was stronger. I persuaded myself that, were it not for her influence . . .' He did not finish the sentence.

'Exactly as you had blamed Frank Devonport for the theft of his parents' money, even though you had known about this, too, in advance,' said Poirot. 'You had agreed to it and profited from it! You are a moral coward, Monsieur Prowd! Do you think that you can kill once and be untarnished? You cannot! That is why it was so easy for you to take another life, when Winnie Lord said to you words that you very much did not want to hear.'

'Do you think I don't know what I am?' Oliver said bitterly. 'I know it better than you. I feel terrible about the way I treated both of them, Frank and . . . the teacher. I feel wretched about Winnie Lord too, and even about your stolen money, Sidney—but I will never regret saving my father from the agony he was having to endure. Never!'

'Please do not torment him, M. Poirot.' There were tears in Daisy's eyes. 'Have you never been afraid of anything? Are you so perfectly moral and pure that you have nothing to rebuke yourself for? I tell you, the killing of Winnie was *my* fault. Let me hang for it instead of Oliver!'

Poirot ignored her. 'Once I had heard this story from Dr Ephgrave, suddenly everything fell into place,' he said. 'At last I was able to explain the most bothersome detail of this whole affair, a detail that appeared to make no sense at all.'

'What detail?' asked Richard.

'Before I tell you that, I wish to ask a question of you, Mademoiselle Helen.'

'Ask it,' she said.

'How did you and Frank Devonport meet?'

'You know the answer to that.'

'Oh, I do. Indeed I do.'

I didn't. From the looks on their faces, neither did anyone else in the room.

'Frank Devonport must have spoken to you of his old friend Oliver Prowd, yes?'

'Yes,' said Helen. 'He talked about Oliver rather a lot,

326

and they were still acquainted in business, though they no longer saw one another.'

'*C'est ça,*' Poirot said. 'Ladies and gentlemen, Frank Devonport did not know about the engagement of Oliver Prowd to his sister Daisy. He was estranged from both of them, so how would he know? And for the same reason of estrangement, neither Daisy Devonport nor Oliver Prowd knew of Frank's engagement to Helen Acton.'

'Why are you telling us this?' Lilian Devonport asked. 'What possible relevance can it have?'

'Mademoiselle Helen,' said Poirot. 'Did Frank Devonport ever tell you that Oliver Prowd was dark-haired and handsome?'

Helen looked surprised. 'No. Men do not generally say such things about other men. He spoke only of Oliver's character and their relationship.'

'Nothing whatsoever about his physical appearance, then?'

'No.'

'Mademoiselle, I have heard now several accounts of how you ran down the stairs, seized Oliver Prowd by the arms and confessed to him that you had murdered Frank. You agree that this is what happened?'

Helen nodded.

'You said to him, according to more than one person who witnessed the scene, "I killed him, Oliver." At that moment there were three men standing in the entrance hall: Godfrey Laviolette, Oliver Prowd and Percy Semley. They had all just arrived from Kingfisher's View. As Frank's new fiancée, coming for the first time to Little Key, *you had met none of them before*. This was the first time you could conceivably have laid eyes upon any of them, yes? I suggest to you, mademoiselle, that you therefore could not have known that the handsome man with the dark hair was Oliver Prowd, or that he was named Oliver. You had not been introduced to him, so how could you have known it was he?

'And yet I did,' said Helen with a small, sad smile. '*Je le savais aussi bien que je connaissais mon propre nom.*'

Why on earth was she suddenly speaking in French, I wondered. Then I tumbled to it all at once. '*You* are the French teacher?' I asked her. 'You . . . you knew Oliver already?'

Helen nodded. 'He was the last person I expected to find at Frank's parents' house. As you say, M. Poirot, Frank also had no idea that Oliver would be here or that he was engaged to Daisy. Then, when I met Daisy and she started to talk about her fiancé, Oliver . . . well, the truth soon became apparent: *it was the same Oliver!* Frank was surprised but not horrified, as I was. He had nothing to fear. I was in such a terrible panic, I had to leave the drawing room and go upstairs. All I could think about was Oliver returning from the other house and telling Frank the one thing I had never told him, the one thing I would sooner have died than have him know—that I was a killer and, even worse, that I had kept it from him. Honesty, integrity . . . Frank valued these qualities above all else. How could I make sure he never found out? I couldn't think of anything!

I was half wild with panic. Then Frank came to my room and I . . . I had to pretend to be perfectly all right. And then we heard the front door, and the voices . . .' Helen stopped and stared into the distance. It was as if she was watching this scene from the past unfold before her eyes.

'And then Frank walked out onto the landing,' said Poirot quietly. 'You followed him and saw Oliver Prowd in the entrance hall below. Now, imminently, it seemed certain that Frank would discover the truth. *And he could not be allowed to know.* The man you loved more than anything in the world could not live to see you hang for the murder of Otto Prowd. And so . . . you pushed him to his death.'

'I did not mean to,' said Helen. 'Yes, I did it, but there was no intention. I was out of my mind—not capable of rational thought in that moment. My hands seemed to move without my awareness. And then Frank was falling from the balcony and it was too late.'

'Mademoiselle, if you had not intended it, it would not have happened,' said Poirot. 'Hands do not move unless minds make them move. Like Monsieur Prowd, you had killed before—on that occasion, you believed that you had an excellent reason for doing so. In the case of Frank, you try to tell me that no reason or choice was involved. *Neither of these statements is the truth!* There can be no justification for such actions. And once a first murder has been committed, the second becomes so much easier. The law against killing our fellow men and women is not there only to protect them, but also to protect us from our worst impulses.'

'You may think and believe what you wish,' said Helen. 'Remember, M. Poirot, I am not trying to escape justice. All I want, all I have wanted for some time, is to die and be with Frank again. I confessed immediately—and I only lied about why I did it to protect Oliver. I did not want him to hang for what we had done to Otto. I agree with him: to end a person's suffering, at their express request, when death is so imminent. I do not believe that to be a sin.'

'The law disagrees,' Poirot told her.

'As soon as I had pushed Frank and he was falling, I . . . I knew that I had made the most appalling mistake,' said Helen.

'Indeed. You made a serious miscalculation,' said Poirot. 'Monsieur Prowd would never have told Frank that the two of you had together killed his father. He wished to protect himself as much as you did.'

'I realized that only once it was too late,' said Helen. 'Until then, all I could think was that Oliver had blamed me for what we did to his father—me alone. Oliver, did you not insist over and over that I had forced that course of action upon you? I thought that at any moment you would look up, see me on the balcony and say, "There's the woman who murdered my father." And then . . . then Frank was falling and hitting the ground—and Frank was dead and I wanted to die too. Only moments earlier I had been desperate to avoid the gallows for the murder of Otto. Now Frank was dead, it was my fault, and suddenly the gallows were all I wanted.'

'So you ran down the stairs and confessed to Oliver Prowd what you had done,' said Poirot. 'He was kind to you then, having been unkind the last time you had encountered him. You could afford to be sympathetic this time, Monsieur Prowd—here was a death for which you were not responsible.'

Richard Devonport had stood up and was walking slowly across the room to where Helen sat by the piano. 'I was so sure you were innocent,' he said to her. 'So sure. Your love for Frank . . . well, I never doubted it. I thought it meant that you would never have killed him. I thought that M. Poirot would find out the truth and . . .' He left the sentence unfinished.

'And what, Richard?' said Helen. 'You thought I would then love you the way I had loved Frank, because you would have been my saviour?'

Violently, he turned away from her.

Poirot nodded to Sergeant Gidley, who rose to his feet and pulled two sets of handcuffs out of his two trouser pockets. 'Miss Acton, you are already convicted of the murder of Frank Devonport and you are soon to pay the price for your crime.'

'Thank goodness.' Helen closed her eyes and smiled.

'Oliver Prowd,' said Gidley. 'I am arresting you for the murders of Otto Prowd and Winnifred Lord.'

'No,' Daisy gasped. 'No! Oliver! Where are you taking him?' She staggered to her feet as Sergeant Gidley and Marcus Capeling led Oliver Prowd and Helen Acton from the room. 'Stop. Stop at once! M. Poirot, this is quite wrong.

Winnie's death was my fault—you know it was. If I had not asked Oliver to marry me, he would not have been at the house when Frank brought Helen here and . . .' She closed her eyes tightly. 'Why can one not undo the past? If only it were possible. Poor, poor Helen. Can't you see that she never intended to harm *anyone*? I thought you were supposed to be clever!'

'Mademoiselle, I am afraid that . . .'

'No! Do not say a word, I don't want to hear it. I don't want Oliver to die! Or Winnie, or Frank. Or you, Mother. I don't want anyone to die. Let us stay in this room forever and never open the door. We can tell ourselves the lie that all is well and that all the harm that's been done can be undone.' I saw an expression on her face then that I had never seen there before: peacefulness. 'I find that I am able to believe it,' she said with a sigh. 'Please, nobody say a single word. Please let me go on believing it for as long as I possibly can.'

Three Weeks Later

'Catchpool?'

I looked up from the papers in front of me. 'Poirot! What are you doing here? Did Blanche Unsworth let you in?' My face felt rather hot, and I did my best to look innocent.

'*Oui, mon ami.*' He smiled. 'How else would I appear in her drawing room to find you here? I do not have the magic powers to move through walls.'

Hastily, I pushed the papers out of the way as if they were irrelevant and uninteresting, and picked up a newspaper instead.

'You did not hear my arrival or my conversation in the hallway with Madame Unsworth?'

'Hmm?' I pretended to concentrate on the news headlines in front of me. 'Gosh, listen to this: it seems we have a new political party. Did you know that? It's called the—'

'I find it interesting that you did not hear,' Poirot interrupted my attempt to distract him. 'You were absorbed in your papers, were you not? Not the newspaper, but those papers there.' He pointed. 'What are they?'

'It's nothing.'

He had started to walk slowly towards them and would see them at any moment unless I leapt to cover them up. I sighed and said, 'Don't laugh at me if I tell you. I'm working on a new board game. Inventing one, I mean.'

'Catchpool!' My friend's eyes sparkled with delight. 'You have been inspired by Peepers, yes?'

'Quite the opposite,' I told him. 'No board game should have rules that look anything like the rules of Peepers looked. They're far too complicated and would make anyone want to run for his life. I am determined to invent a board game that is perfectly simple, yet at the same time immensely satisfying.

'Speaking of satisfying . . .' I said

'Yes, *mon ami*?'

'That whole business at Kingfisher Hill . . .'

'What of it?

'Were you, *are* you . . . satisfied with the way it all turned out?'

'Ah! Allow me to ask you: were you dissatisfied? We arrived at the truth, did we not?'

'Yes, but . . . what if it's true that Helen Acton was momentarily not in her right mind when she pushed Frank over the balcony? And the whole Otto Prowd affair . . . He was in terrible pain and so close to death . . . Dr Ephgrave said so, didn't he?'

Poirot nodded. 'I see what causes you the struggle. Yes,

my friend, it is always easier when the criminal gives one the satisfaction of being very clearly the embodiment of evil with no contradiction in his character—only the badness from top to bottom. Sadly, this is rarely the truth of any human being. It is possible to feel the sympathy for a person who has done something terrible and at the same time hold them responsible for their actions. The satisfaction of solving a murder, in such instances, comes from two sources: the belief that the law must be upheld in even the most difficult of circumstances, and then following that law without allowing your resolve to be swayed by pity for the perpetrators who must now face justice.'

Poirot leaned over and pulled the newspaper out of my hands. He folded it and put it down on a chair. 'Now, tell me more about your board game,' he said. 'What is it to be called? Does it already have a name?'

'No. I have a few ideas, but I haven't settled on anything yet.'

'Then you know what to do, *mon ami*. It is the same thing that I always tell you: it is how your little grey cells function most effectively.'

'What?' I asked him.

'You must make a list!'

THE END

THE AGATHA CHRISTIE COLLECTION

Mysteries

The Man in the Brown
Suit
The Secret of Chimneys
The Seven Dials Mystery
The Mysterious Mr Quin
The Sittaford Mystery
The Hound of Death
The Listerdale Mystery
Why Didn't They Ask
Evans?
Parker Pyne Investigates
Murder Is Easy
And Then There Were
None
Towards Zero
Death Comes as the End
Sparkling Cyanide
Crooked House
They Came to Baghdad
Destination Unknown
Spider's Web*
The Unexpected Guest*
Ordeal by Innocence
The Pale Horse
Endless Night
Passenger To Frankfurt
Problem at Pollensa Bay
While the Light Lasts

Poirot

The Mysterious Affair at
Styles
The Murder on the
Links
Poirot Investigates
The Murder of Roger
Ackroyd
The Big Four
The Mystery of the Blue
Train
Black Coffee*
Peril at End House
Lord Edgware Dies

Murder on the Orient
Express
Three Act Tragedy
Death in the Clouds
The ABC Murders
Murder in Mesopotamia
Cards on the Table
Murder in the Mews
Dumb Witness
Death on the Nile
Appointment With Death
Hercule Poirot's
Christmas
Sad Cypress
One, Two, Buckle My
Shoe
Evil Under the Sun
Five Little Pigs
The Hollow
The Labours of
Hercules
Taken at the Flood
Mrs McGinty's Dead
After the Funeral
Hickory Dickory Dock
Dead Man's Folly
Cat Among the Pigeons
The Adventure of the
Christmas Pudding
The Clocks
Third Girl
Hallowe'en Party
Elephants Can
Remember
Poirot's Early Cases
Curtain: Poirot's Last
Case

Marple

The Murder at the
Vicarage
The Thirteen Problems
The Body in the Library
The Moving Finger

A Murder Is Announced
They Do It With Mirrors
A Pocket Full of Rye
4.50 from Paddington
The Mirror Crack'd from
Side to Side
A Caribbean Mystery
At Bertram's Hotel
Nemesis
Sleeping Murder
Miss Marple's Final Cases

Tommy & Tuppence

The Secret Adversary
Partners in Crime
N or M?
By the Pricking of My
Thumbs
Postern of Fate

Published as Mary Westmacott

Giant's Bread
Unfinished Portrait
Absent in the Spring
The Rose and the Yew
Tree
A Daughter's a Daughter
The Burden

Memoirs

An Autobiography
Come, Tell Me How You
Live
The Grand Tour

Plays and Stories

Akhnaton
Little Grey Cells
Murder, She Said
The Floating Admiral†
Star Over Bethlehem
Hercule Poirot and the
Greenshore Folly

* novelized by Charles Osborne
† contributor

ALSO BY SOPHIE HANNAH

The Monogram Murders

'It is hate that makes people kill . . . not love.'

Hercule Poirot's quiet supper in a London coffee house is interrupted when a young woman confides to him that she is about to be murdered. She is terrified, but begs Poirot not to find and punish her killer. Once she is dead, she insists, justice will have been done.

Later that night, Poirot learns that three guests at the fashionable Bloxham Hotel have been murdered, and a cufflink has been placed in each one's mouth. Could there be a connection with the frightened woman? While Poirot struggles to connect the bizarre pieces of the puzzle, the murderer prepares a hotel bedroom for a fourth victim . . .

'Grips from the very start. Hannah gets it right in every particular.'
THE TIMES

'Immensely satisfying—an ingenious ending'
INDEPENDENT

'A highly readable locked-room mystery with a delectable twist.'
MAIL ON SUNDAY

'Superbly orchestrated . . . as exhilaratingly complicated as anything by Christie.'
SUNDAY TIMES

ALSO BY SOPHIE HANNAH

Closed Casket

'What I intend to say to you will come as a shock . . .'

Lady Athelinda Playford has planned a house party at her
mansion, but it is no ordinary gathering. She announces that she
has decided to change her will, cutting off her children and
leaving her fortune to someone who has only weeks to live . . .

Among Lady Playford's guests are Belgian detective Hercule
Poirot and Inspector Edward Catchpool of Scotland Yard, who
have no idea why they have been invited . . . until Poirot starts
to wonder if Lady Playford expects a murderer to strike. When
the crime is committed, and the victim is not who Poirot
thought it would be, will he be able to solve the mystery?

'Sparkling second outing for Hannah's reimagined Poirot'
SUNDAY TIMES

'Offers a clever twist which the Queen of Crime would have
applauded'
DAILY EXPRESS

'Another satisfying addition to the Agatha Christie canon'
IRISH TIMES

'A novel fizzing with ideas and spikey dialogue'
SUNDAY EXPRESS

ALSO BY SOPHIE HANNAH

The Mystery of Three Quarters

'Murder! Me? How dare you!'

Hercule Poirot's tranquil afternoon is ruined when an angry woman accosts him outside his front door. She threatens to report the famous detective to Scotland Yard for falsely accusing her of murder. Seeking sanctuary inside, Poirot is startled to find that he has a visitor—another stranger claiming to have received a letter from Poirot accusing him of killing the same man.

How many more innocent people have been sent letters? If Poirot didn't send them, who did? And who is Barnabas Pandy, the alleged victim—is he dead or alive? Poirot has answers to find, and quickly, or more lives may be put in danger . . .

'What Sophie and Agatha have in common is a rare talent for fiendish unpredictability. They make you see how the impossible might be possible after all.'
SUNDAY TELEGRAPH

'A literary marriage made in heaven!'
THE TIMES

'Sophie does justice to the Belgian brainiac, both in terms of bringing his character to life and giving him a mystery to solve that is worthy of his talents. It's her best Poirot novel so far.'
SUNDAY EXPRESS

About the Authors

SOPHIE HANNAH is an internationally bestselling writer of crime fiction, published in more than 49 languages. Her novel *The Carrier* won Crime Thriller of the Year at the 2013 Specsavers National Book Awards. She lives with her husband, children and dog in Cambridge, where she is a Fellow of Lucy Cavendish College, and as a poet has been shortlisted for the TS Eliot Prize. *The Killings at Kingfisher Hill* is Sophie's fourth Hercule Poirot novel.

AGATHA CHRISTIE is known throughout the world as the Queen of Crime. Her books have sold over a billion copies in English with another billion in foreign languages. She is the most widely published author of all time, outsold only by the Bible and Shakespeare. She is the author of 80 crime novels and short story collections, more than 20 plays, and six novels written under the name Mary Westmacott.